HOLD
THE
Light

HOLD
THE
Light

APRIL MCGOWAN

WhiteFire
— Publishing —

HOLD THE LIGHT

WhiteFire Publishing
13607 Bedford Rd NE
Cumberland, MD 21502

ISBN: 978-1-939023-87-2 (digital)
          978-1-939023-86-5 (print)

For the loves of my life
~Ken, Madeline and Seth~
&
my sister in faith, joy, and adversity
~Janet~

John 8:12
Then Jesus again spoke to them, saying, "I am the Light of the world; he who follows Me will not walk in the darkness, but will have the Light of life." (NASB)

CHAPTER 1

Unremarkable. Amber glanced out the streaming windowpane at the cityscape below her. The rain washed all the color from the sky, trees, and buildings, covering the world in grayscale brush strokes. She traced a raindrop with her finger as she'd done as a child, watching it gather speed, collecting friends as it went, only to splat useless on the sill, pool, and drizzle away.

There was nothing to be done about it. The world would go to dusk, darken, disappear—and she would go with it not in a rage, but with a quiet whimper of acceptance. Amber twirled her ring around her finger, spinning and spinning, panic filling her until she bit down on her lip. *Hard.* No. Not her. She'd face this as she'd faced everything in her life. She could handle it.

Amber wiped a tear with shaky fingers and pulled her honey-brown hair back into the scrunchie she wore on her wrist before turning to face the doctor, resolute. The exam room seemed to be affected by the same dull gray as the outside world. She guessed the blind really had no use for designer colors or flashy artwork on the walls.

Ironic.

He said something she didn't understand.

"What do you mean, it's genetic?" She waited for him to answer, hoping for some light in the ever-growing bleakness.

The doctor sat back against the examining room table. "Someone else in your family might have this disease."

Her mother would know. Her *biological* mother, that was. Did Mom know, though?

Tiny pieces of torn paper seemed to reassemble themselves before her eyes and tumble apart all over again. The shredded letter, floating down around her like snow, falling, falling into little useless piles she'd vacuumed up four years ago. She hadn't wanted to be in contact with her birth mother, not ever. How dare she try and contact her? Amber's anger at being abandoned, donated, sold like an old car on the Internet, had burned through her for years.

"I'm adopted." The words always brought about a feeling of finality, like the slamming of a lid on an old wooden box, buried six feet under. Except her birth mother wasn't six feet under. She'd just walked away from Amber.

"I see. If there's any way for you to find your biological family, you might want to. It will give us some clues."

"And then we can stop it?" She held her breath, hoping.

Dr. Birkman gave her a pitying glance, his watery hazel eyes full of sympathy. "No, we can't stop it."

Questions raced. "How long do I have? What if we'd caught it earlier?"

Moving toward her, he gave her shoulder a gentle squeeze. He didn't know her, but he comforted her. She felt small in his presence. He had all the answers, held her fate in his medical books. What did she have?

"Diagnosis doesn't do anything but give us guidelines. I'm afraid macular degeneration can't be cured by the medical knowledge we have now."

"Isn't this something older people get? I'm only twenty-eight."

"There are several variations of this disease that affect younger people, although yours, admittedly, has taken longer to make an appearance."

"I guess I should be grateful." The words, like a mantra, tumbled from her lips but made no connection with her heart. "How long?" she asked again.

"At this rate, not long. Your case seems to be moving rather rapidly. You'll start to notice more and more changes. Maybe a year."

Numbness washed through her, starting at her fingertips, racing into her middle, buzzing between her ears.

"Will I lose my sight entirely?"

"It's rare for everything to go black. Most people with your condition lose portions at a time, making their vision spotty until everything goes hazy. Some keep partial sight. But I don't want to give you false hope."

He reached over to a stand of pamphlets on the countertop and handed her several. "Is there anyone I can call for you?"

Dr. Birkman was trying to help, but Amber didn't want anyone with her right then. She just wanted to go home. Alone.

"No. I'm fine. I need to go."

"I'll have my staff call and set up your next appointment." He was aiding in her fast escape.

She nodded in agreement. But what was the point of coming back? He couldn't stop this. Amber pulled on her coat and grabbed her purse, shoving the pamphlets deep within, crumpling them. She headed out of the exam room, past other patients sitting placidly in the waiting area, down the narrow corridor toward the elevator. Her hand glanced over the braille directive bumps on the hall edgeway, and she drew back as if she'd touched something repulsive. She shivered and tried not to notice similar bumps over the floor number, on the nameplates, and then, once the elevator doors opened, on the button panel.

As the elevator met and reached each floor, a ding rang out, joined by a female voice naming every one. Fifteen, ding, fourteen, ding, thirteen, ding, and on and on. People boarded the elevator at the seventh floor, jostling her aside, animated and happy. A shiver coursed through her, and she pulled her sable-brown trench coat closed. Finally, the car reached the ground floor and she pushed past the others, nearly running through the foyer and out the glass front doors. Amber gasped as the chilled fall breeze met the stale air in her lungs.

Rain poured down, and she fumbled with the slick buttons on her coat, raising the collar against the onslaught. Cars sped by as she passed food carts and stepped over jagged, cracked planks of sidewalk. The grass and weeds reached up as if to trip her and pull her down, kicking and screaming, into the crevasse. She swallowed hard and tucked a strand of escaping hair behind her ear. The bus pulled up, and she jogged to catch it but then stopped. The last thing she wanted to do was pile onto the city bus full of rain-soaked, steamy bodies. Instead, she went to the light and waited to cross.

For a moment, she closed her eyes, listening to the patter of rain, the grind and slide of shoes against slick pavement, the call of the vendors, a petitioner desperate for signatures, a homeless man demanding change. Far in the distance the train passed, and farther still a jet plane buzzed the sky. A child laughed.

Dizziness swept over her. Just before she lost her balance and fell onto the street and into the path of a car who ran the red light, she felt a hand grab her arm.

"Careful there," a deep male voice admonished her.

Amber wrenched from the man's hand, startled at being touched almost as much as by the worry she saw in his eyes. He must have only been in his late thirties, but he leaned heavily on a stylish hand-carved cane. His blue eyes matched his raincoat and were framed by jet black hair sprinkled with gray at the temples.

"Sorry. Just trying to help." His glance cast away, and he put up his umbrella. She wanted to thank him for his kindness, not chide him for grabbing her, but the words wouldn't come. Not today.

The light changed, and the telltale bird chirping sound signaled her to cross. Before she could take a step out into the street, a careless driver sped around the corner, not stopping for her or for the light. Amber's heart raced up into her throat, choking off a curse that built. What if she were already blind? She'd be dead. How were those auditory signals helpful to anyone?

Her hand flew to her chest as if to quiet her rapidly thumping heart and catch her breath.

"Not your day?" The man gave her a sympathetic look.

"No. Not my day." Her voice shook and she bit her lip to calm her nerves. "Thanks. For back there." They walked along together now—her avoiding cracks, him limping.

"Glad I could help." They approached another bus stop, and he gave her a warm but uncertain smile. "Have a good day."

She wanted to tell him it was much too late for that. For some reason, she wanted to tell him everything. A stranger's distance from the situation would be lovely about then. *My name is Amber, and I'm going blind.* But she didn't.

"Thanks." She plodded on past, up the inclining street. Twenty city blocks to go.

The rain continued to pour down, chilling her neck, mixing with the hairspray in her hair and running into her eyes, blurring her vision with mascara and glue. She rubbed at them, desperate to clear her sight.

Maybe skipping the bus was a bad plan. Five blocks later, she took shelter under an awning and waited for the next ride to take her home to her apartment. Within a few minutes, another bus stopped by and she climbed aboard, taking her spot in a lemon-yellow molded plastic chair. The door closed and the bus took off into the busy downtown Portland traffic.

Fifteen blocks would have taken her forty minutes to walk—though on a bus starting and stopping for passengers, it took even longer. It gave her time to dry out and take stock. She took out her cellphone and scanned her e-mail. Most were from work or prospective private clients.

Amber's hands shook from cold and the fear building inside. In less than a year, life as she knew it would end. She looked up at the other passengers, caught up in their own worlds. The man in coveralls, the woman in business attire, the student, the skater kid, the group of three girls texting each other and laughing—they had no clue what tomorrow would hold. But she did.

Swallowing her emotions, she put her phone—soon to be useless—back into her pocket and concentrated on the passing landscape of cars and masses of people heading home. Her stop arrived, and she walked past everyone and out onto the street. Two blocks up, she arrived at her apartment building.

Amber stood outside, staring up at the aging red brick exterior of the five-floor complex, the cornice moldings, the framed glass windows and flower boxes on porches. She'd gotten this place because it was within walking distance of the grocery store, the art supply store, and other shopping—not to mention the school where she primarily taught.

Teaching. What a joke. A colossal joke. On her.

She used her passkey to open the outer door and entered, stopping by the bank of copper mailboxes. She used another smaller key to unlock hers and pulled out a bulky wad of advertising and bills. And a postcard from Kyle. She smiled—he'd only been in Hawaii on business and would be home tomorrow, but he'd still sent her a card. Then the memory of the day pressed in, and her smile faded.

She took the junk and tossed it into the recycling bin nearby, then headed up the dark-blue and red paisley carpeted stairs. On the second landing she began counting the steps. Then she tucked the mail into her purse with the pamphlets and went back down to the bottom, panting.

Closing her eyes, she gripped the rail and began to count again.

One, two, three. After she hit the seventh stair, her jarred feet leveled out on a landing, and she cracked her eyes open for a peek. Snapping them closed again, she made the corner, still grasping the rail, and counted again. This time the landing didn't take her by surprise. She peeked again and counted. Up, up, until she'd reached the third floor.

Her breath came in gasps, and blood pounded in her ears. She reached out, waving her hands in front of her, searching for the other side of the hall. She brushed her hand up the wall, passing one doorjamb, then the next, then the next, until she reached what she imagined and hoped was her door.

Searching fingers caressed the beveled surface until she found the number and letter that were her own. 3G. Tears escaped down her cheeks as she rummaged past all the paraphernalia she'd shoved in her purse, past the crinkled and sharp corners of the pamphlets, and found her keys. She clenched her eyes closed, not cheating, flipped to a key and tried it.

Wrong one. Another. Another. Each one clinked against the next. "Please," she gritted out. The sixth one found purchase, and she heard the deadbolt slide back. She pulled it out and felt it, memorized the pointy edges, the rounded spots and shook her keys back together. Then she did it again. Second try. Then again. First.

Only then did she let herself inside, drop her belongings on the table, shrug off her sopping coat. Only then did she lock the door from the inside, lean against it, slide down it to the floor, and cry.

CHAPTER 2

A mber brushed her hair and got ready for work. Her phone rang again, sounding her mom's ringtone, but she ignored it. She'd stopped taking calls for three days now. She got up, ate, went to work, came home. Shannon acted hurt when she didn't answer her texts, but how was Amber supposed to break this news to the sister of her heart? Let alone tell Kyle.

A knock sounded on her door as she gathered her materials for class, and she jumped. Someone must have buzzed in a salesperson because no one who knew her, save Shannon, would ever come over unannounced.

Amber looked out the peephole. *Kyle.* He must have snuck in behind another person entering the building. She'd have to talk to the landlord about that. People should be more careful these days. What was the point of living in a secured building if some stranger off the street could just follow you inside? Besides, what was he doing here? She wasn't ready for this. She needed time to think. The world hadn't stopped with her diagnosis, although a part of her wished it had.

For a moment, she thought she'd pretend not to be home. But then her phone rang and gave her away. Her heart raced with guilt at being caught. This is what she'd come to. Hiding.

"Amber, you in there?" He knocked again. "I'm worried. Do I need to get the super?"

Her shoulders dropped in defeat, and she shuffled to the door, opening it but leaving the chain on.

"Hi."

Kyle's brown eyes squinted questioningly at her through the crack. "Aren't you going to let me in?"

"Sure. Hang on." She shut the door and took a deep breath, smoothed her top and forced a smile as she swung it open.

Kyle breezed by her, gift bag in hand, looking around her one room apartment, suspicion in his eyes. "What's the deal?" He ran his fingers through his blond hair, something she used to find endearing but now rankled her.

"What do you mean?"

"I've been home since yesterday, and you're not answering calls."

She bristled at his accusatory tone. "I've had a lot going on."

He scanned her dinette table, the kitchen counters, her easel in the corner, and then the mantel over her gas-insert fireplace before his eyes brightened. Walking past the couch, he reached up for the postcard on the mantel and showed it to her.

"You got it." He grinned. "Thought you'd like that." He put it back, covering a photo of her parents, and held out the bag. "I brought you a present from Hawaii."

Was it only two weeks ago that Kyle's remembering to give her a gift would have meant the world to her?

Amber reached for the bag and opened it. Inside was a bag of Kona and a coffee tumbler painted with an array of Hawaiian flowers. She *did* love coffee. The aroma filled the room as she pulled it from the sack.

"Thanks." He was being thoughtful. It wasn't his fault her life fell apart while he was gone—in paradise.

Kyle pulled her toward him, keeping his hands on her hips. "I know you have to get to work, but let's have dinner tonight." He kissed her lightly, but it all felt like a routine to her. The passion, the excitement, had faded. Numb.

He deserved to know. She'd tell him tonight.

"Sounds like a good idea. I have some news." Her voice trailed off, but he didn't seem to notice.

"Me too. Big news. Can't wait." He backed away, heading to the door. "I'll pick you up at seven."

"I'll meet you."

His hand paused on the doorknob. "But I always pick you up."

"I need to run some errands first, okay?" Amber forced her voice to be light, her eyes to be bright and expectant.

"Sure. Emilio's. Seven." He blew her a kiss and left the apartment. The walls closed in, the air heavy with overly sweet aftershave and coffee.

Her phone rang again. Mom. She might as well get this over with altogether today. "Hi, Mom."

"Amber? Are you okay? I've called five times. It's not like you to ignore me."

"I know. Sorry. Listen, are you doing anything for lunch?" She wasn't sure how she'd do this, but it needed to be done.

"Something's wrong, isn't it? I can always tell when something's wrong. Fess up."

"Can't I take you to lunch once in a while without something being wrong?"

"Yes. But you never do."

Touché.

After she hung up, Amber headed to the school.

Three hours and two classes later, she readied her desk to leave for lunch with her mother. Her last class was at three and then she could...what? Her fingers itched to dial the number she'd been ignoring for the past few days. Once she called the counseling service, there'd be no turning back.

"Miss Kirk?" Amber looked up at her youngest student—Katie, a fourth grader. Frankly, she was more gifted and intuitive than most of her students.

"Yes, Katie?" Amber tucked her phone back in her pocket, grateful for the interruption.

"I wanted to turn in my assignment early because we're going on vacation." Katie held out a watercolor painting of a still life they'd been working on. Instead of the typical apple and oranges in the bowl, though, Katie had drawn cartoon figures hiding behind the realistic fruits, peeking out with comical expressions. If Amber hadn't known Katie could do a straight painting, she would have gotten after her for not following the assignment. But this was Katie.

As a kid, Amber had been equally imaginative and didn't always do things according to direction. She'd had one particularly discouraging teacher take a red pen to her perspective drawing and mark all over it showing where the lines ought to have been. She'd almost quit drawing that day. She knew how to draw the perspective, she'd done it before—but her imagination had taken hold of her, and she'd turned her picture into an interior primitive. She hadn't known it at the time, but that was fairly sophisticated for a middle schooler.

Once Amber started teaching art, she'd decided she would never quash anyone's creativity. Guide it, yes, but not try to kill it for the sake of ego.

"I love this." Amber held out the painting and tacked it up on the wall. "It's really imaginative." She glanced at Katie and saw her consternation. "Not what you wanted?"

"I'm not sure on the shading." Katie pointed to the banana with a small boy hiding behind it, sticking out his tongue.

"It's not the shading, it's the highlights. You have to really pay attention to the light. It will make or break a piece." Amber turned to her desk and made a fast sketch of an apple and used the eraser to dramatize the highlights.

"But that's much brighter than it really is."

Amber grinned. "It is. Sometimes we have to highlight things more dramatically to make them seem as real as they are to us in person." She took the eraser and lightened it even more.

"That's too much, though." Katie sounded disappointed in her. Amber squinted at the drawing. She was right. Instead of trying to fix her error, she pushed the sketch away from her.

"You get the idea."

Katie bobbed her head. "I'll do it better next time."

Amber brushed back Katie's hair as it fell from her pony tail. "How about when you get back, you can work on this some more and make it just right?"

"Really? Thanks, Miss Kirk." Katie gave her a huge hug. "We'll be at my grandma's all next week. I'll take lots of pictures."

"Pictures?"

"She lives in the desert, remember? There's all kinds of things with shade and shadow there." She grinned and skipped from the classroom. Amber had no doubt that someday Katie would make a tremendous artist.

As long as life didn't interfere.

The restaurant bustled with activity. Maybe this wasn't such a great idea after all. Too many witnesses. Before she could make her escape, her mother blazed in, sporting a bright pink jacket, turquoise pants, and big gold earrings.

Then again...

Jennifer Kirk was a woman to be reckoned with. At least, that's what she told every one of her real-estate clients. The only proof she needed was owning her own business, Rose Gate Realtors. Never mind that it was a small company—her mother could sell a house a day when the market was bright even if the weather never was. Again, that's what she told all her prospective sellers.

Her mom leaned down and gave her a kiss on the cheek, leaving the sticky imprint of bright pink lips. Amber felt the urge to wipe it off, but resisted while her mother could see.

"Oh, I love this place. The salads are to die for." Jennifer grabbed her menu and put it down again, certain of her choice. Amber kept her eyes trained on her own menu, trying not to meet her mother's discerning eyes. The small café bustled with more and more of the lunch rush. The aroma of onions and garlic streamed from the kitchen, whetting her appetite.

"We've been coming here for ten years," Jennifer urged as she clacked her perfectly manicured fingernails against her glass of water expectantly. "I'd appreciate it if you'd hurry and order. I've got a two o'clock."

Amber motioned toward the waitress and ordered the house salad and clam chowder. Her mother ordered a cobb salad, hold the egg, the ham, the cheese, the bacon, the croutons, and the dressing. Amber bit back a sarcastic remark, dying to know why she didn't just order a chopped turkey salad. But that was Mom. If she could make it complicated, she would. The waitress gave Jennifer a quizzical look but wrote down the order and gave Amber a sympathetic smile.

Once again, she felt secure in her choice of meeting place.

"Okay, spill. Something wrong with your apartment?" Her mother straightened the silverware, glanced at the door, and looked at the couple cuddling at the next table before her gaze fell back on Amber. "I can get you into a house for the same monthly rate, you know."

"No. My apartment's great." And it was. She loved her Victorian apartment in the heart of downtown. The plumbing and heating had been upgraded three years ago. She got to paint it whatever she wanted as long as she agreed to pay a fee if the manager didn't like it when she moved out. Sure, it was small, but she had everything she needed. Now even more than before.

"Then your job. What's happened, sweetie? Are they laying you off? I knew this would happen. Art teachers are a dime a dozen."

"That's not true, Mom. Just stop. My job is fine." Though *that* wasn't true either. Soon, she'd be out of a job.

The waitress brought their food, and they both began to eat—at least, Amber pretended to eat. Her mother took a few bites and put down her fork.

"Amber, the only time you can't eat is when something's gone wrong. Now, I won't take another bite until you tell me what it is." Worry laced her mother's eyes. Jennifer had been her mom for most of her life, and although Amber had been rushed, and cajoled, and sometimes forced to do things she didn't want to do, she'd always been loved. Unconditionally loved.

Amber put down her soup spoon. "I had an eye doctor appointment on Tuesday."

Jennifer gave her a smile. "That's good. The next thing you need to do is get a physical. You never know when your insurance may be canceled these days."

Panic and fear welled up inside her. She had yet to say it aloud. To anyone. Even herself. She swallowed hard. "Maybe sooner than we'd like."

"What's that supposed to mean? I knew your job was in jeopardy."

"Sort of. But not the way you think. Let me get this all out, okay?"

Jennifer took a sip of water and sat straight in her chair, looking intently into Amber's eyes. Amber took a deep breath. Now or never.

"Mom, I'm going blind."

Her mother's face went ashen, and she took another sip of water, tipping the glass and spilling some on the table. She dabbed at it with her napkin, not making eye contact with Amber. "Are they sure?"

"Yes. Very."

Jennifer looked up at her. "How long?"

"How long? Not 'How can this happen?' or 'What disease is it?'"

Jennifer's eyes welled, as Amber expected. But that was it. Something was off in the studied way her mother took the news. And the guilt in her eyes.

"You're not surprised?" Amber leaned closer. "Wait, why aren't you surprised?" Anger and confusion quickly pushed aside the fear, tamped it down, and lit it on fire.

A tear slipped from her mother's eye. "I never wanted this for you. I thought once you were past your teens then the likelihood diminished, and even more so into your twenties." Her voice broke. "Chances were slim."

"Chances?"

"All the evidence suggested..." She stopped and wiped at her eyes with a tissue she'd produced from her sleeve. "It'd be so rare." The waitress came by with more water and looked worriedly between them before her mother waved her off.

Amber shook her head in denial. This wasn't happening. Her mother couldn't have known about this. There was no way. If she'd known, she would have told her. The atmosphere went cold and dead quiet around her as a ringing filled her ears. The restaurant crowd slowed as all their movements became exaggerated and happy, eating as if nothing out of the ordinary had happened. Nothing was happening to *them*.

Her glance focused back on her mother's mouth and the words she was forming. Then, as if someone turned the volume back up, she heard Jennifer's confession.

"When your eyes were fine through middle school, your dad and I decided to stop worrying. We couldn't gain anything by it. We never knew exactly when your birth mother lost her sight." She took a shuddering breath. "When Dad died, I just decided not to revisit the past. I couldn't emotionally do anything else."

She couldn't?

"Wait. My birth mother was blind?" Amber started rapidly twisting the ring on her finger.

"Yes." Jennifer sent her plate to be boxed and asked the waitress to do the same for Amber's. Amber would have protested, but she knew there wasn't a point. She was done.

"And you knew this but never said anything?"

"You need to remember how angry you were at her for giving you up. Years of counseling. We decided to just keep all the information to ourselves. There wasn't any reason to bring up new heartache."

"So you lied." Why did her mother have to bring all that up as if Amber's anger was her own fault? If people would quit leaving her, she could stop being angry about it.

Her mother leaned across the table. "Watch your tongue. We never lied. We just didn't tell you. Any time we tried to explain about your mom, you were livid and near violent in fits of anger. Or have you forgotten?"

No. She hadn't forgotten. The rage renewed itself when Dad died of a heart attack. She'd ripped the arms off her favorite stuffed animal. She'd endured three years of grief counseling after his death. They'd never gotten to the heart of her anger, but it cooled enough to satisfy everyone that she'd recover.

"What about my birth father?"

"He'd died previously. We really don't know anything about him. But his death did force her into giving you up for adoption. She just couldn't raise you."

Amber had always wanted children and a family. If her birth mother had to give her up, what chance did she have?

"I have a letter from her at our bank."

"I ripped that up, remember?" Amber palmed the wetness from her cheeks.

"No. Not that one. From when we adopted you. I saved it in our safe deposit box. For some day."

Amber shivered and pulled her sweater closer. This was some day.

CHAPTER 3

Amber collapsed on her sofa, listening to the traffic passing outside, watching the beams from the sun shift from blazing yellow to an orange-pink haze and sepia. Light flickered around her like she was the subject of time-lapse photography. Her cell phone rang. Part of her would be glad to rid herself of that device. The other part feared what being cut off would mean. She'd get a landline, sure—but what would she use for emergencies? It was like she was heading back to the Dark Ages.

She groaned aloud at the bad pun. The cell phone rang again. Amber extracted it from her pocket and saw Kyle's contact picture smiling back at her. Dinner with Kyle. There was no way.

"Hello?"

"Hey. Where are you?"

"I'm not feeling great. Had a rough afternoon. I'm sorry, but I'm going to have to cancel." She pulled the pillow from under her hip and covered her face.

The line went silent a moment. "Let me bring you something. You've got to eat, right?" She could hear the hurt in his voice. She really should have let him know earlier, but sorrow stole her memory.

"I really need to be alone. Tomorrow, okay?"

"I've got something." He cleared his voice. "I'm bringing you food. Minestrone and breadsticks. I'll be there in thirty." He hung up.

She let the phone drop against the sofa and pushed the pillow against her face, screaming into it until her throat burned. After her fit, Amber straightened her apartment, tossing away empty containers and pushing her laundry into the hamper. Kyle liked everything just so. As she washed dishes, a buzz sounded from the panel near her door. She wiped the suds from her hands on her apron and hit the call button.

"Yes?"

"Emilio's delivers, *signora*. You order the soupa, yes?" Kyle did his best fake Italian accent, and she laughed despite herself. She hit the entry door release buzzer and took off her apron, opening the door just as he arrived.

"Hey." He leaned in and kissed her before handing her the takeout bags. "Sorry you're feeling low."

"Thanks." Amber took the bags over to the table and started unpacking them. He moved to the cabinets and got out the plates, bowls, and silverware. They set the table together in silence. She used to dream of this—a man to share her life with. But when confronted with the worst situation she'd had since her dad's death, she couldn't bring herself to share it with him.

"What's your news?" He sat down across from her and began ladling soup.

Her hand froze on the breadsticks. "That's okay, you go first."

"You sure?"

Amber nodded at him.

"Let's say grace." He bowed his head and thanked God for the meal. She said amen but didn't feel it.

He blew on his soup before taking a spoonful. "I'm getting a promotion."

She grinned. He'd worked hard for that. "Accounting supervisor?"

"You got that right. Maybe I'll be accounts manager in a year or two. The only way to go—up, up, up." He took a triumphant bite of breadstick.

"I'm so happy for you."

"For us." His voice took on a new level of seriousness.

"Us?" They'd been dating for six months, and she'd always assumed there would be an *us* someday...until Tuesday. Now *us* wasn't on her radar.

"Yeah, us." He took her hand. "I wanted to do this right, at our place"—he motioned to the takeout bags—"but I can do it here." He slid out the chair, still holding her hand.

No. He wouldn't. Not now. She watched in horror as he started to go to one knee, but she jumped up.

"Sorry, bad manners. I forgot the drinks." She opened the refrigerator, her voice shaky. "Orange juice or milk?" She gave him goofy look. "I guess I need to go shopping." She really did. Condiments and a rusty head of lettuce were the only things keeping the drinks company.

Kyle sat back in his chair. "Did you have to do that right now?"

"Sorry?"

"It's just that... Look, what's going on?" He put his hands on his legs, propping himself for bad news. Maybe he knew her better than she thought. Than she wanted.

Amber closed the fridge door and took a steadying breath.

"I got some bad news, and it's really hard for me to wrap my mind around it."

Standing, he came and took her hands in his, leading her to the living room. He drew her down next to him on the couch.

"You can tell me, you know. I'm totally here for you."

Amber wiped at the tears already threatening to spill. Why hadn't she called him first? He could have been with her, mourning the loss alongside her.

"Is it cancer?" He squeezed her fingers. "Don't worry. We've got that battle beat."

"No, not cancer."

"Well, what then? What could be worse than cancer?"

"I'm going blind." The words escaped in a whisper. She hoped he'd heard her. He leaned back. His eyes filled with shock. He'd heard. Kyle pulled away from her. Apparently, *that* was what was worse than cancer.

Her hands felt empty, so she grasped them together in her lap, waiting for his response.

"This doesn't make any sense. People don't just go blind."

"Some do."

"But..." He grasped for words and then got to his feet and started to pace. "How did this happen?" His tone sounded accusatory. "What can we do to stop it?"

"Nothing. There's nothing." Tears spilled and she swiped at them, looking away.

"Well, I just can't accept it. God wouldn't do this to us."

Us again. He'd said he loved her that one time, and she'd said it back. But she hadn't been thinking of them as *us* yet. Somewhere along the line, Kyle had jumped a few steps. And God?

"God didn't do this to us. He did it to *me*."

"But we're a couple. I mean, I was about to..." He swallowed. "I've prayed for a wife for a long time, Amber." He went to his knees in front of her. "We both love God. I got the promotion. It's the logical next step." He took her hands in his, leaning his head against hers. "We're in this together, right?"

Were they? Had God brought Kyle into her life right before she lost her sight so she'd marry him and be taken care of?

"I really can't think about that right now."

His eyebrows furrowed. "What do you mean?"

"It's just too much all at once."

"Look." He stood and began ticking off plans on his fingers. "First, we'll get a second opinion."

"I already did."

"Then we'll find another doctor." He dismissed her. "We'll go to the church, and the elders will pray over you."

She wasn't crazy about his church. She'd gone with him for a few months now, but everything felt sterile. Something was missing, but she couldn't put her finger on it.

"Kyle." She reached out to him, but he stepped away.

"No. I won't accept it. We have plans. You have a career as an art teacher. What are you supposed to do if you go blind?" Again, he seemed to be demanding an answer from her. She didn't have one. "And what about kids?"

"I don't know."

"How can you take care of our babies if you can't see?"

Babies? "We're not even engaged, let alone married."

He stopped his pacing. "But you're sure about us, right?"

"I need time to think."

Kyle nodded slowly, his teeth grinding back and forth. "What's there to think about? We're getting married."

Had he actually asked her? He'd swept into her life six months ago, rushing her along the tracks, serious from the get-go. At first she'd found it charming. But now?

"Aren't we?"

"This is hardly the proposal I imagined." She sniffed and grabbed a tissue. No dashing man telling her he loved her more than life itself, no ambiance, no flowers. Just a crushed blind girl desperate for someone to take care of her? No. Not this.

"We've got to roll with this. You'll see. We'll get married, move you into my place, and I'll take care of you. You won't have to worry about anything." He sank down on the sofa and pulled her into his arms. "It's all going to be okay."

Right.

"Kyle, I need time, and you can't force this. And I want a real proposal. Later. Right now..." She pushed him away. "I just need space."

"*Then* we'll get married?"

"I don't know."

"You have to know. God told me we were going to get married."

Anger surged through her. "Did God also tell you He was going to steal my sight from me? Did He tell you I was going to be disabled for the rest of my life? Did He tell you what I was going to do with my career? Because. I. Didn't. Get. The. Memo!" She was in his face, daring him to disagree with her.

Instead of answering, Kyle pulled on his coat and headed to the door.

"Where are you going?"

"I'm giving you space." He didn't look at her. "I'm going to be praying that God will heal you, Amber. He loves you, and He's not going to let us go through this. He doesn't want you to suffer." With that, he pulled the door closed.

Amber's heart raced, rage still thrumming through her system. She'd attended church for the whole of her life. Even when she moved out of her mom's house, she'd continued going. She'd sit in the same row every Sunday, listen to the sermon, attend a Sunday school class, go through all the motions. She was kind, she tried to love others, and she supported missions. She'd done everything right. It sure hadn't gotten her very far.

She moved to the dinette and began cleaning up Kyle's side of the table. As a little girl, she'd imagined being proposed to many times—but it had never been like this. There'd been a man with dark hair and sparkling eyes who loved her for who she was. They'd married in a church in the countryside on rolling hills, flowers trailing in the air as she and her husband ran to the car, laughing. The car—a convertible—would race down a dirt road, covered over with arbors of great oaks, the sun setting in the distance. They'd honeymoon in Australia, see the Great Barrier Reef, swim with dolphins, and go to the Sydney Opera House. He'd hold her hand as if she were a precious gift.

Never in all her life had she imagined her husband holding her hand to keep her from tripping over an unseen object, or fixing her meals, or her being a burden to him. The image brought on a case of chills. Instead of dwelling on her shattered dreams, she loaded Kyle's dishes in the sink, then sat back down and tried to eat. Nothing settled right in her stomach. She pushed the bowl away.

The only thing that sounded good was ice cream. Mint chocolate chip. And she had none.

Instead of crawling back onto the couch, she headed out to the grocery store. Along the way, she watched an older woman pull her belongings in a cart. Amber would need to get something like that. And a cane. Dark glasses so people would know to help her. Or pity her.

Her shoulders sagged, and she tucked her hands into her pockets. She needed to call the number on the pamphlet and meet with the counselor. There were too many decisions to make, and she didn't have any information to base them on. As she neared the grocery store, she saw a young girl and her mother sitting outside with a box. Instinct told her to keep moving by, but she stopped and peeked inside. Wrong move.

Two kittens rolled and mewed inside. One black and one silky brown. Her hands betrayed her and picked up the brown one. It stuck its pink nose into her neck and began to purr. She giggled. For the first time in a week, her heart lightened.

"You can name him yourself." The little girl's lilting voice filtered through to her ears, and warnings went off in Amber's mind. She had no business getting a kitten. Not now. She held the ball of fluff away from her, and it mewed and clambered up her arm and into the crook. She began to pet him, running her fingers through the soft fuzz.

"I've never seen a brown kitten before."

The woman smiled, but she let her daughter do all the talking. "He comes from good parents—our neighbor's black kitty and our Siamese. A Havana brown. We just can't keep him, and we don't want him going to the pound." She handed Amber a piece of paper with a list of things to do when buying a cat. "We also don't want him to go to just *anyone*. You need to agree to get him his second round of shots, and please try to keep him indoors." Her bright, hopeful face shone, and she spoke as if the deal were done.

Amber continued petting the kitten, and he calmed, nestling in. She looked down the list. Shots. Cat box. Litter. Kitten food. Water and food dishes. Brush. Glancing at the grocery store, she knew she could get everything she needed.

Before she realized what she was doing, she nodded. "I'll take him."

"Good. That's fifty dollars."

Fifty dollars? She must have looked surprised because the little girl's eyes narrowed at her.

"I'm sorry, but I thought they were free."

"No, you need to pay for the shots he's already had, and I'm saving for a bicycle."

The mom intervened. "Also, people tend to care more for pets if they pay for them."

That made sense. Amber reached into her purse, but came up empty. "I'll have to get cash out. Can I carry him with me in the store?" Suddenly, letting the kitten go back into the box seemed like the worst idea ever. "I need to make sure we're a good match."

The little girl's eyes lit up. "Sure."

Thirty minutes later, Amber exited the store, complete with a shopping cart, all the items on the list, a sleeping kitten, and fifty dollars in cash.

The little girl wrote out a receipt that had the vet's office number on it and her family's name—the office was only five blocks from her place. "Make sure to take him in a few weeks for his check-up."

"Okay."

The little girl reached up and kissed the kitten reverently. "What will you name him?"

Amber looked down, concentrating on his silky brown fur. "Mocha. His name is Mocha."

"I like that." The little girl's eyes twinkled in approval. "Be good, Mocha."

Amber moved back up the street, Mocha in one arm, the cart's handle in the other, feeling more hopeful than she had in days.

CHAPTER 4

Staring at the phone didn't appear to help. Mocha skittered across the kitchen floor and raced to the couch, all a-fluff, startled by something new. Probably the moth in the bedroom he couldn't kill the night before. Amber had tried to catch it in a bag to release it outside, but all she'd ended up doing was wearing the sparkly dust off its wings. And then it had mysteriously disappeared.

The kitten leapt from the couch and pounced on an escaped piece of kibble. After that, he proceeded to snuffle the floor, searching for tidbits of leftovers and crumbs. He licked up a dust bunny and sat down to ponder the texture, tongue licking out over and over until it tumbled back onto the floor in front of him. He batted at it before moving on. Mocha spied Amber's mug on the table, full of coffee with milk, and started to lap it up before she could move it away from him.

"Oh, no you don't." She laughed as he raced away in guilt. Amber made a face at the leftover liquid, wondering if that was the first time he'd tried her coffee or if she'd been sharing her cup with him all morning.

"I guess I gave you the right name if you like coffee." To distract him, she held out a treat, and he raced to her side, tumbling over the pillows until he reached her fingers. He gently removed the treat and swallowed it whole before settling down beside her. She petted his ears, running her fingernails gently back and forth over his head and neck until he flopped flat, spent from an hour of hunting.

Tiny purrs emanated from him, rumbling against her leg, and she didn't know how she could have lived so long without a cat in her life. Besides, she'd never realized how lonely she'd become until now. It was nice to have someone to talk to that didn't want anything from her except for the necessities of food and companionship.

Amber pulled her phone toward her to check her e-mails. She squinted and turned up the screen brightness all the way. It helped. Some. Four messages from her mother. An e-mail from Shannon. Nothing from Kyle. He seemed to be honoring his promise to leave her alone. She had mixed feelings about that—but mostly relief. Her mind, ever so slowly, was coming to grips with her diagnosis. It felt possible to tell Shannon tonight when they met for dinner, but not anyone else at work. Not yet. The term would be finished in a few weeks, and she'd let them know then. She couldn't deal with the sympathy looks and pity glances.

Leaning back against the sofa, her thoughts crushed her. She didn't know how to apply for disability, how to help retrofit her apartment, how to arrange for rides, or how to learn to read braille. None of that. Her mind spun and her breaths came in gasps.

"Why me?" she questioned aloud. "I thought I'd done everything right." She choked back a sob and decided to take a shower and not think about it right then.

After she bathed, she pulled on a pair of jeans and a blouse, slipped in some dangling earrings, and added a spritz of her favorite perfume—it smelled like roses and cloves. As she put on her makeup, she found herself getting closer to the mirror than before. She looked into her reflection.

"What a mess, right?" Her reflection's eyes filled with tears and agreed.

●————• • • •————●

Amber could see Shannon sitting in a front booth of the bustling Chinese restaurant, sipping her wine and searching her phone. Her flashy black, purple-tipped hair hung perfectly around her shoulders. She wore a loose sweater, which slipped over one shoulder, revealing an intricate, vibrant magnolia flower tattoo that perfectly set off her Asian skin tone. At least Amber knew it was a magnolia from past experience—today it looked like an impressionist painting. Everything was starting to look like that.

Amber plopped down opposite her.

"Hey, you're late." Shannon tucked her phone back in her pocket. "That's not like you." Her black eyes sized up her friend.

"Sorry. I had to feed my cat."

"No way!" Shannon was a lifelong cat lover.

"I know, right? Me. A cat."

"Psssh," Shannon blew past her lips, not quite a whistle. Amber tried not to smile. Her friend never could figure out how to do that. "I can't believe it."

"He needed me." Amber picked up the menu.

"Let me guess—the black little fuzz balls outside Safeway?"

Amber nearly dropped her menu. "The brown one."

Shannon laughed long and loud. Amber ducked her head, hoping they weren't being too noisy.

Shannon fiddled with her silverware. "I saw them out there. Cute little guys. And that girl with the big puppy-dog eyes. I just averted mine and hardened my heart." She took another sip of wine. "Is that your news? I'm so excited to be a kitty-aunt. What's its name?"

Amber's countenance must have changed, because Shannon's tone shifted. "Uh oh." She leaned in. "Food first or news first?"

"Let's order, at least." Amber felt emotion build and needed to change the subject.

Shannon's head nodded in understanding, and she motioned the waitress over. Once they'd ordered she sat back, waiting. Amber suddenly felt like she was making much too much out of this. It wasn't like she was dying or anything. People suffered from cancer. Children starved in India. Really, her trial was nothing on the grand scale of the entire world.

Unfortunately, knowing that didn't make her feel better. It just made her worry about the entire world.

"You know I've been complaining about my eyes for a while."

"Yeah, so you went to the doctor."

"Right. And he sent me to another doctor with a diagnosis that the specialist confirmed." Her gaze locked on Shannon's. "I guess..." She swallowed. "I guess I'm going blind." The words lingered in the air between them, and Amber wished she could take them back. They didn't sound right coming from her mouth. They didn't sound like anything she'd ever say. Right up there with, *I had my oil changed on my Ferrari.* Or *I had the Vanderbilts over for dinner on my yacht.*

A sniffle brought her back to the conversation and the horrible words she'd never imagined speaking but had now said three times.

Tears welled in Shannon's almond-shaped eyes, pain flickered over her features, and she reached out to take Amber's hand.

"Oh no." As she gently held Amber's hand, tears streamed from her eyes. "Oh no. This," Shannon choked, "it can't be. I mean..." She took a breath as if she were drowning. "I'm so sorry." She came around to Amber's side of the booth, scooted in and put her arms around her. Without warning, Amber began to sob.

Amber never got emotional in public, she never cried openly, but here she was, like a baby in her friend's arms. After several minutes, she pulled away and Shannon offered her a napkin to blow her nose.

"How long until it's gone?"

"A few months. The specialist said maybe a year, but I've noticed some dramatic changes in the past few days. Maybe I'm more aware of it, but I don't think that's it. This morning I had every light on in my apartment and it still seemed drab and dim." Amber blew her nose.

"Okay, so I saw this movie about a seeing eye dog. You'll need to get one of those." Shannon could go from emotional to practical so fast that sometimes it was hard for Amber to keep up.

"I just got a cat." She felt like slapping herself for not thinking of that before.

"I don't think they have seeing eye cats." Shannon bumped her shoulder and snickered. "They're not really about serving *others*."

Amber wiped at her eyes and chuckled along. "No, I guess not." She sighed. "It was a knee-jerk reaction to get Mocha. But I really needed him. I don't feel so alone now."

"You've got me."

"So, I've got you and Mocha."

Shannon leaned away. "What about Kyle?"

"Oh." She exhaled. "He's really putting on the pressure to get married."

"I thought you wanted that. A husband, family, the works?"

"Yeah, but not like this. He kept saying how he'd take *care* of me." Amber shivered for dramatics.

"Like overly protective?"

Amber nodded. "The more I told him how I needed space, the more he pushed."

"Okay, well, no control freaks need apply. Dump him."

Shannon had never really liked Kyle. Hers wasn't the objective opinion Amber needed right then.

"And your mom?" Shannon flipped her hair around her finger and began to chew on it—a self-comforting technique from childhood. She noticed right away and stopped before Amber had to remind her.

Her mom. Amber hadn't spoken to her since their lunch. "I'm really ticked at her right now. She knew my bio mom had this disease, but she never told me."

"Crud."

"Yeah."

The waitress returned with their food, and Shannon moved back to her side of the booth.

"So not talking to Kyle, not talking to your mom. Got it."

Amber gave Shannon a grateful smile. She should have called *her* first. Shannon always knew the right things to say. And what not to say.

"I should take you along when I talk to my mom or Kyle. You can be my mediator."

Shannon guffawed but then grew serious. "You know, that's not a bad idea." She put her hands up as Amber began to wave her off. "Not only with them, but from now on, at your doctor's visits. You'll need someone to think objectively and write stuff down. You're too close to this."

"Sure." Amber took a bite of her meal.

"I mean it." Shannon's level tone and narrowed eyes told Amber she did.

"Okay. Will do." They ate in silence for a while. "What do you think about my marrying Kyle?"

Shannon put down her fork. "It's not my life."

"Maybe it's God's will?" Amber held her breath, waiting for the answer, knowing Shannon wouldn't hold back.

"Maybe. But God knew this would happen all along, Amber. Don't put Kyle's ideas on Him. Pray about it." Shannon didn't go to church, but she was very spiritual and talked a lot about Jesus. She seemed closer to God than most of the people at church.

"This whole thing is too much right now." Amber took a sip of hot green tea.

"I get that." Shannon took a bite of her food. "I'll give you a couple more days, but then you've got choices to make. The sooner you find something concrete to hang on to, the sooner you'll feel better."

Amber gave her an incredulous look.

"How long have we known each other?"

"Forever."

"Right. Trust someone who knows you, okay?" Shannon reached over and pressed her hand again. "You know you've got me by your side no matter what, right?"

"I know." Emotions threatened to overwhelm her, so Amber started stuffing Chinese food into her mouth, flavorless as it seemed right then.

An hour later, Amber hugged Shannon good-bye and headed back to her apartment. She closed her eyes after she opened the entry door, as was her new custom, and counted the steps to the mailboxes, then used them to guide her to the rail and up she went.

Once inside her apartment, she looked over the pamphlets Dr. Birkman had given her and tossed them aside. Later. Tomorrow. Instead, she turned off all the lights, changed into her pajamas, and opened her curtains wide. Mocha jumped on the bed, then off to eat and back again. Amber crawled under the covers and stared out at the city skyline, memorizing every light, every shape, until she fell asleep, the kitten purring at her back.

CHAPTER 5

Rubbing her fingers against the pain building at her temples, Amber looked out over her empty classroom. It'd been a long day. More paint spills than usual, two grumpy boys, and a new student who kept crying when she couldn't paint as well as the girl next to her. It didn't help that the room grew fuzzier and more out of focus by the day.

Amber closed her eyes against the stress and tried to take deep, relaxing breaths. Despite her best efforts to ignore the situation, she had more and more trouble juggling her work schedule and her emotional state. Nearly everything reminded her of the impending loss of her sight. The boats on the river, late blooming flowers, waves of weather, shifts of sunlight and clouds, and black sky to blue. All of the things she loved so dearly brought her pain and regret. And resentment.

"Miss Kirk?" Amber looked up at the principal of her school, standing in the doorway of her classroom. Brandon Glass moved inside and pulled a chair near her desk, settling his heavy six-foot frame into the creaky seat and tossing his braided ponytail to one side.

"Yes, sir?"

"I wanted to check on you. Everything going okay?"

Amber felt a sigh escape. She'd been moody and impatient with the kids. She'd snapped at another teacher in the break room. She'd even missed a couple appointments with her independent students.

Maybe she should tell Brandon. He'd keep it close until she was ready to tell everyone else. He deserved to know.

"No, not really." She straightened the papers on her desk. "I'm facing a rather large life change."

"I hope you're not leaving us." He gave her a warm smile that faded at her lack of response. "Are you unhappy here?"

"No. Not in the least." She felt her emotions twist up into her chest, so she began to walk the length of the room, checking windows to make sure they were locked, glancing at supplies, and straightening paintbrushes in cups. "I've been putting this conversation off for a while now, though."

"That doesn't sound hopeful."

"It doesn't feel too hopeful, either." She swallowed hard, glanced over her shoulder, and saw his form stiffen as if waiting to be hit. He was an excellent boss, but he hated conflict.

"Is there anything I can do?"

Amber turned to face him, unable to make out his features clearly from where she was. His graying beard merged into his overalls. Maybe not seeing his face would make it easier. Best to get it over with.

"I've been diagnosed with early onset macular degeneration."

"Oh dear." The words carried over and thudded at her feet.

"I don't really have long before my sight will be gone. I'm afraid"—she choked on her words and cleared her voice to cover—"you'll have to find another teacher to fill my place next year."

He shuffled in his Birkenstocks over to her. "I can't imagine what you're going through. What can I do to help? Have you filed for disability?" The aroma of herbs and turpentine emanated from him, a mix of sweet and bitter.

"I'm not sure how that all works. I need to call this counseling service. There are classes to take. It's all so overwhelming."

He reached out and squeezed her arm. "Let me know if I can help with anything. Why don't you take a week off?"

She could tell by his tone it wasn't really a suggestion. She'd worked for him for seven years. She hadn't always agreed with his methods, but he put the students first. For her, that made all the other incidental disagreements unimportant. He was right. She'd been pushing through this too long.

"Thanks, Mr. Glass."

He gave her shoulder a little squeeze. "I'll see you in a week. I'll take care of your private lesson clients too. I'll reschedule them if they'd like."

She'd still get paid for the time off from school, but not for her private clients. The reputation of the school rode on her performance, though, and she knew how important that was to him.

"That sounds fine." It didn't. Nothing about any of this sounded fine. Every day she was giving up a part of herself and she didn't know what, if anything, would be left when it was all over.

He wandered out after giving her some advice on breathing exercises and vegetable drinks that could help her heal. Amber had done enough research to know there was nothing in the physical realm to heal her eyes—the Internet attested to the evidence of those trying and failing.

Last week she'd found a page with holistic suggestions, eye exercises, and tinctures to mix and take. Hope swirled for a few days and then, after finding no evidence whatsoever of any of those methods working, she felt more depressed than ever. All the advances of the modern age, and not one to really help in slowing this disease. Sure, it was rare and not epidemic on the cancer scale of things, but the disease impacted her nonetheless.

Amber grabbed her things, fumbled with the keys to her classroom, and locked the door. Brandon leased the building out to community functions, and she'd learned long ago that if she didn't lock her room, people from the outside would come in and break her things and steal supplies. The use of her equipment didn't bother her if only they'd clean the brushes and put things back where they found them.

Her feet shuffled against the carpeting as she headed up the dark hallway to the blurry green light at the end guiding her to the exit. She put her hand out and ran it up along the wall, feeling for the breaks, the gaps of the doorways—that empty, floating feeling when she found one. The ever-present scuffling sound of her shoes against the stubs of commercial grade carpeting haunted her. She wondered how long she'd been walking like that, insecure and afraid. Amber lifted her feet, trying to walk like a ninja, without trace or sound, moving over the floor with stealth and confidence. The game lasted only seconds before she heard a sickening thud and felt pain alongside her face. Then blackness.

Her head pounded. As Amber opened her eyes, she could see the shape of a couple of other teachers at the end of the hall, wandering out. They looked back over their shoulders, checking for stragglers. Amber waved at them, unable to gather her wits enough to call out, but they didn't see her lying on the ground, mid-hallway. They flipped the last light switch at the entry and locked the doors.

Darkness enveloped her. She could see the vague outline of an old pay phone jutting from the wall above her. She'd walked right into it, blindsided. Amber lay back, taking stock, wondering how long she had been out. Reaching up, she gently fingered the growing bump on the side of her face. The ache pounded every time she blinked. She pulled her phone from her pocket, trying to read the time, but the contrasting glare blurred all the numbers.

The HVAC system turned off with a clunk, and everything around her went still. She lay and stared up at the blurry grayness of the ceiling tiles, watching the light fade. The sour smell of old carpeting and aging dust filled her senses. A dog barked somewhere outside.

She shook her head. "I can't. I can't do this. I don't want this. No. No. No." Sobs wracked her frame, every muscle contracting until she lay in the fetal position, knees drawn up, arms curled against her chest. Wave after wave of incapacitating grief washed over her.

A key in the door alerted her to another presence, and she took a deep breath, quieting her cries, not wanting to be found so compromised.

"Hello? You here, Amber?" Shannon's voice reached her like the piercing horn of a ship through the dense weather over the river in winter.

She mustered a cry with her last ounce of hope. "Help."

CHAPTER 6

Amber sat in her apartment, ice pack held against her pounding eye with one hand, coffee warming in her other. Shannon handed her a napkin to wipe the tears still betraying her. Mocha jumped up on Shannon's lap and began to knead and purr.

"Well, he's a cutie. I don't remember seeing *him* in that box, so you must have gotten there before me." Shannon scratched him under the chin before he leapt to the floor, off to chase his toy mouse.

"I'm so glad I have him." Amber's voice exposed her desperation. Her emotions turned on her every chance they got lately. She chewed her lip.

"Want to tell me now why you were laid out on the floor?"

"I didn't see it."

"Didn't see what?"

"The phone. The stupid pay phone. Why do they even have one in the school? I don't think it works. Everyone uses cell phones." Except, soon, not *her*. She took a shaky sip of coffee.

"Listen here." Shannon put her hand on her shoulder. "You're not alone in this."

"I know."

"No, you don't. You're not listening to me." Shannon paced the room. She motioned to the piles of clean laundry lying unfolded on the floor near the couch, the sink filled with dirty dishes, the over-full garbage can. "This isn't like you. You're depressed."

"You think?" Amber tried to joke, but it didn't work. Instead, her voice cracked and a sob escaped. If she could stop the crying, that'd be good.

"Oh, sweetie." Shannon sat down next Amber, tipping her chin ever so slightly to make eye contact. "I'm here."

Amber let the icepack slip from her grasp and fall to the floor. "What's going to happen to me?" It was the one question she hadn't dared ask before, but with Shannon, she didn't need to worry about pat answers or empty platitudes.

"I don't know. But we're going to figure this out." Shannon stood before her, arms akimbo. "Where are those brochures?"

"I'm not sure..." Amber knew exactly where they were. And she could tell from Shannon's accusing glare *she* didn't believe her. Her shoulders sagged in defeat. "Under that pile of laundry."

Shannon scooped up the clothes and dumped the pile on the sofa, retrieving the pamphlets about services for the blind. One pamphlet in particular seemed to draw her attention.

"Okay, this sounds like just the thing." She flattened out the glossy trifold and scanned its contents. "This place assigns you a mentor to walk you through the process. They help you do everything from retrofitting your apartment to job training. They'll get you plugged into a support program."

"Ugh. No." Amber turned away from her. The last thing she wanted was some lame support program where everyone went and lamented their losses and whined. That wasn't what she was about.

Shannon sat back down at the table. "Have you ever been blind before?"

Amber's head stiffened to attention, and she glared at Shannon from her good eye. "What kind of crummy question is that?"

"Have you? Because I haven't. And lots of people go blind every year. If the doctor gave you this brochure, then I think it'd be in your best interest to follow up and see what it's about before you shut me and them down."

Amber's chin sank against her chest, her lip quivered, and huge tears dripped down onto her jeans. This wasn't what she wanted. She wanted to go on teaching little people how to discover their art inside. She wanted to live independently and in peace. She wanted to finally get a showing for her work and be discovered by the art world. She wanted to get married someday and have a family—to move through life as unobtrusively as possible. She didn't want to connect with anyone else, or need help, or be... "Crippled."

"What?"

"I never understood what that word meant until now. Crippled. Severely damaged, unable to function, helpless..." More blasted tears.

"Hey."

Amber didn't look up.

"I'm talking to you. Look at me."

"And looking. We use that all the time. *Look* over there, *look* over here, *look* at me. What's to see? What?" She began rocking back and forth in her chair. "Nothing. There's nothing."

Shannon pulled her up, hugging her as she cried. "Now you listen to me, Amber Kirk."

Amber's body shook, her face buried into her friend's shoulder, probably snotting on her.

"Can you hear me?"

She shook her head no. At least she didn't want to.

"Good." Shannon ignored her. "You're going to have a good cry, and I'm going to listen to all of your fears and then we're going to call this place and make an appointment. Do you understand?" It was Shannon's no-nonsense-all-business tone that got stuff done and moved obstacles.

"Do you?" Shannon could be very commanding when she wanted to be.

"Yeah." Amber's face mashed against her friend's shoulder. "I need a tissue."

"I probably do too, huh?" Shannon leaned back, checked her shoulder, and they shared a slight laugh before she handed her a tissue. Amber gave her nose a good blow.

"What would I do without you?" Deep appreciation and sisterly love washed over Amber.

"You've been there for me countless times. Let me be here for you, okay?"

Amber nodded. "Okay."

They sat together, watching the kitten play with a crumpled piece of paper, jump and leap on it, and then bat it to life again.

Shannon's voice broke the silence. "What's the worst thing?"

Amber didn't want to play Worst Thing because *this* was the worst thing. She interacted with her environment through sight and light and an expression of such through her work.

"I don't want to think about it." Amber blew her nose again and sank back into the armchair. Mocha jumped on her lap, and she began to pet him, stroking his back, running her fingernails gently over the top of his head, and fiddling with his pointy little ears. He batted at her fingers and clamped down with his needle-like kitten teeth before he bounded off again.

"Tell me. Come on." Shannon plopped down near the laundry on the couch.

Amber sighed. "I lose my sight."

"At least *try*." Shannon coached her with her hands.

"I live the rest of my life in abject poverty without a purpose and die alone." She'd meant it to sound sarcastic and flippant, but it was true. Every word.

"How likely is that?"

More sighing. "I can't do my art anymore. And I won't be *me* anymore. I won't know who I am." Tears, uncontrollable, streamed down her face. She wiped angrily at them. "And the crying? This has to stop."

"You're a child of God."

Amber's head shot up. "I don't want to talk about God."

"I get that, but one of these days, you're going to have to. He knows you're mad."

"That's right. I'm mad. He gave me this gift." She pointed to her canvases, the stacks of finished paintings in the corner. "I'm teaching kids, loving my job, growing in talent and ability, and now He's taking it away. What's the point of that?"

"I won't pretend to know what's going on here, or to know how to read God's mind. But maybe He's got a different plan now?"

Amber shook her head and wiped her face. "I'm not talking to Him right now, and I'm certainly not talking about Him or His plans."

Shannon waited for Amber to calm down. "Okay, what else?"

"I'll never get married or be able to have kids."

"I won't let you go there. You can't know that. Lots of people with disabilities have families."

"My birth mom gave me up because of her blindness. What would make my situation any different?" Amber pulled Mocha up from the floor and tucked him under her chin.

"You don't know what your birth mom's situation was, so don't put yourself in her shoes."

They went quiet for a while, and then Shannon nudged Amber's foot with her boot. "That's all you got?"

"Yeah." Amber tipped her head back, and the blood pounded around her eye. "My head is killing me."

"You think you should go to the doctor?"

The pain didn't subside even after she held perfectly still. She put a hand to her temple. "Kill me."

Shannon went and got her some ibuprofen and a glass of water. Amber took them.

The phone rang in her pocket. She pulled it out and squinted at the name. Kyle. They'd left things badly, and true to his word, he'd given her space. She tipped the phone so Shannon could see. A dissatisfied expression crossed her face, but Shannon held her tongue, grabbed her coat, and headed toward the door.

"I'm going to go now, but I'll be here early in the morning and we're going to call that number together. Got it?"

"Got it." Amber waved at her as she left and cleared her throat before answering her phone.

"Hey."

"Hey. How are you?" His voice sounded tenuous in her ear.

"Doing okay." She sighed and took a leap of faith. "That's a lie. I'm not okay."

"Do you want me to come over?"

At least he'd asked this time instead of pushing. That was a good sign. "Yes. I'd like to see you." *See you.*

"Great. I'll be right there. Can I pick up anything?"

"No, I'm good." Actually, she needed to go to the store and buy more kitty litter and some other things. But she wasn't going to ask Kyle to do that.

As she waited for him, she made a salad and spooned part of a can of kitten food onto a little plate for Mocha. He sat near her feet, making smacking sounds as he ate and purring loudly. After cleaning up, she sat on the couch near her laundry and then realized what a mess her place was. Part of her didn't care, but the other part still worried about what Kyle thought.

She raced around and tossed the clothes onto her bed, closing the door behind her and hoping he didn't need to use the bathroom while he was there. He'd have to maneuver through scattered papers and piles of towels in her room, and the toilet wasn't clean either.

Shannon was right. None of this was like her.

The door buzzed and she pushed the release switch so Kyle could get into the building.

As she washed the last dish, she heard a knock on the door. Instead of feeling comforted, her stomach knotted. She put on a fake smile.

"Come in." She motioned him toward the couch and shut the door behind him. He held out a bouquet of flowers.

"What are these for?"

"Get well flowers." He gave her a boyish smile that she found hard to return.

"I'm not sick."

"Right. Cheer you up flowers."

Her grumpiness embarrassed her. Instead of apologizing though, she turned to take care of the bouquet. After trimming their stems and placing them in the vase, she carried the wildflower mix to the coffee table.

Mocha jumped up and began batting at the blooms.

"When'd you get a cat?" His tone suggested he should have been consulted.

Amber gave him a smile and shrugged.

"And a black eye?" He brushed his finger over her cheek, and she winced.

"I had a little accident, but it's nothing. I'm fine." She related the story, minus the panic attack and all the crying.

Kyle took her hands. "No more worries about that. I'm here to take care of you."

She pulled away. "I can take care of myself." Despite her confessions to Shannon, she didn't want to be seen as helpless, even if she felt that way on the inside.

"I beg to differ." He motioned to her eye.

"It was an accident. It could have happened to anyone."

"I'm saying you don't need to worry about things anymore. I'm going to take care of everything."

He might have stayed away, but he hadn't changed at all.

"Kyle..."

"I get that this is hard. But I'm trusting God's going to heal you."

This wasn't the first time in their relationship that he'd made her feel as if her faith were inferior to his.

"And I'm not?"

"You've already given up, but I've got enough faith for the two of us. He's got this."

Amber shook her head but regretted it when hammering pain reminded her of the unexpected victimization by the pay phone. Instead of feeling more helpless, though, it spurred her spirit to life.

"My relationship with God is as real as yours." She sat back, away from him. Truth be told, she was mad at God at that particular moment, but that wasn't any of Kyle's business.

"We don't have to get into this now." He backpedaled. "When you join my church, you'll see."

"Who says I'm joining your church?"

"That's what a wife does—she follows her husband."

Amber stood, shaking in anger. "Did I say yes to your proposal? Because I sure don't remember saying yes. What I said was back off." She shoved her hands deep in her pockets.

"Wait, I only meant..." Kyle appeared dumbfounded, but Amber saw things in a clear light, clearer than they had been in a long time.

"We're done." Calmness resonated in her voice.

"I'll come back in a couple days. You'll see things my way."

"You know what I've noticed the most in the past month?" Her voice dipped in sadness, and she moved to stare out the window, taking in the shapes and colors blending under the bright sun in a kaleidoscope of vibrancy and shadow.

Kyle came up behind her. "What?"

"How often we use *see* or *saw* in casual conversation. I'll be *seeing* you. You'll *see* it my way. Can you *see* that? We take it for granted that not everyone does...even if they're sighted." She turned to him. "This isn't going to work. I need someone in my life who can walk alongside me, and you're not that person."

CHAPTER 7

Amber and Shannon sat in the outer room of Tapestry Counseling, amongst older steel-framed chairs with orange seats and a variety of large print and braille reading materials. The receptionist gave Amber a clipboard and a form to fill out, all the text in large print.

"You got that okay?" Shannon whispered to her.

"Yes, thanks."

Shannon could always get her to let down her guard. Amber knew that even once her sight was completely gone, Shannon wouldn't treat her differently or expect any less from her.

"How'd your mom take it that she wasn't invited along today?"

"I didn't tell her."

"Huh." Shannon picked up a magazine.

"Huh, what?" Amber quit filling out the form.

"She's going to find out, you know."

"I know. Somehow, she knows everything. She even knew I broke up with Kyle before I told her." Amber chewed on her pen and went back to writing.

"How'd she find out?"

"She saw him in the grocery store, and he told her I was distraught and he was going to give me time to come to grips with everything."

"Seriously?"

"Seriously." Kyle didn't know when to say *enough*. She did, though.

An office door on her left opened and a man and woman exited, smiling. They headed to the receptionist counter and made another appointment. Another man came into the doorway, flipping through a file.

"Amber Kirk, please." He turned back inside his office.

"Ready?" Shannon nudged her.

"I guess." She entered into a brightly lit office of warm tones and bold Monet prints. She sat down in one of the guest chairs as the man behind the desk shuffled some papers. He had black hair and he wore a green dress shirt. He didn't seem to care at all that there were people waiting in his office.

"Can I have your clipboard please?" he asked her without looking up. So far, he had yet to make eye contact at all. Amber handed her clipboard to him, and he flipped through the paperwork, spending extra time on her health notes. Then he glanced up and his eyes registered a kind of recognition. Amber felt it too.

"I'm Ethan Griffith." He put out his tawny brown hand and took hers warmly. His head cocked to the side, and his crystal blue eyes crinkled at her under his furrowed brows. "You've been here before?"

"No. Have your kids ever taken an art class at the Maxfield School?"

He shook his head. "I don't have kids. No worries, I'm sure we'll figure it out." He scrutinized her face, motioning to her eye. "I hope the other guy looks worse."

Amber didn't explain. She wasn't about to admit she'd run into a phone.

Not noticing his joke fell flat or Amber's lack of an explanation, Ethan greeted Shannon. "It's excellent that you have a friend with you at our meetings. When you go to group support, you might consider going on your own—sometimes anonymity allows people to share more openly, be more honest."

"Shannon knows how I honestly feel about this." Anger,

unexpected and hot, surged through her. How dare he assume she'd attend a group meeting? No one was making her do anything she didn't want to do, and group confessionals were not even a blip on her radar.

"That's great." He gave her a disarming smile, and her anger ebbed away. "Since you're feeling honest, how are you doing with all of this?"

Amber hadn't expected him to get to the point that quickly. "I'm sorry?"

"We don't have a lot of time in this first meeting, and I want to give you as much information as you need to get started. How to do you feel about all of this? Do you feel prepared?"

Her eyes locked with his. "Prepared? To lose my sight? No." She snorted. Colossal waste of time.

"You feel like you'll need help?" He began rummaging through his desk as if searching for something.

"Why else would I be here?" She leaned forward in her chair, outrage building at his bold assumptions and lack of preparedness.

Ethan came up with a pen and a wink. "Thought I lost this. I try to keep a good stock of my favorite pens, but people keep walking off with them." He chuckled as if he'd made a joke and then his eyes glanced over at Shannon and back to Amber. "To make sure we're on the same page, why don't you tell me what you expect Tapestry to do for you."

"This is ridiculous." Amber began to gather her coat and purse. This guy dealt with tragic circumstances and disabilities all day long? Insensitive much?

"Humor me." He motioned for her to stay. "What do you want?"

Fine. "I don't want to be here."

"Go on."

"I don't want to lose my sight. I don't want to need help."

"Okay. So you need help." He spoke calmly, evenly, straight at her as if coaching her to get to the head of the issue.

"I need to know what's going to happen. I need to find a new job. I need to..." Fear threatened, but she swallowed it down. "I don't really know what I need."

"That's okay. I have some ideas, and we'll work from there." He handed her a packet. "Can you read those?"

She glanced over them. There weren't any fancy graphics—simply a list of large print phone numbers and services. Black type on white matte paper. "Yes."

"Those are helpful services that you are under no obligation whatsoever to use. However, I strongly suggest you chose one or two. There is also a phone number for the organizer of the local support groups. She's a great gal, Maggie Floros."

Amber found Maggie's name. She nodded but didn't intend on calling the woman, no matter what.

"I would like to tell you everything is going to be okay, that this will be easy, and you've got nothing to worry about. But I can't." He gave her a soft smile. "What I can tell you is that you aren't alone, and you don't have to feel alone. At the bottom of that list is my cell number. You have my permission to call it, and I'll get back to you as soon as I can."

Okay, maybe not as big a jerk as she thought.

"Further, I suggest activating accessibility tools on your phone as soon as possible and familiarizing yourself with how they work. Practicing now can save you a lot of headaches in the future."

Amber looked up, eyes wide. "You mean I can keep my phone?"

He chuckled at her excitement. "Sure. Here's a sheet of apps that will make it work better. You may want to consider upgrading your phone and transferring data while you still have your sight. Both Android and iPhone have come out with a lot of tools to help the blind. I always suggest buying whatever you feel most comfortable with."

She took the sheet from his hand. "Shannon or my mom could help me with this, I guess."

Shannon laughed. "Your mom?"

"Okay, *Shannon* can help me. My mom is technologically challenged." *To say the least.* How a woman could be so brilliant with real estate and not understand how to use apps other than Solitaire on her phone was beyond Amber.

"The third number on that list is a service that will go through your whole house to help you retrofit things and look for issues that might be dangerous later. Call soon and get on their schedule."

"I'll think about it." Never. As if she'd let strangers in her apartment to rifle through her things.

"I've walked clients through this process countless times. Everyone is an individual, but you all share something in common. You're starting over. It can be challenging and often terrifying, but you can do it." He gave her an encouraging smile that made her believe he knew what he was talking about. "Go ahead and make another appointment for next week. We'll meet somewhere public, like a coffee shop, and talk about how to maneuver those kinds of spaces."

He wasn't going to send her off into the world on her own after all. She felt her neck muscles begin to relax.

Ethan stood up and tripped by his chair. He reached over and grabbed a cane leaning against his desk before putting his hand out toward her. "It was great meeting you both."

Amber recognized the cane, his stance, everything. That day in the rain.

"You saved my life," she blurted out.

"I'm glad to help." He gave her an uneasy smile.

"No, really, a few weeks ago. I'd just gotten my diagnosis and was devastated. I was about to fall onto the street when a car ran the light. You grabbed me and pulled me back before it hit me."

Ethan's eyes widened. "That's right. Wow, you really were having a bad day."

Amber laughed for the first time in a long time, and there wasn't a hint of bitterness left in its wake. "I really was. Thank you."

Their eyes locked for a long moment and then Shannon broke the silence. "Well, we should probably get going."

"Right. Thanks again." Amber stumbled over herself and they left his office, moved past the reception area, and out into the hall to wait for the elevator.

Shannon teased. "Saved your life? You never told me about that."

"I was caught up in losing my sight." She tried to redirect the conversation.

"Yeah, yeah. He's cute. Nice eyes."

Amber didn't give her an inch. "Is he? He was also rude. Lousy people skills."

"He's trying to get you into fighting mode. He did a good job. I like him."

"Ask him out, then."

"Can't."

They rode the elevator to the bottom before Shannon's words registered.

"Why can't you?"

They exited the elevator and headed outside, starting to walk the twelve blocks home. The brisk fall air cut around them but carried the scent of aging leaves, burn piles, and newly lit fireplaces.

"I'm seeing someone."

Amber stopped short. "Who? When?"

"Justin. For a couple weeks now. We've not said anything about exclusivity, but I'm not interested in seeing anyone else." Shannon had never said such a thing before.

"Wow. Why didn't you tell me?"

"You'd recently broken up with Kyle. I didn't want to bring you down." She flipped her fuchsia tipped hair out of her eyes.

They walked for a while. "I'm happy for you. Really. I like Justin." She did. Working with him at the school was a breeze—his teaching methods were similar to her own. Shannon and Justin suited each other, both eclectic and artistic. They could get matching tattoos or gauges in their ears. Her smile faded as another thought brought reality down on her head, chilling her inside.

"He'll probably take over for me at the school." She swallowed hard, wishing she was home and alone so she could process everything. Sometimes being out with lots of people in the bustle of the city made her feel alive—and sometimes it made her feel more isolated and alone than ever. Especially lately.

"He'll be really good with your kids." Shannon no doubt intended it to comfort her, but her words only served to remind Amber of how replaceable she was.

"I'm sure he'll be great." For the first time, she pictured herself saying good-bye to her students. Amber blinked rapidly, turning her head away so Shannon wouldn't notice the hurt in her eyes.

"He invited me to his church a couple weeks ago. I checked it out."

That knocked her out of her reverie. "Okay, wait. Organized religion and a serious guy?"

Shannon jabbed her in the ribs. "Don't overreact. I'm going slow. You know how I feel about church."

"I know. And I know how you feel about God." Shannon loved Jesus more than anyone Amber had ever met. But she couldn't get over what happened.

Amber couldn't blame her.

CHAPTER 8

"How do you feel about that?" The voice echoed in Amber's ears, sending a jolt of helpless anger throughout her. Even as she bolted up in bed, sweat tickling down her neck, the question reverberated throughout her body. Her ragged breath and the kitten purring next to her were the only sounds in her apartment.

A car drove by, its tires sloshing in the rain and spinning wet against the road. Somewhere a few blocks away, the garbage truck was collecting. She glanced at the red LED lights of her alarm clock and squinted against the blurred red splash. She leaned in closer and made out the time. Four a.m.

Sinking back against the pillow, pulling the covers up tight, she forced herself to relax and fall back to sleep. But sleep wouldn't come. Instead, the memories of countless counseling sessions flipped through her mind.

How do you feel about that? It'd been a question she'd pretended didn't count, because no matter how hard she tried to change her circumstances, it didn't do any good. What was the point of *feeling* about anything? It wouldn't bring her father back. It wouldn't have made her birth mother want her again.

And it sure wasn't going to save her sight.

Amber had survived the counseling sessions by pretending and nodding along while agreeing to things she didn't agree with. She drew what they expected, played with the toys the way they wanted, smiled when they smiled, cried when they thought she should cry. Whatever it took for her to get through her thirty-minute session, she did.

Mocha jumped on her shoulder and began kneading before sliding down toward her neck and landing in a floppy heap under her chin. Tiny claws left a stinging trail over her chest, but it was nothing compared to the ache inside. She tried to pet him, but he leapt off the bed, ignoring her.

Abandoned. Over and over again. First by her biological mom and then by her adoptive father, who'd worked himself to death. And then, strangely, by her adoptive mom, who'd thrown herself into work in the name of saving their house from the creditors. And now?

Kyle didn't count—she'd tossed *him*.

But what if she'd not been losing her sight? He'd never actually wanted her—he wanted the idea of her. *How do you feel about that?*

"You want know how I feel?" She whispered at first but then spoke boldly at the ceiling. "I'm sick to death of doing it all right, and it never being enough. Not only isn't it enough, but now"—she choked on the words—"you've taken the one thing..." She stopped. She didn't want to talk to God.

Amber turned over, scrunching the pillow up under her neck, burying her face, trying to quell the ideas before they began. *Sleep, just sleep.* But sleep didn't come, so at six o'clock she gave up and showered, fed the cat, and headed to the coffee shop around the corner from her place.

As she entered the café, tablet computer tucked in its case over her shoulder, she ran into a man. She hadn't seen him at all.

"I'm so sorry." Maybe she needed a seeing eye dog after all.

"Amber?" Kyle's voice. He stood there with a woman. "You doing okay?"

"Yes, fine." She smiled and moved past him. She thought she made out his arm around the woman's shoulders as he passed by.

She'd opened her tablet and was sketching a scene she had in mind to paint. She blocked it out with colors, studying the effect. Now her mind wouldn't let go of Kyle with another woman. Not that she had a say, but it'd been so fast. Once again, she was expendable.

"That's very pretty." Another male voice. She looked up and saw Ethan from the counseling agency.

"Thanks." She should have chosen a different coffee shop.

"Can I join you?"

"I'm actually..." She paused. Why not? She should probably get to know him better anyway. "Sure."

He pulled up a chair, the metal legs scraping against the tile, setting her teeth on edge. She grimaced as the sound cut to her eardrum.

"Sorry about that. I'll be more careful."

"I think I need to have my ears checked." She shook it off, but the sound of metal scraping still seemed to hang around her in the atmosphere. "Seems like every little sound is amplified lately."

"Actually, that will probably get worse before it gets better."

"What do you mean?"

"As your sight dims, your ears are going to take up the slack. I'm surprised it's happening so soon." He leaned closer, and his hazy features sharpened. "Are you noticing any change in your sight?"

Amber chewed the inside of her cheek. "Yes, in the past couple days especially."

"Having trouble sleeping?"

"Yes." She sat at attention. "You mean this has something to do with my losing my sight?"

"Emotional and physical changes can cause a swift change in your perception and sleep habits." His clinical ease put her on edge.

"I'm depressed, you mean?" Figures. *It's all in my head.* Why not? She went back to blocking color, blocking him as well.

"Sure. I mean, wouldn't you be?"

Her brows knit and she lowered the tablet. "What?"

"If you were in your place."

"I...uh..."

"I've never liked comparisons to others. It doesn't seem to work as well as comparing to yourself in any given situation. Listen, if you came up to you and said you weren't sure what was going on, that you couldn't sleep, that you were awakened by mundane sounds, that you were edgy, what would *you* tell you?"

Her lips moved to the side in an incredulous look. "Seriously?"

"Seriously. Give it a try. Counsel yourself."

"And if I do, will you go away because I'm cured?" Her biting sarcasm lately even surprised her. She started twisting the rings on her fingers to release the stress.

"Harsh." He put a hand over his heart, laughing, but then his jovial attitude faded. "Go on."

"I guess..." She stopped. What he said made sense, more than she wanted to admit it. "I guess I'd tell me that..." She paused as he put up a hand. "What?"

"Amber."

"Really?" He nodded toward her, so she continued, speaking of herself in the third person now. "I'd tell *Amber* that the stress of losing her eyesight, her profession, her only means of purpose"—she swallowed and tried to keep her voice light—"was stressing her out and she should probably see someone. Professionally."

He pursed his lips together. "That's a lot to carry by yourself."

"Well, that's what I've got. Myself."

"What about your friend? Or a boyfriend?"

Was he fishing? "Shannon is wonderful, but she's got her own life. I can't expect her to continually drop everything over and over again to help me. She'll get sick of me." Really, Shannon would stick by her through anything. And that was why Amber didn't lean on her as much as she wanted—she didn't want to wear her out. She would, too. Everyone got tired of listening to whining at one point or another. "I don't have a boyfriend. I mean, I did, but not now."

Amber felt a presence near her and looked up. Kyle. He was glaring down at Ethan. Amber took a sip of coffee and ignored him.

"Is everything okay?" Ethan glanced from Amber to Kyle.

Kyle held out his hand. "Nice to meet you. I'm Kyle, Amber's fiancé."

Amber nearly spit her coffee out. "Since when?"

"Since I ran into your mom the other day in the store. She explained how independent you are, and how this whole blindness thing is messing with your head." Kyle started to pull up a chair, rough tile and metal clashing once again in her ears.

"Blindness thing?" Amber's teeth were already on edge, and she could see Ethan's hackles rise as well. "Did my mom call it that, or did you?" She pressed her fingers against her temple, feeling her pulse thump back under them.

"I get that this is bad, but that's no reason to shut me out. I can take care of you." He took her hand in his, but she yanked away. "You didn't see me earlier, did you? You walked right into me. How long do you think it's going to be before you walk into the street and get hit by a car or get lost or mugged? How will you support yourself?"

Ethan, his voice trembling with what Amber assumed was rage, interjected. "Amber is going to be fine. She can, with training, support herself."

Amber nodded along, although she hadn't figured out how she'd support herself just yet.

"Well, she doesn't have to." Kyle took measure of Ethan. "Who are you, anyway?" His voice claimed her as property. She'd had enough. Kyle's smothering, controlling ways were too much for her to handle.

Amber gathered her things together, snapping the lid on her coffee and packing her tablet. She'd find a nice quiet place by the river to finish the blocking and then go home to paint. That's what she should have done in the first place.

"Wait, where do you think you're going?"

She ignored Kyle. "I'm sorry, Ethan. I need to go. I'll call the office again soon." Amber pulled on her coat and headed out of doors, leaving the men behind to figure things out themselves. *The nerve.* As soon as she left the darkened space of the coffee shop, however, the sunlight, so well hidden by the clouds, burst through, and she froze to the spot, unable to see. Her heart beat a wild tattoo. Bodies bumped against her, and her coffee, crushed against her chest, popped its lid, spilling hot liquid over her hand and down her front.

"Ouch." She stumbled against another body, and her tablet flew from her hand. The bag skidded away in front of her and another passerby kicked it. All her work! She had to get her bag.

Another person pushed past her and picked it up.

"Please, don't, that's mine." The desperate tone in her voice frightened her. The panic seemed to affect her vision even more. The shape moved closer, limping and leaning to the side. He handed her the bag.

"It's okay. You're okay." Ethan, his low voice, his spicy cologne, all served to calm her. She reached out with shaky hands and claimed her work. Her life.

She couldn't speak. She felt him brushing napkins down her coat. He reached into his pocket and pulled out a white and yellow packet. As he tore it open, the instant citrus scent of Wet Ones filled the air. He handed it to her, and she wiped her hands. The aroma was overpowering but strangely comforting.

"Whew, I never realized how lemony these things were. My mom"—she choked back her emotions— "used to wipe my face with these after we'd eat out. Words of advice: never lick your lips after that."

"Yuck. Yeah, my mom did the same thing." He took the used wipe from her and picked up her lost coffee cup from the ground. "Can I buy you another?"

"No. I'm fine." Her voice told another story. The last thing she wanted to do was go back in there. Or wait.

"Let me walk with you."

She looked behind her but didn't see Kyle.

"He's busy with another friend who came in as you left."

She wondered if it was the same woman from earlier. Ethan didn't elaborate. She didn't care. She wanted him to leave her alone. It was *her* coffee shop, *her* neighborhood. Kyle had no right to encroach.

"That's for the best, believe me. He's certainly not going to facilitate my new way of life. If you're not for me..." She cut a finger across her throat to demonstrate and stopped, realizing she might be over confiding in someone who didn't really care.

"I get it. That's the way it should be. Always."

"I guess so." They started walking. "I'm glad I found out before things got serious."

"Sounds like things were plenty serious."

Amber glanced in his direction. She didn't know him well enough to tell if he was being judgmental or curious. Or both. They passed a couple on the street, kissing as if the world didn't know they existed. She'd never done that with Kyle. She'd barely felt comfortable holding his hand in public, let alone showing PDA.

"No. At least, not from my side. We'd been dating, but as soon as all this happened," she said, motioning toward her eyes, "he ramped it up. I won't be pushed."

Her parents had never been outwardly affectionate. She knew by the way her mom grieved that she had loved her dad. Jennifer had thrown herself into her job, leaving the occasional real-estate work for more serious commercial findings. She had been at seminars and classes until late in the evening. Amber was left to figure out her grief on her own.

Their walk took them down Front Street, by the river. Ethan paused near a bench, shading his eyes from the sun with his hand, and looked out over the sparkling expanse, the bridge, the busy travelers going from Oregon to Washington and back again.

"It's quite peaceful here." Amber followed his gaze, watching the white blur of sailboats make their way up river, imagining the sea birds dipping and floating into the winds.

"I love it here. I...I come here often." He gave her a soft smile and ducked his head as if embarrassed to reveal this fact to her.

Amber made mental note of the location and decided this would be a good place for another one of her studies. She'd never come to this particular place. Despite the busyness around them, this spot was tranquil. She saw the appeal.

He motioned them on, back up the hill, past the homeless men and women squatting alongside buildings, begging for handouts. Amber stopped to give one a nutrition bar from her pack. The young woman gave her a smile that Amber would carry with her the rest of the day.

"That was nice of you." Ethan's voice broke into her thoughts.

She shook off his compliment. "It seems like no one sees them anymore—they've become a fixture. But they aren't. That girl is someone's daughter. I don't know why she's sitting there in her filthy clothes, in the open air, putting herself—her very life—at risk. But she must have a reason not to be somewhere else." *But for the grace of God.* If her mom hadn't chosen her and she'd ended up in foster care and become a runaway as so many had... Well, who was to say that wouldn't have been *her* sitting there feeling unloved and unwanted? Or Shannon.

"A lot of people would scowl and call them drug addicts and leave them on their own." Ethan sounded like he was quizzing her. She didn't take the bait. Exactly.

"Fine. So she's an addict. Why? Addicts become who they are

to hide from the pain. That's hardly a life they would choose on purpose, even if they have chosen it by circumstance. I wouldn't invite her into my home because that puts me at risk. But feed her? Yes. Give her clothes? Absolutely. Point her to help if she wants it? Every day." Shannon even carried what she called grace packs. They were the size of ice packs, but instead held socks, a toothbrush, several protein bars, a pair of mittens, a comb, and lotion. Inside one sock, she tucked a map to the Portland Rescue Mission.

Her response apparently gave him something to ponder—they continued on their walk in quiet. Before she knew it, she found herself in front of a stand of food carts, and the spicy Middle Eastern food smells beckoned her over. Amber's stomach growled.

"Sounds like lunch is in order?"

Amber felt her face go hot. "Sorry. I was up so early, I didn't really eat much before heading out."

"That's fine. There's a great falafel truck right up the street near the park." He tucked his hand in the crook of her arm and began to guide her. She didn't feel guided. Instead of feeling helpless or controlled or led, she felt...escorted.

"Do you like eastern cuisine?"

"I do."

"Do you mind if I order for you?"

She shook her head. She really didn't.

He moved away from her to the window. "Two falafel gyros, vegetarian style." The man mumbled something, and Ethan paid for their food. Within moments, he handed her a delicious something and a wad of napkins. He escorted her again to a picnic table where a couple and their kids were at the other end.

"Do you mind if we sit here?"

They assured them it was fine. He handed Amber her food as she got settled into her seat, and they began to eat. Heavenly. She made a happy sound and hoped he didn't hear it.

He did. "I know, right? Best thing ever."

They didn't speak again until they were both finished. Instead, they ate and people-watched—or rather, Amber people-listened and pondered the day. Did God know how hard things were getting for her? It was a question that wouldn't leave her mind. She didn't ask Him though. They still weren't speaking.

The colors of the fall oak leaves were brilliant splashes of orange and yellow against the cool blue of the sky. Amber knew the blurring colors were the leaves rustling in the wind, crackling against the setting chill. They shuffled against one another, like the hands of an old person being rubbed for warmth. The beauty of it, even from her limited vantage point, overwhelmed her. It had a message for her. Not all change was scary. She still wasn't sure what she was going to do with her life, or if she'd have to live it alone, but maybe one day someone would come alongside her.

The wind picked up and blew the napkins off the table. She reached after them, but they escaped her grasping fingers. Ethan leapt up, staggering to the side, leaning heavily on his cane, and did his best to gather them together, laughing. "I keep retrieving things for you today."

She took them from his hand and thanked him. "Sorry about that."

He shook his head. "Not a problem." He grinned at her, and then his phone rang. "Excuse me a moment." He moved away from the table, and she watched him as his form meshed into a crowd, until she could no longer pick him out of the bustle of customers surrounding the food carts.

Fear washed over her as she realized she didn't know which food carts these were and which street she was on. How far away was her apartment, and where was the river? She used to be able to look down the street and orient herself. But now?

As fear threatened to overtake her, Ethan returned. He came

closer, his form becoming more recognizable and his face more lined with worry.

"Are you okay?"

She let out a shuddering breath. "Yes. I couldn't see you, and I realized I didn't know where I was."

He sat down next to her. "I'm so sorry." His voice took on the grave tone of someone who really understood—who really was sorry.

"It's okay. I was..." Amber couldn't complete the sentence. *Afraid.*

"There are going to be these times, Amber. Don't store them up. Breathe them out and move on. That's what's going to keep you going, keep you level."

She nodded, took a deep breath, and let the tension go. He gave her an encouraging thumbs-up. "There you go. You're going to be okay."

For some reason, when Ethan said it, she almost believed it. Amber had embarrassed herself in countless ways today in front of him. Normally she'd be beating herself up over her stupidity, scrutinizing her every error. Normally she'd feel ashamed of her imperfections, her weaknesses. Not today.

CHAPTER 9

Amber turned away and sighed as her mother's secretary, Debbie, answer yet another phone and gave her an expression that begged for patience. What had started out in her mind as a justified rant had turned into a deflated kind of frustrated fatigue. Her mother was tied up with a client and more waited to talk to her. On hold.

Amber folded her arms and moved to the window, staring through the frilly white sheers to the busy street one floor below. She ran her fingers over the lace and parted them to see more clearly. The white glare of the sun barely made a dent in the fog. At least she pretended it was foggy out. She let them drop again, moving away, choosing to focus on what was nearer instead.

The modern art in her mother's office used to instill in her a sense of wonder with their bold splashes of oranges, reds, and moody blue undertones. As she moved in closer though, she realized the blurred slashes and pixilated blobs were looking all too familiar. Giving up, she sank into a chair and closed her eyes to wait.

Debbie's pleading voice mixed with the fax machine's whining and buzzing another contract to life. It all echoed into her auditory nerve. She clenched her eyes, and the sounds intensified. What once was comforting white noise now blared, each sound becoming more independent and competing for her attention. Not to mention the smells.

A burnt, metallic coffee aroma permeated the office, growing in intensity with the brewing of a new pot. She expected to hear the fire alarm go off at any moment.

Ethan said this would get worse?

To distract herself, she thought back to that morning's meeting with Ethan at the Tapestry counseling office.

Instead of balking at everything he'd suggested as she had on their first meeting, she had Shannon take notes.

"Write that down," Amber directed.

"I am, okay?" Shannon had given her a look that warned her of crossing a line.

"Sorry. It's a good idea." She bumped shoulders with her, trying to tease.

Ethan smiled. "I gave you most of this in our first meeting. In the handouts. And don't worry, we'll cover it again. They'll cover it in your group, too."

That very word *group* brought up those same unhappy memories of her previous counseling sessions in childhood. All the other kids would sit and talk about their feelings. Except for the one boy she was both attracted to and frightened by. He'd defiantly say nothing when questioned, would scoff when the others answered, and broke the toothpicks from the deli sandwiches into tiny pieces while everyone else spilled their guts.

Amber never shared her real feelings. She'd make things up or agree with the counselor. The boy would always stop breaking toothpicks when she spoke. Then he'd give her a nod of approval when they moved on to the next kid. They were a front in the rebellion, stalwart companions, fighting the battle against parental tyranny. Outside of the group, though, his imposing size and tattoos frightened her. His gruff manor, and the way he cussed at his parents when they came to pick him up, made her uneasy.

One day he'd quit coming back. Months later, she'd heard he'd beaten up his father so badly that the man had been taken to the hospital. The boy had been sent to juvenile detention.

"Group?" She'd pretended not to understand when Ethan asked her again.

"Right, where you can get support in all of this. No one understands what you're going through like those who are also going through it."

Shannon had piped in. "I think that's a great idea. I'll drive you. I can wait outside and write or sketch."

And just like that, she'd been sentenced. The memory of it all made her nauseated and panicky. She could have sworn she heard the clanging of a metal jail door slamming shut. Instead, it was Jennifer slamming the copier's lid and complaining about paperwork.

"Amber?" Her mother's perplexed voice jarred her from her thoughts. "What are you doing here? Is everything okay?"

Amber tried to summon the anger she'd had only moments ago. But for some reason, the thought of that group pushed it all away.

"I'm fine. I can see you're busy." Shaking her head at her silliness, she started for the door. "I'll call you later."

"I'm never too busy for you." Jennifer caught her arm and guided her into what Amber had mentally dubbed the inner sanctum. The hub, the answer to the mystery surrounding her mother's late nights, missed plays and dances, and other important events. The walls here were a pastel lilac, and the artwork took on a decidedly more homelike appeal. The filing cabinets were hidden behind artistic screens and a pot of melting wax scented the air with baking cookies. No real cookies, though—they were too full of calories.

Jennifer motioned toward one cushy armchair across from her desk. Amber sat. The phone rang, and Jennifer answered it, and then asked Debbie to hold further calls.

"Let's catch up. Want to have lunch?" Her mother clearly had lunch at her desk—a bite of a sandwich was missing, a baggie of veggie sticks was opened. Jennifer must have seen her looking. "Oh, that was breakfast. I've got two houses closing, three showings this afternoon, and a bunch of interest in a new listing. It's been one of those days." Jennifer gave her one of her real-estate maven grins.

"I'm glad things are going well for you." Amber admired her mother. She'd always been a hard worker. Successful. At everything.

"I'm sorry things are so hard right now, sweetheart. I was thinking, maybe you could start filling in here in the office. You know, where I could help you if you needed it." Her mother shifted gears from professional to caring mom so fast, Amber didn't quite follow. Work in an office? Then her mother's eyes narrowed.

"Oh my heavens, what have you done to your face?"

Amber reached up and pulled her bangs lower to conceal the bruise she'd gotten from what she'd started thinking of as the wall-phone-incident.

"I'm fine. I walked into an object at school." The complete explanation sounded so stupid in her head, she couldn't imagine relating it aloud.

"Well, that confirms it. You need to be somewhere where I can help keep an eye on you." She could hear the I-told-you-so tone and the ramping up of reasonableness and argument in her mother's voice.

"No, Mom. I appreciate it, but no." It's what Kyle wanted to do—keep her close, protect her. Control her.

"Well you can't sit around your apartment and hope things get better. Kyle told me you're at odds with everything. He said you were disoriented when he saw you the other day at the coffee shop, that you dropped your tablet, that your apartment's a mess, and that you were wearing mismatched shoes."

The shoes seemed to be the part that worried Jennifer the most. Not that she'd bruised her head or dropped her computer. However, Amber latched onto another idea first.

"Wait. You've talked to Kyle since then?"

"Well, sure I have. It's not as if *you're* calling me. I figured that's okay since you're engaged."

"Wait, what?" The blood pulsed in her ears. "We're not engaged."

"Kyle told me you were but wanted to keep it low until things settled." She motioned to Amber's eyes. "It would have been nice had *you* been the one to tell me."

Amber ignored her mother's tone. "You mean until I'd lost my sight entirely."

"Yes, because it's just too much at once. He's so sweet, willing to wait to announce it like that."

"Stop."

"And you can imagine how comforting it's been to know Kyle will be there for you." She leaned closer. "You know, when you were first diagnosed, I kept picturing you all alone out there, in the rain of all things, lost. Now I can picture you with him." Jennifer squeezed her hand as if to say all was right with the world.

Nothing was right. Anywhere.

"Mom, I broke up with Kyle. Please don't talk to him again." Amber stood, gathering her things, doing her best not to drop anything or trip over an unseen obstacle.

"When did you break up?"

"When I told you I did. Weeks ago." Kyle hadn't any right to talk to her mother or hang out in Amber's coffee shop.

"So my calling him and suggesting we all meet for lunch was a bad thing?" Her mother let the last word hang.

"I'm leaving."

"Amber, wait."

Amber headed to the door but suddenly couldn't find it. There were two shapes outlined. Right or left? The last thing she wanted to do was stomp triumphantly into the bathroom. Her hands shook with rage and fear. She couldn't even storm out of an argument like she used to.

"Which one?" she demanded.

Her mother sighed. "He seems like a really caring guy. Whatever he's done, I'm sure he's sorry."

Spinning around, her fear absorbed, she gave her mother all she had. "It's hard enough losing a part of myself every day without you or Kyle reminding me how helpless I'm going to be. Without you worrying about my well-being as if I'm going to end up destitute and alone. I've got an excellent vision-loss counselor, a support group, job training. All of those things."

"I keep thinking how your birth mom could barely take care of herself..." Jennifer trailed off, leaving Amber to jump to her own conclusions.

"That was decades ago, Mom. People are more open-minded about hiring employees with disabilities."

Her mother's blurry expression and silence betrayed nothing.

"I don't want your pity."

She heard her mother's gasp and decided to leave before either of them said anything else they'd regret. Amber made for the door on the left, hoping it was the right choice. It was. She charged from the inner room, past an aghast Debbie, her mouth agape in mid-sentence on the phone, slammed the door, and headed toward the outer door and the steps in front. Too fast again. The sunlight flooded her eyes, washing everything out like overexposed film, and she lost her footing, catching her elbow on the rail right before she tumbled down the steps.

A scream from inside the building told her that her mother saw the whole thing. Her pounding left leg and the knife-like pain shooting to her knee told Amber it was most likely broken. Her mother racing outside, shouting panicky orders into her phone at the 911 operator, demanding they rush an ambulance, told her she'd most likely be spending the next several days in the hospital.

Spectators came and gave less-than helpful advice, standing over her, gawking. Amber lay back against the gritty cement, fed up with sensory mysteries and interfering people.

Why even try anymore?

CHAPTER 10

"You've really got to get to that support group." Shannon walked into Amber's hospital room, canvased in bright flowers, with a bunch of get-well balloons to add to her collection. The last thing Amber wanted was backward advice, especially when her head and knee were trying to outdo each other in the pain department.

Amber moved to sit up. The room spun, and it stirred her stomach with the same spoon. She clenched her teeth. "Well, if it hadn't been so uncharacteristically sunny out, I wouldn't have fallen in the first place."

Shannon's eyebrows went up. "It was overcast all afternoon."

"I said what I said." Amber flicked her hospital sheet and looked away, out of the window and into the glare. A definite glare, like yesterday on the steps.

A baby cried in the distance. In the bed next to her lay a woman who'd had some kind of major surgery. Amber heard the nurses talking to her husband when she'd been asleep. For now, the woman flipped through some file folders and messed with her phone, tapping away at something.

"Why are you in the baby wing, anyway?" Shannon straightened the heavy blanket over her legs.

"I guess they ran out of bed space. Lots of stuff going on in the ER." Amber wasn't looking forward to listening to screaming infants all day. And night.

"Well, no worries. Your mom is out there pitching a fit with the head nurse about moving you to a private room."

"Oh no."

"What? You expect her to do anything different? She's your mom."

"No. Not that." Of course her mom would be using her powers of magical persuasion to override whatever got her in way. It was what she did best.

"What then?"

"Mocha. He's all alone. You've got to go feed and water him and give him lots of petting. I don't want him to think I've abandoned him."

"Got it covered. I grabbed your keys earlier from your mom while you were in surgery—she's got your purse, you know. Anyway, I already know the little fuzz ball. He's great." She sniffed. "Changed the cat box too. You know, you've really got to get your laundry put away, or he might..." She paused to make a stinky face.

"Yeah. Everyone's real concerned with my laundry lately. Kyle, my mom. Probably her secretary too. Unfolded clothes, a pox on humanity."

"Hey." Shannon took her hand. "It's me, okay? I'm not after you because your place is a mess. I'm trying to keep the kitten from a bad habit." She sat down next to her. "What's really going on?"

The room spun a different direction this time as she tried to concentrate. The pain meds were doing their job but good. "I have a torn tendon." Her words mushed at the end as the sleepiness built.

"Not any longer. The doctors fixed you up. You're lucky you didn't break your neck."

"What's that supposed to mean?" Amber pulled her hand away and crossed her arms.

"You're acting like superwoman, that's what. You've got to quit trying to handle this on your own."

"I'm going to counseling."

"That's not enough. He's a preparation counselor. He's not going to talk to you about your feelings."

"I'm talking to you."

"I'm not blind. You need to talk to someone who gets this. I don't."

"Fine then." Amber looked away.

"Look at me."

Amber didn't.

"You're not serious." Shannon's voice told Amber she was treading dangerously close to the edge.

Instead of backing down though, she kept her eyes focused on the far wall. She didn't want to be admonished. She didn't want to be reminded. She wanted to be as alone as she felt.

"Okay then." Shannon stood and pulled on her jacket and left.

She left? Amber turned back to see her bedside empty.

Shannon really left. *Perfect.*

Another baby down the hall began to cry. She'd never get rest at this rate. Her head pounded, her eyes ached. She needed to sleep. A group walked by holding huge teddy bears of pink and blue and a balloon with blurred words on it. The woman next to her started to sniffle and curled into a ball.

She tried to ignore her and was almost asleep when her mother arrived. More flowers. The biggest, gaudiest bouquet of lilies she'd ever seen. Weren't lilies for deathbeds?

"Oh, you poor thing." Her mother put the flowers on the table nearest to Amber's head. The overwhelming sweetness of the orange and gold flowers—her mother's favorites, not *Amber's*—triggered another bout of nausea.

"I'm painting bright yellow stripes on those steps as soon as I can find a contractor to do it. And I'm installing a sturdier handrail. I feel awful. And this room. They say they can't do anything about it. Overbooked. Like a hotel? Ridiculous." Her mother paused and glanced over her as if remembering Amber was in the room. "How are you?"

"The doctor was able to repair the tear and I have no broken bones, so I'll be out of here tomorrow and then off to physical therapy."

"Tomorrow?" Her mother sounded so hesitant. "I hoped you'd stay."

"Nobody wants to stay here, Mom. I'll get no rest. I want to be in my own place with my own stuff."

"Alone."

"I've been alone for most of my life." Her voice sounded edgy, cutting. First she'd taken off Shannon's head and now her mom's? This wasn't like her.

She was about to apologize when her mother asked, "Do you want me to call Kyle?"

"Never. Don't ever call him. He's not who I thought he was. I don't want you to ever speak to him again." *Wow. Where'd that come from?*

"Amber." Her mother paused, pressing her lips together and squinting at her as if sizing her up for sale. Was she too ruffled? Did she need a coat of paint or a complete remodel? "I'm going to let you rest, okay?" She gathered a few things together and straightened the flowers. "I've added this to the prayer list."

"This?"

"Well, and the other thing." It was as if Jennifer couldn't say it.

"My blindness."

"Yes. We're praying for your healing."

Amber swallowed hard. She'd been praying. Well, in between bouts of anger. Sort of. And what had that gotten her? Tossed down the stairs.

"I'm not sure I'm on His good list right now."

"I wish you wouldn't talk like that. He's not Santa Claus." Her mother frowned at her. "I'm going to go. I can see you're out of sorts."

"Mom..." Amber started, but stopped. She really did want to be left alone. Lately, all she craved was peace and quiet. She didn't need to be constantly reminded of her own weaknesses and helplessness either. Her mother gave her a sad look and shook her head as if it were too late to make amends now.

"I won't be made to feel guilty over this, Amber. It was an accident, pure and simple. You need to think about your attitude."

"Why can't someone else feel bad for a change? Why is it always me having to bite my tongue and say the right thing and never show how I feel?"

Her mom sighed and headed toward the door. "I've got your purse—you really can't trust these places for security." Before Amber could protest, her mom left and the woman in the next bed started to cry again.

"You okay?" Amber whispered, hoping she hadn't heard her, not really wanting to get involved with anything. She was desperate for solitude.

"Why would they put me in here?" The woman's voice filled with anguish.

Amber took stock of her. "What do you mean?"

"Nothing. Leave me alone." Her sobs were full on, and she turned away.

A nasty thought filled Amber's mind, and she caught herself rolling her eyes. Then, a wave of disgust roiled through her. What was wrong with her lately? She used to be kind to others. She used to be empathetic. If people would quit telling her how to feel about losing her sight, things would undoubtedly improve. A baby cried loudly in the next room. Not to be outdone, the woman in the bed stepped it up a notch.

Amber pushed the call button. Maybe the woman needed pain meds or antidepressants. Whatever it was, she hoped she'd get them. Soon. Maybe the nurse could bring her some ear plugs. *Ugh.* Amber's own bitterness soured in her mind. She'd become hateful.

A nurse came. "How are you feeling?"

"Can you check on her?" Amber motioned toward the sobbing woman.

"Sure." The nurse moved over. "Mrs. Wellington? Is there anything I can do? Are you having any pain?"

"Get me out of here. Put me someplace else."

"I'm so sorry. I wish I could. As soon as a bed is free, I will."

"Anywhere, please." The desperate tone knocked all selfish thoughts from Amber's head.

The nurse shushed her and then pulled the curtain, giving Mrs. Wellington more privacy. Amber tried not to listen, but her super-power ears were kicking in overtime.

"It's not right. I've had a hysterectomy. I'll never have babies of my own now. Please." Her voice broke off again.

Shame and anger filled Amber. She agreed, that woman should be anywhere but there. As the nurse passed by to leave, she waved her down. "If I'm assigned a room first, you give mine to her. Okay?"

"That's not how it works, but I'll keep that in mind." The nurse gave her a patronizing look of mock understanding and headed toward the door.

"Could you close that door at least?" Amber couldn't begin to imagine how her roommate felt, although she understood about plans hoped for and lost.

The door closed and the outer hall sounds faded. The woman's cries subsided into a barrage of nose blowing. Amber was about to fall asleep when the woman cleared her voice.

"Thank you." She spoke through the curtain.

"It's okay. I hate hospitals."

"Me too."

After that, the noise died down and Amber thought she heard

her breathing deeply. She glanced at the flowers and cards near her bed. They'd arrived fairly quickly. Someone from the school had been notified, probably by Shannon, and the place activated. Her coworkers were good at organizing for parties, private and governmental. She wondered how many of them knew of her impending blindness. That'd sure rate a higher-than-normal flower cascade. Amber figured there should be about two bouquets at most for a knee surgery. But blindness? Yeah, better get that girl a bunch of colorful things to look at while she still could.

Amber stared at the ceiling, noticing the misshapen tiles, the out of place cracks and holes, the emptiness and darkness on the other side.

In her heart of hearts, she wanted so badly to talk to God. And that annoyed her. If she hadn't been sure before that He was real, she was now. You couldn't *not* talk to someone who wasn't there. In fact, His presence seemed stronger, surer than ever before.

Then why was she still so mad and getting angrier by the day?

"I'm not really talking to you, right now, if you've noticed. But could you please help this lady, God?" She sighed. Being out of communication with the one person she talked with on a daily basis was exhausting. If only He hadn't let her go blind.

CHAPTER 11

The elevator jolted under her, knocking Amber off balance, and she bumped into the wall. The car rattled at the very shift of her weight. She held her breath, clenching her eyes closed and willing the machine ever upward as it inched slowly toward her floor.

Having been able bodied until now, she'd never given the elevator a second thought. Now she wondered if she shouldn't have checked it out better when she moved in. Thank goodness she had an elevator to ride in.

Suddenly everything wavered around her, the sound of scraping, the clang of metal. Wait, she didn't have an elevator in her building. Did she? The brakes shuddered, and then the car twisted down and around, and she was tumbling through space like a pumpkin bouncing inside a dryer. The car was suddenly full of water and floating bits of flowers. A lily went by her. Her crutches floated past her in slow motion. She screamed, but only bubbles came out. Over at the old-fashioned control panel, a man appeared, mouth agape in burbling laughter, cranking the machine faster. It was Ethan.

She bolted awake, her heart thumping, head aching. Amber scanned her hospital room. Her roommate had been moved, or so she assumed from the empty bed. Or had she moved to a private room? Everything was a blur. Over to the side of her bed sat Ethan, eyes fixed on a magazine.

Right. He'd come to drop off some paperwork and a suggestion for someone who did physical therapy for his other clients. Someone nearby her house. He glanced up at her.

"Did I wake you?"

Her heart still thumped, but she kept her voice calm. "Uh, no." She pulled the covers closer. "Why are you still here?" Her cutting tone should have embarrassed her. Despite getting sleep, her anger had returned, tenfold. So had her headache.

"We were in the middle of a conversation, and you dropped off. I have a meeting scheduled in a while, so I grabbed a magazine and stayed. I hope that's okay?" She could tell that while he was secure in giving advice about blindness and therapies, he wasn't comfortable in dealing with people in general.

"Yes. Sorry." Amber lay back against the pillows, drawing up her covers, suddenly self-conscious of her appearance. She ran her fingers through her hair, trying to work out the tangles. Those pain meds were sure doing a number on her. She hadn't felt self-conscious until now. Maybe she should call the nurse in to give her another dose.

Ethan pointed to the paperwork on the tray near her bed. "Those are two different physical therapists near your address. I took the liberty of calling, and either can see you. They're both really great people."

"If they're both so great, why didn't you pick one?" Did every word emitting from her mouth carry a dagger?

Ethan sat back a minute, and Amber heard him sigh. She was sighing at herself.

"Sorry. I can't seem to say anything right lately. To anyone. Go ahead and escape while you can." She turned toward the window, staring out at the gray expanse of sky, above the pink and gold setting sun. The light cast through over her bed, shining on her. She imagined the warmth she might feel outside. But then rain pelted the window and the sun faded, blocked behind the new storm blowing in.

She shivered.

"I don't want to escape, but I do have a meeting." He moved closer and she saw his smile, always genuine. Guess it was easy to smile when everything was going your way.

"I suppose now I'll need to get a second cane. I'm going to be crippled two ways." The words, heated with disappointment and frustration, tumbled out before she remembered whom she was talking to. That did it. The smile faded from his face.

"Take care, Amber." He limped away, leaning on *his* cane, and was out of the room before she could form an apology. How hateful she'd become.

She lay in defeat against the bed, wishing with every ounce she could disappear. What was left for her? The elevator dream images returned, the terror, the helplessness. The fear of being out of control hung around her as if in a shroud. The ridiculousness of it all compounded. If her building had an elevator, this was the kind of nightmare that would keep her from ever using it again.

The doctor came in, a wizened man with graying hair and a kind face. He checked her stitches. She looked away, not wanting to see the discoloration and ugliness—it was bad enough in her imagination. "Looks really good. I don't see any reason you can't go home tomorrow. I'll want to see you in my office in a week, and then we'll take it from there." He saw the physical therapy papers on her table. "I don't know this one, but I can recommend Dr. Blythe. Samantha did her internship under me before she decided to go into physical therapy."

"Thanks." A lady physical therapist sounded like a good bet. "Are stairs okay?"

The doctor raised his eyebrows at her. "Stairs?"

"My apartment has a couple flights."

"Uh. No. Not yet."

Her heart sank at his words.

"Well, then, when?" The sense of freefalling washed over her again.

"As soon as you can safely use crutches."

"Oh, if that's all, I can totally use crutches." Amber had used them for quite a while after a sprain.

"Even so. That's a lot of stairs. I'd feel better if you got your information directly from the physical therapist."

Amber groaned. "I'm fine. Really."

The surgeon looked at her, long and low like the principal at her high school. "Make sure you have someone with you. I don't want you tearing out those stitches. Or falling and messing up your other leg."

"You'd make more money."

He glared. She deserved the glare.

"Got it." At this point, she was willing to ask a total stranger to watch her rather than call Shannon or her mother. Or anyone else.

"Did I see Ethan coming from here earlier?"

"Yes. He's...helping me. He gave me the recommendations." How did the doctor know Ethan?

"That makes sense." The doctor nodded.

It did? Before Amber could ask, a nurse came in and interrupted them, handing him Amber's file. "I'll see you next week, then." He made a note on her chart and left. The nurse followed him and then came back in.

"The doctor will release you under the condition that you choose one of the physical therapists today, call them, and tell them your plans. And make sure they know you're sight challenged."

"Going blind, you mean?"

"Yes, that's exactly what I mean." The nurse gave her a scowl. Score total for the day: one hurt, one glare, one scowl. "Listen here. Being blind is one thing. Recovering from knee surgery is another. It's highly unlikely you'll recover from a broken neck, and Dr. Porter would hate to have wasted all that time and energy on the knee of a dead girl."

"You're blunt." Amber felt her face go hot.

"Sounds to me like you could use some bluntness. And the next time you insult Ethan, you'd better be ready for me."

The temperature in the room went up another ten degrees. "I didn't mean..."

"No? Well, it's time you started to mean something, young lady. I've heard you verbally attack three other people today. You've got a lot of work ahead of you. Quit trying to do everything yourself. Lean on someone. You couldn't start with better than Ethan Griffith."

The nurse gathered her charts, handed Amber the papers and the phone, and walked out, closing the door behind her.

Ire built. Who did that nurse think she was? But the steam compressed quickly and released in a flood of her own self-pity and tears. As she wiped them away, she took a shuddering breath and made the call.

The next morning, Dr. Samantha Blythe dropped by her room with a set of crutches. Amber wasn't sure what she expected, but the beautiful redhead not much older than herself surprised her. She wore jeans and a navy long-sleeved top.

"You must be Amber." She held out her hand and moved closer. "I've talked with Dr. Porter, and he's explained your situation."

"My increasing blindness and the two flights of stairs?"

"Exactly. We're going to go to the therapy room and practice on a set of stairs there this morning. I want you to go back later this afternoon and then again this evening."

"But I'm checking out."

"I looked up your insurance, and you can stay another day. I think that's best. I want you to feel safe using these things"—she lifted the crutches—"in any situation. Have you started using a cane yet?"

"You mean for the blind?"

"Yes. Not everyone does, or even has to. Some like it, some don't."

"You help with that kind of therapy too?"

"No, not directly. But I have some blind patients. And Ethan was my patient."

This perked up Amber's ears. "I didn't know that."

"Yeah." A strange shadow passed over Dr. Blythe's face and then she changed the subject. "Now or never?"

Amber sighed. "Now."

CHAPTER 12

Amber reached the top step, sweat trickling down her face, arms shaking, wrists pounding, and armpits burning from the pressure of the crutches. Her good leg bent and pulled her up onto the landing, and she hobbled to the wall, gasping for breath. Down the hall toward the glowing light, her apartment waited. Desperation filled her.

"What do you think you're doing?" Kyle's reproachful voice surprised her from behind.

Clenching her eyes closed, she kept moving. "I'm going to my apartment."

"What's so bad about asking for help?" She heard him mounting the steps behind her, coming up quickly.

As if to betray her, her hands dropped her bag of personal items she'd packed at the hospital. He grabbed it and headed past her before she could stop him. As she reached her door, he held out his hand for her keys. Against her better judgment, she handed them to him.

Amber fully expected an angry kitten, a messy apartment, and the aroma of an overused litter box. Instead, she smelled something pleasant and lemony, and all her laundry was folded on her bed. Mocha lay curled on the couch, some toys next to him. A bouquet of fresh flowers sat on her table in a canning jar. She loved flowers.

Shannon did this. A mixture of thankfulness and guilt raced through her. She hadn't spoken to her since the hospital incident. At least, that's what she called it in her head. She was collecting a lot of these experiences lately. She also owed Ethan an apology. A big one.

Kyle's voice cut into her self-recriminations. "I'm glad to see you've got your place under control. I was worried about you for a while. It's good to know this thing isn't getting to you." He came over and put his hands on her shoulders as if he had a right.

"This *thing*?" Amber moved back and crutched her way to the couch, falling into place next to Mocha, who stretched and began kneading her good leg.

"Yeah, the whole blind thing."

Something twisted her in her back. "What can I do for you, Kyle?" Amber scratched Mocha and acted as if she hadn't a care in the world.

"I wanted you to know there's no hard feelings."

She blinked up at him. He mistook her amazement at his obtuseness as an inability to see him, and he moved into the chair nearest her. While she was having trouble making out his features, she didn't need him to sit next to her so closely. She scooted away, and he took it as a clue to move closer onto the couch.

Kyle took her free hand in his. "Listen. I know I've said some really dumb things. I only wanted to protect you. I mean, Amber, look at you. You need my help more than ever." His tone, his gentle touch, and the lagging hangover of her meds lulled her into a false sense of comfort. Maybe...

"Please, don't shut me out. I want to be with you through this." He pulled her into his embrace and the familiarity of him, his warmth, made every one of her objections seem silly. *I can't face this alone.* Even as she thought it, a still small voice reminded her she was never alone. She turned away from it.

Kyle caressed her hair, ran his hand down her back in tiny circles, massaging her worn out muscles. "I love you, you know that, right? I only want what's best for you. I didn't mean to push you away."

Amber nodded into his shoulder. She did know that, didn't she? A flash of an image from the coffee shop last week went through her mind. Kyle was with a woman, and he didn't seem eager to be seen by Amber. And then when the woman was gone, he'd acted jealous and overbearing. Amber shoved the doubts aside.

"I think we should get married right away. You can move into my place, and I can get the best PT guy on this for you. You'll be back up on your feet in no time."

"That's okay, I've already got a PT person. I really like her."

"You'll like mine better." He dismissed her again. It was then that the fatigue-induced haze lifted and she realized she was in the arms of someone she shouldn't be, listening to him once again insist on marriage and imprisoning her in his house.

"But you've never had a PT person. Ethan recommended Samantha highly, and I really like her. She's the one who got me home early and ready to be on my own."

The atmosphere around Kyle shifted. "Ethan?"

"My blindness counselor. The one helping me adjust to all of this and get set up with services and classes and training. At the hospital he said—"

"How did he know about your accident?" His tone went from curious to suspicious.

"I'm not sure." She'd never asked Ethan. She'd only demeaned him.

"But he was with you at the hospital? You didn't even call *me*." Now he'd turned accusing. This wasn't like him. Or it never used to be. "You were with him in the coffee shop, too. Spending a lot of time together, aren't you? Don't forget, we're engaged."

Amber leaned back. "I told you, Kyle, I don't want this pressure. And we're not engaged."

A blaze of anger even Amber could see flashed in his eyes.

"It's what's best for us. Your mom agrees. Why are you being so stubborn?"

Her brain prickled to life at the hint of danger in his tone. Mocha leapt from her lap and hissed at him.

"Kyle, I think you need to go."

He ignored her. "You can't take care of yourself like this, Amber. Soon you'll be completely blind. You can't even walk down the street without knocking into people. Once we're married, you'll move into my place. I'll even let you keep that cat." Kyle chuckled, but it sounded hollow and false. In all their time together, he'd been happy—maybe overly so—and careful. Attentive, saying all the right things at all the right times. But since she'd put him off, that sweet side was masked. Could it be it'd never been real in the first place?

Her heart thudded, as if her subconscious could tell something was incredibly wrong. Amber shifted toward her crutches, to move away, but before she could, his grip on her hand tightened.

"You asked me to be patient, and I have been. We're right for each other, you're my soul mate, and I'm not going to let you out of this engagement, Amber." His voice frightened her, but then he lightened again. "I've been talking to my pastor. He agrees we couldn't pick a better time for our wedding. Right now, before your sight is gone entirely, while you can look on the flowers and decorations and guests with your artist's eye. Now is best."

The phone rang. She reached for it in her pocket.

"Do you really need to answer that now?" He chuckled again, but she didn't see the joke. "It'll wait." He held her hand down.

She had never wanted to answer her phone more. Instead of obeying him, she reached into her pocket and began to hit the button. Kyle's hand gripped her knee in its brace, and she gasped in agony. The phone skittered away and Mocha chased after it, batting at it with each ring, perplexed.

"Oh gosh, I'm so sorry." He went to the floor before her. "I didn't realize that was your bad knee."

It took a few seconds for the words to make sense through her pain. Kyle had gone from irritating to frightening. Her mind raced for a way to get out of there, but with her knee out of commission and her arms worn from a day of hobbling around, there was no way. How had this man she'd dated gone from overly kind to intimidating so quickly?

"I'm okay. Really. I'm tired." Her mind raced, trying to find a way, an excuse to get him out of her place.

God, help. She inwardly cringed. Going to God only when she was desperate for help made her feel like a coward. Especially when she'd shut Him out for the past couple months.

"I'll get you some ice. When you tear your ACL, they recommend lots of ice." He moved into the kitchen, opening her fridge. "No ice?"

How had he known about the tear? Had her mother told him? "Maybe you could get me some?" She could get him out and—what then?

"Sure. And I'll pick up dinner. You've got nothing decent to eat in here at all."

"You don't have to do that." She didn't want him spending any more money on her. Nothing to obligate her to talk to him again. Nothing.

"I love taking care of you. Besides, my job is going really well."

"Right, your promotion." She acted interested.

"Actually, that fell through." He shrugged. "A misunderstanding. Something happened in Hawaii that my boss completely misconstrued. I'm working it all out. I should have that promotion in no time." His voice was slick, cool, nonchalant. But Amber wondered what could have happened, and whom did it happen to?

Her phone rang again. This time she lunged for it and scooped it up, nearly falling off the couch in the process. Mocha skittered into her bedroom and darted under the bed.

She was never happier to see the photo of Shannon's face light up her phone.

"Hey. Thanks for calling."

"I wanted to check on the cat. And make sure you got home." Shannon's cool tone told Amber she was still miffed.

"Sure, that sounds great. Dinner? That's so sweet of you. Can you bring extra? Kyle's here."

Kyle went around, searching in her kitchen for something, opening and closing the cabinets. Then he went into her bedroom. All the hair on the back of her neck rose to attention. He came back, with a pad of paper and pencil that she kept in her desk drawer, sat at the table, and started writing.

"Kyle, *dumped* Kyle?" Shannon's voice went on alert.

"Yep, that's right." Amber's singsong voice went unnoticed by Kyle.

"You want me to call the police?"

"Uh." Did she? He hadn't really done anything wrong. She just didn't want him here. Ever again.

"I'll come now with food. Then we'll figure this out. I'm bringing Justin."

"Great, see you soon." She lay the phone down but didn't hang up. Kyle came back in with a cool towel.

"Here you go. That should help." He folded it into a plastic bag and put it on her knee. The kindness had returned to his eyes, but she didn't trust him this time. "I've got a list of things you need." He held up the paper he'd been writing on. "I'll head to the store, too."

"Actually, you know, I'm super tired. Maybe we could continue this another day?" She leaned on the arm of the couch as if to signal him to leave.

"Not too tired for Shannon, though?" He motioned toward her phone.

"Yeah, actually, I'll call her and let her know." She gave him a weary look, willing him to go. Instead, he stood staring down at her with an indiscernible look.

"Sure. How about tomorrow?"

"I'll have to let you know."

A knock on the door surprised them both. No one buzzed anyone in, but instead of being annoyed, relief flooded her. Shannon couldn't have been that quick.

"I'll get it." Kyle headed to the door. He peered out the peephole. "Some guy with a lot of tattoos."

"Does he have black spiked hair and gauges?"

"Yeah. Who is he?"

Amber shifted on the couch, feeling relieved. "Shannon's boyfriend."

Kyle looked over his shoulder at her, disapproval etching every line of his face. "You really need to find better friends. This guy's a thug. No Christian girl should be hanging out with him. Not even Shannon. No worries, though. Once we're married, you'll have my friends."

The subject of Shannon was sacred territory. No one in her life had stood by her like Shannon.

"Let him in." Her voice sounded commanding in her own ears, and she could see by Kyle's widened eyes, it did in his, too. Instead of dismissing her, though, for some reason, he unlatched the door.

Justin pushed past the door and sized up the situation. His worried expression landed on Amber. "You okay?"

She nodded.

"Why wouldn't she be?" Kyle put out his hand to shake Justin's, a congenial and welcoming look on his face. "I'm Kyle. I can't remember if we've met." Amber had never noticed before today how well Kyle lied.

Justin ignored Kyle's hand and took a deep breath to respond, but Amber interrupted him. "Get out, Kyle. Don't come back. Don't call me, and don't contact my mother."

Her words took a minute to register with Kyle. Justin, on the other hand, clenched his fists, ready for a brawl.

"Wait a minute." Kyle put on his most disarming smile. "I know we've had our disagreements, but you can't throw away our relationship like that. It's your fear and pain talking."

"I will admit I'm in pain, but I'm not afraid. And I'm not throwing away anything. From my side, there wasn't much of a relationship to begin with."

Kyle's countenance shifted, and the energy in the room filled with a palpable rage, but she could see the shadow of a smile plastered on his face. "I'll call you tomorrow."

"If you do, I'll call the police. You're not to contact me or my mom or my friends. You're not to come by here anymore." If she needed to file a police report, she could use Justin as a witness. Amber pulled herself up on her wobbly foot, bracing against the crutches, looking as determined as she could. Her eyes were tired and she couldn't see all of his features at this distance, but she needed to make it clear, he wasn't to ever come back again.

He opened his hands as if begging for money. "I told you that God wants us together, Amber. You can't go against His perfect will."

Maybe a couple weeks ago, he might have swayed her with his talk of the Lord's will and plans and how well he knew Jesus. But right then, even as angry as she was at God, she knew full well that Kyle didn't know Him at all.

CHAPTER 13

"You're serious?" Kyle's voice, jagged and dangerous, cut through his teeth.

"Very. Get out. Don't come back." Amber pointed to the door.

Kyle crumpled the list in his hand and threw it across the room. He yanked his coat from the chair, toppling it in a loud thump on the floor, and slammed the door open so hard that the doorknob embedded into the sheetrock of the wall. Leaving it open, he tore down the hall.

Justin went over and pulled the door free of drywall, and dust cascaded to the floor. After wiping off the handle with his hand, he closed the door and flipped all the latches, each click making her a tiny bit more secure.

"Does he have a key?"

Amber shook her head.

"He could and you might not even know it. As soon as Shannon gets here, I'll head to the hardware store and get you a new deadbolt."

Anger pounded in her temples, and she tried to speak but instead started crying. Justin came over and patted her shoulder awkwardly. They both jumped at a knock on the door. Justin looked through the peephole and visibly relaxed. "It's Shannon."

As soon as Shannon came in, she raced to Amber's side and held her while she cried.

Justin shuffled behind them. "I'll, uh, head to the hardware store.

Be back in a few. Shannon, lock this while I'm gone and don't let him in if he comes back."

Shannon disengaged herself from Amber and locked the door. She paused at the hole in the wall.

"Did he do that?"

Amber could only nod. She'd never seen Kyle so enraged. Until today, she'd never seen him angry at all.

"Well, you're not staying here alone, that's all there is to it. I'll take the couch. Once Justin is back, I'll go get my stuff."

Somehow, Amber found her voice. "No, I can't let you do that. Once Justin changes the lock, I'll be fine."

"Whatever. I'm staying." Shannon righted the chair and picked up the crumpled paper. Then she retrieved the broom and dust pan and swept up the mess. "You need to call the police and report this, so there's a record."

"He was angry. This wasn't really like him."

Shannon didn't respond right away. Instead, she went on cleaning and then came and sat down next to Amber.

"I haven't had a good feeling about him from the start—he's too happy." She shivered.

"What, you don't like happy people?"

Shannon pursed her lips in thought. "I like real people. People that put on that salesman type attitude? I don't trust 'em."

"He says he's a Christian."

"When people try to sell Jesus, I trust *them* even less."

Amber sat quietly for a while. "Aren't Christians supposed to be bubbly and happy?"

"Bubbly? Maybe. Twenty-four seven? That's phony. We've all got trials and hardships, Amber. God never promised we'd have an easy time on this earth, and anyone who sells a version of Jesus promising you that life's going to be all flowers and sunshine once you accept Him as your savior is a liar. In fact, I'd go so far as to say, your life might get harder once you align yourself with Him, because the devil really wants a bigger team." She sighed. "False teachers come in all shapes and sizes. So do abusers." The last sentence was pointedly said.

"Abusers? Kyle never touched me." Her knee begged to differ.

"But he scared you and manipulated you. And he used God as a guise to do it. Stay away from that man, Amber. He's no good."

Amber shook her head. Had she misjudged Kyle's intentions from the beginning? She didn't know.

"You saw how he acted when you turned him down. He's not listening because you're not telling him what he wants to hear. Don't let him in here ever again. Promise?"

Amber promised, but at the same time, she couldn't grasp the events of the day. It all seemed ethereal and remote. She felt herself slipping sideways.

"Let's get you to bed." Shannon went ahead of her into her bedroom and pulled back the covers. "You need to use the bathroom before you lie down?"

Nodding, Amber hobbled into the rest room. When she came out, her bed was full of fluffy pillows and Mocha waited for her. The bedroom door was almost entirely closed with enough room for Mocha to squeeze out when he tired of playing nap with her. Amber smiled and crawled in, falling asleep as soon as her head touched the pillow.

A while later, a buzzing sound followed by hammering filled her ears, and she woke to a dark room. Her heart thudded, and she wondered if Kyle had returned, if the encroaching darkness was nighttime or if the blindness was winning faster than she'd expected. She pulled her alarm clock close and saw that it was only seven at night. She'd been out four solid hours.

She heard the high-pitched shriek of power tools. Justin must be fixing her door. He spoke to another man, and Shannon laughed.

Amber pushed herself to her feet, slid the door closed entirely, and went into the bathroom to clean up—there was no way she'd see them in this condition. She sat on the edge of the tub and pondered how she'd take a bath. If the faucet was on the other side, she could leave her knee elevated and get clean that way, but that wasn't going to happen. Plus, she'd probably get stuck down there and Shannon, or poor horrified Justin, would have to lift her out. She opted for sticking her head in the sink and washing her hair. Easier said. She smacked her head multiple times on the faucet.

"Seriously? As if this wasn't hard enough already." She gritted her teeth and continued, cupping handful after handful of water over her head to get the soap out. She nearly slipped twice and tossed a towel on the floor. That'd be just the thing—break a hip. After taking off her soaked shirt, she sponged off everything else and put on deodorant.

Pants were another thing altogether. She opted for her sweats that had the lower knee cut-off. But underwear? That was tricky. Leaning down, she looped one leg hole over the end of her walking cast and then got her other foot through the other. They were so pulled out of shape, she knew they'd fall down after she got them up. A tearing sound told her the elastic wouldn't survive this kind of treatment again.

Grunting and rolling from side to side on the bed, she nearly fell off. Sweat broke out over her body. Her heart pounded and breath came in gasps like she'd raced up twenty flights of stairs. Good thing she wore that deodorant. Her T-shirt was easy. She brushed her hair one last time and prepared to leave her room. Amber tipped to the side, the fatigue from all the activity clobbering her with invisible hammers. She leaned against the door a moment, composing herself. Sliding back the pocket door, the three in her apartment turned and welcomed her. One of them was Ethan.

She was doubly glad to have cleaned up.

"Hey." She waved past her crutches at them and hobbled to the living room.

"Sorry if we woke you. Got the door finished." Justin showed off the new deadbolt, locking and unlocking it.

She squinted. "That looks really nice." Amber caught a whiff of something cooking and glanced at the kitchen.

"I made a hearty beef and veggie stew." Shannon knew how Amber loved soup when she wasn't feeling well. "Let me serve you some."

Amber limped to the table. "I'll wait for you guys to finish. We'll eat together. That is, if everyone can stay." Her comment was pointed at Ethan.

"I don't want to intrude. I called earlier when you were asleep, to remind you of our appointment in the morning, and Shannon told me a bit about what's been going on. So...I brought this for you." He motioned to a binder on the kitchen table. "There are some handouts on the service dog offerings in our area. And an application along with some other things. A dog would be great protection for you too."

"That's really nice of you." Especially after how she'd behaved. She saw he was leaning extra heavily on his cane, and her own knee throbbed in empathy.

"No trouble. I figured you wouldn't be making our appointment." He started moving toward the door.

"Please stay." She wanted to apologize to him but didn't feel she could in front of Shannon or Justin. "We've got enough, right Shannon?"

Shannon tried to hide her smile. "Yeah, plenty. I need Justin to run me to my place, but if Ethan's going to be here, then I won't worry." Shannon grabbed her sweater.

"Oh, I couldn't..." Amber started, wondering how such an easy invitation to dinner had turned into something uncomfortable and complicated.

"That's fine." Ethan smiled. "I'm done for the day anyway." He pulled out a chair and sat at the table. "I'll show you the brochures while we wait."

"I'm ready." Justin cleared away his tools and came over to hand Amber the shiny new key. "I rekeyed the knob lock, too." He'd put a little decorative cap on the key as well, one that was bumpy with a painting of a house. She'd pick that out from her ring easily. She gave him an appreciative smile.

"I put myself through art school as a locksmith's assistant. Paid good." He grinned. Shannon motioned for him to leave with her.

"I'm going to grab some rolls, too, and a few more groceries. I'll get my things and we'll head back here."

"You don't have to stay the night. I'll be fine."

"Really, having just been released from the hospital, it's a good idea to have someone with you for a couple days. Not to mention this thing with your boyfriend." Ethan motioned to the newly repaired wall.

Both Amber and Shannon spoke at once. "He's not my boyfriend."

"He's not her boyfriend."

Ethan shrugged. "Okay, well with this guy. It's a good idea."

As Shannon and Justin headed through the door, Amber studied the patch on her wall, nearly invisible aside from the paint being wet. She smiled, glad she had people she could count on. As Shannon closed the door she said, "And don't worry, I took a picture of the damage so we can put that in the police report too. And a copy of the estimates of what it cost to replace your locks and repair the hole." She waggled her fingers in Amber's direction and closed the door.

Ethan smiled. "It's good you've got such loyal friends."

"I've known Shannon most of my life. She's been by my side for a long time."

"She and Justin seem like neat people." He fiddled with the flowers on the table and then opened the folder and rifled through it, looking for something. There was more than just a couple pamphlets inside.

"My—" She stopped and thought for a moment. "I mean, Kyle didn't care much for their appearance."

"In what way?" Ethan seemed truly baffled.

"I don't know." Frankly, if she'd met Justin on a dark street corner at night, she might be worried until he flashed his toothy grin at her. But Shannon's changes had been so gradual, she'd never even thought about it until Kyle objected. She'd gone from second piercings in her ears, which she and Amber did at the same time, to matching hoops on both upper ears, a nose ring, more hoops, tattoos, colored hair. It was all part of her expression and the appreciation of beauty and adornment that spoke privately to her.

"There's the seeing eye dog school. I think you should make an appointment as soon as possible to get acclimated while you still have your sight. I hope you don't take this the wrong way. Your gradual loss is a blessing."

"Some blessing." The cynical bitterness, swept away by loving friends, came whooshing back in, nearly taking her breath away with her own anger.

"Hear me out, okay?"

"Fine. But I won't *see* it your way."

If Ethan heard the poison in her tone, he ignored it. "That's a good one." He chuckled. "You've got a chance that most people don't. They're either born without sight or lose it in an accident."

"And?" Nothing he could say would make her feel better about this. Nothing.

"And you have the chance to see whatever you want before you sight goes." His enthusiasm confused her. He had his sight, so why was he animated and excited?

"Yippee."

Anger flashed in Ethan's eyes, and the tips of his ears went red.

"You're acting like a spoiled child. You've got a chance where so many don't. Take it." He sounded like someone ordering her rather than making a kind suggestion.

"And do what?" Her voice softened.

"You're an artist, right?"

"For now." Angry again.

He waved off her objection. "Don't 'for now' me. You're an artist. God made you to appreciate the beauty of things around you and to interpret and share that beauty with others to show off His grand creation. Truth?"

She'd thought so until two months ago. She couldn't find the words to answer.

"You have the chance to see everything you're not going to see again." He pulled out a clean sheet of paper and wrote *Sights She Must See by Amber Kirk* at the top.

"I don't have the money to go traipsing off around the world." She sniffed. "I barely have enough money to pay you for your services. I'm about to be an unemployed disabled person. I probably can't even afford one of those helper dogs."

He shook his head. "You don't have to see it all in person. But you could see some. And if not in person, videos of it. Look, don't give up." He reached over and squeezed her hand. His squeeze wasn't anything like Kyle's. He wasn't trying to change her mind for his better, but for her own. "There are assistance programs for service dogs, so don't go there either." He waited for her to speak, pen poised at the ready.

Something in his eyes, the excitement in his tone, wore her down. It was like the hope he carried around with him was sloughing off on her. She relented.

"There are these blue caves around this island in Greece I've always wanted to see. And I want to swim with the dolphins. I'd like to head out to the high desert and watch the sunrise." Her voice grew wistful and a terrible sadness descended on her, regret washing through, casting its black, shadowy fingers on every good idea.

"Keep going." He pulled out a handkerchief from his pocket, handing it to her. "Don't worry, it's clean."

She dabbed at her eyes and caught a trace of his spicy, woodsy cologne. It reminded her of her dad and the cozy way they used to sit together, watching old movies and eating peanuts. A new wave of grief pushed over her.

"What's that face?"

"I miss my dad."

"He'd dead?"

She nodded. "For a long time now. He always said we'd go ocean fishing. He never took the time off to schedule it, though. And then he died."

Ethan wrote *ocean fishing* on the list.

"I can't go fishing."

"Why not?"

"I get seasick."

"But you want to?"

Amber thought about it. Why not? "Yes. I'd love to be out there on the expanse, feeling the roll of the ocean under my feet, the wind whipping around my face, and the sea spray."

"Not really to catch anything?"

She frowned. "No. I like God's ocean creatures right where they are. I don't even like the taste of fish. Oh." She stopped and took a glorious breath. "Whale watching. I'd love to go whale watching."

He put a line through the fishing one and replaced it with *whale watching*. "Now that's something we can do."

She liked that he'd said *we*.

When they were done, there was a list of twenty things written down that she'd like to experience. A knock on the door announced

Shannon's and Justin's return. They all enjoyed fresh fluffy rolls and hearty stew, and she laughed at silly jokes.

For the first time in two months, she laughed.

It wasn't until hours later, when she lay in her bed listening to Shannon snore softly from the other room and Mocha purring at her own back, that she realized she'd never apologized for the thoughtless things she'd said to Ethan.

She'd do that when they crossed paths again. In her mind's eye she saw the word *sunrise* on her *Must-See List*. In two weeks, barring any more accidents, she would ride east with Shannon and Justin to camp in the high desert. They'd intended to only watch the sunrise. But now, a new plan formed in her mind.

CHAPTER 14

Justin climbed into his tent, giving them a last look. Well, at least giving Shannon a last look. "Good night, ladies. See you at dawn."

Shannon waved at him, and Amber snickered and jabbed Shannon in the ribs with her elbow.

"Shut up." Shannon moved away, mumbling something she couldn't quite make out but she'd definitely touched a nerve. Amber bet if the sun was still out, she would have seen Shannon blush. It was fun seeing her friend, who'd practically taken a vow of singleness, fall for such a great guy.

Amber shivered against the cool desert air and zipped her hoodie closed, pulling the drawstrings tight and nearly dropping her crutches in the process. She'd been on them for nearly three weeks, but they still flummoxed her. Shannon doused the campfire with old coffee and grounds, filling the air with the aroma of burnt toast and something elusive Amber couldn't quite discern. An earthy, bitter smell that took her back to mornings when her father would rise early on Saturday and work on a project in his garage. Sometimes he'd invite her along.

Shannon climbed into their tent, motioning for Amber to follow.

Amber attempted a side crouch, maneuvering her healing knee the best she could, and knocking herself under the chin with her crutches as she climbed through the opening. She collapsed back against her air mattress with a whoosh and fumbled into her unzipped sleeping bag. Sweat broke out across the back of her neck. Who knew getting into bed could be so hard?

She sighed aloud. Somewhere, deep down, tomorrow frightened her.

"You okay?" Shannon zipped the flap closed and faced her.

Talking about it didn't seem like the best idea. "Not canoodling with Justin tonight?"

"Canoodling? Who says that?"

"The Brits." Amber turned off the overhead lamp.

"You watch too much television."

"Not for much longer."

"Hey." Shannon's tone dropped.

Amber didn't respond.

"You can pull that garbage with someone else, but please don't try to joke me out of this thing. Okay?"

Amber shut her eyes. "Okay." She went still, hoping Shannon would fall asleep instantly. No such luck.

"You nervous for tomorrow?" came her friend's sleepy voice in the darkness.

Swallowing hard, she could only nod. Then she realized Shannon couldn't see her. "Is that dumb?"

"No, not dumb. I get it."

Shannon usually did. Which reminded her of a conversation they still hadn't had. Amber was never one to avoid an apology, but the shame she felt at her behavior kept stealing her words.

"About the hospital." Amber chewed her lip, searching for the right things to say.

"I told you to forget it."

Amber reached up and switched on the lamp again, making them both wince against the brightness. "I don't want to forget it. I was a creep."

"It's over."

"Can you lay down your cooler-than-thou attitude and let me apologize, please?"

Shannon's eyes narrowed at her. "What's that supposed to mean?"

"Let me say I'm sorry."

"Fine." Shannon waited.

"I'm sorry."

"Good. Now turn off the light."

"Fine." Amber switched off the battery-powered lamp and lay back against her air mattress. Every time she moved or breathed, the air in the mattress seemed to breathe along with her. Shannon's mattress matched it, echoing louder and louder. The wind rattled the tent flaps and sent debris peppering across the outside. She pulled her bag tighter and dug into her sweatpants' pockets for a pair of ear plugs.

Sometimes they worked. Sometimes they'd drown out the sounds. More often than not, though, they'd amplify the beating of her heart. Each thump reminded her of the seconds passing into minutes, into days. Days before she'd lose her sight. Anytime now, really. She'd open her eyes in the morning and it'd still be night. Forever night.

As a little girl, she'd closed her eyes and wandered around her house, bumping into walls and giggling, trying to get from the kitchen to her room and back. Didn't most kids? It was a game. Sometimes she'd carried food, and sometimes she'd end up in the wrong room altogether. But then she'd opened her eyes and there were her things, the world, right where she left them. Nothing to fear.

Amber turned on her side and counted her heartbeats, trying to let her mind wander, but it didn't do any good. The thumping grew louder and faster until she tugged the plugs from her ears. Her breathing slowed, and rather than fight it, she let the night sounds in.

They were one of three groups camping in the loop. All the other campers had apparently gone to bed, because she couldn't hear any chatter. The hiss of sand being chased by the wind increased. An animal skittered by, rubbing the tent. Then the scrub grasses outside shifted. The smell of pine and earth filtered through the tent wall. She pictured the desert in her mind, the dry crumbling ground, the river off the trail they'd seen earlier, cutting through a barren but colorful landscape. So much beauty.

Why had it taken so long for her to take time to go camping? There were always excuses—good ones. Things to do, a day to relax, because camping was such work. Packing and shopping and setting up and cooking. Hiking. After working with kids all week, the challenges, the triumphs, the mess and tears, she needed downtime. This was some good downtime, though. Something she'd always wanted to do.

Tomorrow she would hike and search and absorb, like the ground absorbed the heat of the sun, bearing up under the relentless winds. She closed her eyes, imagining riding such a wind, letting it carry her along to someplace else. To be *someone* else.

The alarm on her watch went off, and she silenced it. Time passed much faster than she'd expected—somewhere along the way, she'd gotten a couple hours of sleep. She'd thought about having Shannon see the sunrise with her, but now that the moment was here, she needed to be alone. She reached into the corner of the tent and grabbed a flashlight and her canvas and paints in her backpack. She unzipped the tent, each tooth of the zipper clicking in her ears, but apparently not loud enough to wake Shannon. Crawling through the opening, shoving her crutches ahead of her, her stiff leg caught on the inner flap, and she more fell out than made a graceful exit.

Groaning in pain, she clamped a hand over her own mouth, waiting to see if she'd be caught, but all she heard were the sounds of Shannon shifting in her sleeping bag and Justin snoring away in his tent.

A sense of guilt washed over her at leaving her best friend

behind, but she also knew Shannon would understand this. She closed the tent and flipped on the flashlight, trekking to the cooler for a can of iced coffee and a bagel, stashing them in her pack, and then heading to the rest room. The scrape and grind of her boot and the walking cast, and the drag of the crutches on the parched earth echoed around her in the still predawn. She tried to imagine what a restless camper might think if they heard her. She sounded like someone dragging a dead body. How apropos.

After using the toilet and cleaning her face in the frigid water of the bathroom sink, she got her bearings, seeing the first hint of light over the plain before her. She found the trail and started out, glad the snakes were still in their burrows. Rocks skittered away as she kicked them, and the occasional something shifted in the scrub near the trail. A group of bats dove above her, chirruping their echolocation calls, catching insects. She'd always admired bats for the way they survived, their cute little fingers, their fuzzy little wings. Their resilience.

Blind as a bat. Except they weren't. They could see but had been blessed with an extra measure to find food and make their way. If only. She pushed away the jealousy that threatened and refocused on the task at hand.

As Amber topped the hill, she found the folding chair near the log she'd set up the day before, her easel tucked safely under it, wrapped in a sheet to protect it from the sand. She scanned the set up with her flashlight, wary of dangerous invaders. A small scorpion teetered away, and a race of shivers went up Amber's spine. As much as she loved God's creation, there were some creatures she had little use for. Snakes and scorpions and centipedes found themselves lumped together in a category best avoided. And mosquitos. Oh, and yellow jackets. No one needed those.

She unfolded her easel, unpacking her things, setting it all out. Amber had always routinely put the same colors in the same place on her palette, and now she appreciated that ritual. She squeezed tubes of cadmium yellow, cadmium red, raw umber, cerulean blue, Phthalo green, titanium white, and ivory black into quarter-sized mounds in a semi-circle. She ran her fingers over the hair paintbrushes, feeling the soft and coarse bristles. She turned to the sky and the promise it held of a new light, a new day.

Without realizing she was doing it, Amber began to hum "Morning Has Broken," and tears blurred her vision for a moment. She hadn't heard that song for years—the old tunes were out of vogue in church these days—but it had been her favorite hymn as a child. The imagery it brought to mind still flashed in her memories. The harsh fabric of hard pews beneath her, the banners hung so precisely on the wall, high above the congregation, near the organist as she dramatically played. The cross. The stained-glass bits molded into pictures that came blazing to life as the sun hit the windows.

Then, as if rising from her imagination, the first rays of dawn broke over the hill, and she began to paint in large, dramatic swaths. The gray-blue of the sky creased with pink and orange and coral reds. Slips of ragged white clouds emerged, and desert birds filled the air, competing with the last of the bats for the nighttime insects. Sounds of life rose around her. She could have sworn she heard the desert flowers shift their faces toward the life-giving light.

"Mine is the sunlight, mine is the morning," Amber sang past the ache in her throat. The sunrise blazed to life under her brush. Flowers dotted the landscape, and she swiped in a spindly, thirsty pine.

Her brush hovered over the pine, and her eyes watched the clouds. The vapor there couldn't be enough to satisfy it, but somehow, the pine found enough liquid to survive. The Provider did what He did best. And it hit her. If He could provide for this lonely pine, He could provide for her needs too.

"I'm sorry." Her voice trembled. "I'm sorry." She sobbed. "I've been so angry."

She couldn't say anything more yet. Instead, she caught the glow of the sun as it poured its radiance over the earth, chasing back the darkness. It lit on the flowers, the ground, the tree. Not the enemy, scorching the moisture from their beings, but life-sustaining, nourishing.

Two hours passed. Amber breathed in the last of the cool air, clearing her lungs and filling her with a peace she'd not realized was missing. She sipped at her coffee and ate her bagel, tossing a crumb here and there to some ants. As she finished her painting, she heard footsteps grinding up the path behind her, followed by a gasp of pleasure and surprise.

"That's your best work so far." Shannon put her hand on her shoulder, giving it a squeeze.

Amber stared at her canvas. She hadn't been sure she'd imbedded the depth of feeling or captured the shades and shadows, but she could hear the honest admiration in Shannon's voice, and that was all the confirmation she needed.

"You've made your peace."

Amber looked over her shoulder at her friend. "I'm working on it."

Shannon leaned down and hugged her. "You're going to blow Justin's mind. Seriously."

Amber glanced up at Shannon, sporting the worst bedhead she'd ever seen. "Your hair is going to blow Justin's mind."

"Shut up." Shannon ran her fingers through the mop of spiky black and purple. "I was worried about you out here by yourself. Although"—she motioned at Amber's painting—"I shouldn't have. You weren't alone."

Amber stared off into the distance and then smiled gently at her friend, who always seemed to know what she was thinking.

"Besides, Justin isn't even awake yet."

Amber glanced at her watch—it was barely seven a.m. Fatigue fell heavier over her with each ray of the sun. Soon it'd be too hot to rest in the tent, and she knew she needed to sleep. And she needed to get off her leg.

"Help me clean up? I think I'm going to go back to bed."

"Good plan."

"And then, *you*'d better clean up. Because..." Amber motioned to Shannon's head.

"He loves me for me."

"Does he now?"

"He hasn't said as much but I can tell." Shannon kept walking, nonplussed, as if it was the most natural thing in the world to say a man loved her. As long as Amber had known Shannon, she'd kept men at a safe distance. Somehow, though, Justin had broken the barriers.

As soon as they were back in camp, Amber maneuvered into her tent, collapsing on her sleeping bag, and was asleep in seconds.

CHAPTER 15

The alluring aroma of camp-cooked food tickled her senses and woke her from a deep, dream-filled sleep. She blinked against the glare of sun on the tent and heard Shannon and Justin talking, the fire crackling, and something sizzling over the fire. Bacon. Or ham. Definitely burnt eggs. She uncovered and turned into her pillow as dreams, full of color and imagery, pulled her back, lulling her to sleep once again.

The next time she awoke, the tent blazed with sunshine and sweat trickled down her face. Her head pounded from the heat. Somehow, she'd covered herself back up. She extricated herself from her sleeping bag and once again fell out of the tent, blinking back against the bright light, only to find the campsite empty.

Amber plopped down in a folding chair near the smoldering campfire pit and saw a note taped to the coffee pot. They were off on a hike, and her breakfast was inside the cooler. Coffee in the thermos. She grabbed her clothes and headed to the showers to sponge off and wash her hair. Refreshed, she trekked back to their site, glad for the privacy. After breakfast, she loaded up her easel and supplies, left Shannon a note, and tromped off to the river.

Nature around her, a breeze at her back, the sun beating down on her head, she felt a sense of completeness that had been missing in her life these many months. Maybe longer. Regret again threatened to steal the joy she'd carved out this morning. She pushed it away.

Today she'd be grateful to be here and not wonder why it took her so long to arrive.

After placing her shade umbrella and chair strategically, she set up her things and began to block out her painting. This morning's painting needed to be captured, but this afternoon's could be lulled onto the canvas. She watched as the blue-green river twisted its way through the barren country. A fly-fisherman waded far upstream, waving his arm back and forth, as if casting a spell rather than casting a line. A bird flew to the edge and bathed, flipping water over its back, ruffling feathers and shaking its head. The slight breeze rattled the scrubby grasses.

Amber dabbed blue and green and white onto her brush and drew the stream, the sparking sunlight, the rambling rapids and deep bubbling pools. She cut the river through the canvas as it did through the rocky hillside. Then swept up tawny walls of impenetrable strength and immoveable magnitude. Dark crevasses and mighty splits of rock and earth were the only touches besides the river on the far side. No brush dared grow, no animal dared live, save those that hid deep in the darkness.

Under it all, appreciation built, as it did for Amber whenever she took time to study the form and function of nature or object or man-made monument. One creator admiring the Creator—a true fan. How anyone could decide this beauty and majesty were random accidents was beyond her. On everything shone His mighty fingerprint.

Art school taught her to distinguish between creative genius and forgery. She could see a piece, study it, and know not only the time period but the artist. With the great artists, their gift and mastery grew, but you could always see the progression, the pattern. Like the style of great musicians, or the study of handwriting, their themes and personalities always pointed back to their creator.

An hour passed and then another. She stood and stretched, glancing downriver and finding the fisherman had gone around the bend, leaving her in solitude. Leaning over, she did some minor exercises to keep her knee limber. She ate again, her eyes never far from her painting, glancing back and forth to make sure everything was correct. As she got closer, she noticed her own changes. Her brush strokes were wider, more encompassing. After a few finishing touches, she put up a second canvas.

Then, she closed her eyes. A wave of fear passed over her, but she forced herself to let it go, breathing out like her PT therapist trained her, against the pain and anxiety. It lessened, and she moved ahead.

Feeling the canvas with her fingers, feeling the paint on her palette, she began. The temptation to cheat and look grew, but she fought against it. She did her best to see it all in her head, every cut, every glare, every mellow tone and harsh reality. Sweat trickled down her face, but she kept her eyes clenched, the shush and scratch sounds from her brushes her constant companions. Fear welled. What if she failed? What then? A final swipe of paint and she dropped the brush into her water glass. And then—then she opened her eyes.

It wasn't what she'd expected. She'd lost track here and there, leaving white space where there shouldn't be any. But the emotion. Amber had caught the emotion.

Tears of gratefulness streamed down her face. It would be hard. It would be unimaginably hard. But it could be done. It could be.

She looked up to the blue sky, the wispy, near-transparent clouds, and nodded.

"I'm still mad, God. I'm so mad." She took a ragged breath. "I don't understand this. I don't know why this has to happen to me. I mean, you're God. You can do anything." She sobbed and then spoke up, toward the sky, where her heavenly Father hung, somewhere suspended, invisible, yet not. "You're not going to fix me, are you?" Her voice sounded more like a child's than her own.

This truth had been settling into her for some time now. Her mother prayed for healing, she'd prayed, Shannon prayed. Justin probably prayed too. All those people at her church.

Deep in her heart she knew even if no one else prayed but her, God could answer. Because of what Jesus had done, because of her belief in Him, God would heal her if He wanted.

But for some reason, He didn't want to.

Trust me.

The voice came inside her head, ringing clear.

Amber stank at trust. She trusted Shannon. Shannon had proved herself trustworthy. She'd never betrayed her, never lied to her, never shared her secrets, and never left even when Amber gave her reason to.

She'd trusted her birth mother, but she'd abandoned her. She'd trusted her father, but he'd died. She'd trusted her mother, but she'd thrown herself into work and emotionally checked out after Amber's dad died. And now God wanted her to trust Him? The One who was taking all that she was away from her?

Her eyes focused back on the paintings. She put them near one another. Before and after.

From now on, that's what her life would be summed up as. Before she lost her sight, and after. Like a war or catastrophic event. Before, when everything was great, and after, when everything was hard. Bone-crushingly hard.

"I don't want that." But sometimes you didn't get a choice.

She stared at the pictures. She took the sighted one and leaned it up against a rock. She took the one she'd painted with her eyes closed and set it up on the easel. What would she tell her students, sighted or not?

"Colors are brash but true. Shading needs depth. Some of the colors are mixed up. The light is all wrong." She squinted. "Maybe not all wrong." Amber sighed. *Not bad for a blind person.*

She shook her head. Where had that come from? She squinted

again, remembering her first real painting and her father's unique criticism. Amber had carried her watercolor up to her father as soon as he'd arrived home from work. He sat everything down and stared at it, turning it this way and that. Finally, he gave her a smile.

"What were you trying to communicate?"

Amber, age nine, hadn't a clue what he meant. "Communicate?"

Her father, a novice but talented painter, pointed to her work. "Yes, what emotion?"

"It's just trees and mountains."

"But how do you feel about them?"

She'd never thought of that. How did she feel about trees? "I love them."

"Okay. You're communicating love. What else?"

Amber chewed her lip. She'd only wanted to show off her amazing painting, not explain her motivation for what she'd painted. "I don't know."

Her father nodded. "It's important to know. Before you start anything creative, think about how you feel about it. And then think about what you want to share with others. Art is for sharing. Always start with your emotions."

He'd patted her head and walked away, leaving her to her thoughts. Four hours later, she approached him with another painting. This time, she was nervous.

"Can I show you?" She walked up to his chair and held out her work. It was the same trees and mountains she'd copied earlier from a book.

He waved her closer and pulled her up into his lap.

"Tell me about it."

She took a deep breath and started. "I love the colors of the hills and trees and how they match, but how they are different enough so we can see them all. I love this tree"—she put her finger on the tallest—"because it's pointing up."

"Up?"

"To God. Up."

"You love God."

Her tiny eyes sparkled. "Yes."

"I can see it." He pulled her into his arms and gave her a hug. She'd slipped down, out of his lap, and tacked the second painting up on the wall in her room. The other painting found its way into the recycling bin.

Amber stared at her imperfect painting. The emotion was raw, untempered, full of pain and loss, but still beautiful. She moved the canvas aside and put up a fresh one. She stared at the palette, seeing how she'd missed the colors. Reaching into her pack, she pulled out some gum and chewed several pieces all together. Then she broke them off in lumps, each one a differentiating size that related to color. She felt them with her fingers and her eyes closed, memorizing their correlation. Once she got them all right, she replenished her paints. After filling her glass with fresh river water, she closed her eyes.

Feeling for the lumps, she mixed the colors and began, wide swaths of paint splashed over her canvas for the river. She notched the edge with her fingernail so she could feel its width and not misjudge where to put the land and sky. As she was almost done, she painted a tall tree. It'd been the pine from that morning, nowhere near the river before her, but still, it belonged.

Amber held her breath, afraid of letting herself down, of letting God down. This was it. She cracked her eyes open and then, wider, took in the colors, the feelings, the awe and wonder. The river cut through the land, splashing up on the hillsides, more rapid than it ran now. The earth and sky rose up around it, cradling it. And there, in the middle, not to the side where she'd imagined she'd placed it, was the tree. Not the one she'd painted this morning at all. This was the pointy tree she'd once made for her father. Tears dripped down her cheeks.

Nodding in approval, she cleaned her brushes, covered her palette, and packed away her things. She folded the easel, the umbrella, and her chair. Slipping her pack over her shoulders, carrying everything on her back, she gripped her first "blind" painting in one hand and the second in the other. Glancing over her shoulder, she spied the original leaning against the rock, mirroring its surroundings. Then she looked down at the canvases in her hands.

It's a start.

CHAPTER 16

It'd been months since she'd gone to church. She used to drive herself, but now, her mother drove her. Jennifer told her it was because of her knee, but Amber didn't kid herself. She knew.

And her mother was right. She didn't want to be one of those people who had to have their license torn from their grasp as they fought kicking and screaming in court. Or worse, like her grandmother, years ago, who promised she wasn't driving any longer but then ran her Oldsmobile onto her neighbor's porch and took out their award-winning apple tree in the melee.

Amber, nearly ten at the time and a deeply reflective child, wondered why mommy and daddy hadn't taken Grandma's car away from her before she'd crashed. When she'd misbehaved on her bike, they took *that* away. Over the years, though, she discovered what family discord really was: Grandma reminding them of how they stole her freedom at every visit, every dinner, every holiday get-together. Miserable, bitter Grandma.

Amber searched the ceiling of the car, wondering if God had an Olds in heaven for Grandma.

They arrived, and Jennifer parked and got out. She started to walk away but noticed Amber hadn't followed, and so she came back by her side. Amber tried to roll down the electric window, but without the key in the ignition, it didn't budge. Instead she motioned for her mother to go inside without her.

"Aren't you coming?" Jennifer spoke rather animatedly while

trying to tuck a strand of blowing hair back behind her ear. The hair whipped around her face in the wind, covering her mouth and sticking to her lips.

"Soon," Amber yelled, hiding her grin behind her hand as her mother disentangled herself.

Jennifer seemed to understand and left her alone, heading away toward the front doors.

Amber, watching her mother enter with the rest of the late arrivals, waited. She didn't want a big production of pity and sorrowful words. She wanted to enter unobtrusively and sneak out before anyone noticed her.

She felt a tingle in her knee and flexed it. Her natural-wood cane knocked against the car door, and she squeezed the handle, running her fingers over the wood grain textures. Justin had found it on their trip, sanded it, and gifted it to her when the cast came off. It was the perfect reminder of that day.

After a few minutes, worship music filtered out of the building and cars stopped arriving, so Amber figured it was safe to venture inside. She climbed from the car and limped her way across the parking lot. Scattered here and there around the foyer were stragglers getting coffee and a few haggard moms trying to keep their little ones quiet. All seemed safe. Amber took a relieved breath.

Too soon.

As she approached the double doors to the sanctuary, a woman waylaid her. Amber didn't remember ever meeting her before, but she seemed to know all about her situation.

"You poor thing." The woman gripped her arm. "I'm praying for you. God told me to tell you He's going to heal you if you have enough faith."

Amber's stomach clinched. "I have faith." In fact, she'd made peace with the Lord. Hadn't she? They weren't on cozy terms as of yet, but things were better. She'd started to accept the situation. She'd begun to wrap her brain around things.

"It's not enough. And if that's not it, then you have unconfessed sin in your life."

Don't we all?

"I'm sorry, do I know you?"

"No, I don't think so. I'm on the prayer team, though, and know all about you."

Amber pulled her coat closed and backed away from the woman. "I need to go in... My mother's waiting." Amber's voice faltered.

"I see." Condemnation filled the space between them. "Well, dear, let me know when you're ready to be healed." Judge, jury, and executioner whisked away down the corridor toward the lady's restroom, leaving a hollowed-out Amber in her wake.

Her leaden legs moved through the sanctuary doors and somehow found the seat next to her mother. Jennifer's questioning gaze couldn't be answered yet. Instead, Amber felt her spirit fold in on itself as the songs of worship bounced off her newly erected forcefield. Coming today had been a huge mistake.

Even as the pastor spoke, the woman's words reverberated through her. Ready to be healed? Hadn't she prayed for that very thing and been coming to terms with the answer? God seemed to have spoken words of acceptance to her during her sojourn to the desert. But now?

Could she get in the way of healing poured out by her loving heavenly Father? Amber fought for a steady breath but it caught in her chest, burning. Maybe what the woman said was true. Maybe she wasn't good enough and that kept God from doing anything for her.

The idea that the power of Almighty God could be hinged entirely on what she thought or how she behaved didn't sit right. This put her in control and made God a fearful being, unsettling and tempestuous. Unreliable. At that moment, an old verse she'd memorized from Jeremiah 32:27 came to mind. "I am the Lord, the God of all mankind. Is anything too hard for me?"

The verse tumbled in her head around and around until it found purchase, though tenuous. As the service let out, many of her mother's close friends approached her and spoke comforting words. None could quite erase the spiteful ones from earlier, though.

As Jennifer drove her home, Amber remained cloistered by her thoughts.

"You were so hopeful this morning. What happened?"

She shook her head, not sure where to begin. What if her mother agreed with that woman?

Jennifer pulled the car over into a parking lot overlooking the Columbia River. It'd been a favorite spot of Amber's to investigate as a child. Now the rocky outcroppings felt more like a threat than an adventure.

"You can talk to me." She heard the doubt in her mother's voice.

Regret doubled in her spirit. What made her so badly bent that she held her family and friends so far away? Her mother challenged her, sure. Jennifer was flashy and outspoken and driven. They were very different people.

"This woman came up to me at church and said something."

Jennifer frowned. "What woman?"

"I'd never seen her before. She seemed to know her way around, knew all about me and my blindness. I didn't get her name. She..." Amber stopped. *Accused* was the word she wanted to use, but maybe that wasn't right. "She said I could be healed when I was ready, if I only had enough faith." Or enough repentance. Or enough of anything. The atmosphere in the car went from hesitant to charged. Her mother's cheeks flashed red.

"Describe her to me."

"She had dyed blond hair and wore a hat. She was dressed in

blue." And her eyes. "Dark eyes." Reproachful eyes. "Do you think she's right? Can I get in the way of God healing me?"

"No."

"But how do you know? God blessed people all the time in the Bible for their faith. Maybe I don't have enough."

"You listen to me, Amber Kirk. If God only blessed those who deserved it, there'd be no blessings at all in this world."

Amber's head shot up, and she watched her mother's expression change from anger to adoration, tears filling her eyes. She reached over, caressed Amber's cheek, and tucked her hair behind her ear.

"God has compassion on those He loves. And I know He loves you. I've seen it over and over in your life. Blindness comes from this broken world." Jennifer shook her dismayed head. "We're all blind in one way or another." She gathered Amber in her arms. "Don't you dare take this on yourself. You keep praying and trusting Him." The warmth of her embrace and the aroma of her perfume, so much her mother, wrapped around her. "I love you, sweetie." Deep emotions were not one of her mother's natural gifts, but today Jennifer was in rare form. "Whatever happens, I'm here for you." She squeezed her tighter. "And if I see that woman in church again, I'll box her ears."

A strong vision of her mother slapping the ears of that hateful woman made Amber giggle. She pulled away. "Thanks, Mom."

"Will you promise me something?"

"Sure." Amber settled back into her seat.

"Don't ever mistake the love of God with the way others act. We're only human. Imperfect. Even in the church." She pursed her lips. "Especially the church. He draws the broken to Him, but that also draws predators. There are people in this world that live to ferret out the hurting and hurt them more. Unfortunately, the openness of church to the broken also opens the doors to those. I'll be praying for that woman. God knows her name."

"She said she was on the prayer team."

Jennifer's eyes sparked with recognition. "I'll take care of it."

Amber had no doubt she would.

Her mom pulled the car back into traffic and took her home, dropping her off in front of her apartment. Amber returned to her sanctuary, finding warmth and peace inside and the love of her kitten.

She might still be cracked, and today left her bruised, but her brokenness was mending.

CHAPTER 17

"Amber, do you have a minute?" Amber looked up to see the principal standing in her classroom doorway.

Even though things had been unremarkable since her return from the desert, she was still waiting for the bad news. As much as she tried to be nonchalant about her position and hopeful for the future, she still worried. Her sight could be gone any day, without warning. It was like waiting for a bomb to go off in a movie. The clock countdown went faster with every day, but she couldn't see the numbers anymore. She tried to steel herself for whatever made Brandon walk so stiffly and hesitantly.

"Sure." She motioned for Brandon to sit near her desk. He pulled over a stool and perched on it, looking every bit the part of an aged artist.

"Here's the deal. I've been talking to Justin Rameros."

Amber's heart began to thump in her chest. "And?"

"I feel he's ready to take over your class, but he's resisting. I know you're good friends. I'd like you to make this easier for him."

Easier for *him*? "I'm not sure..." Every kind of retort fought to the surface, but none escaped.

"We all know this is coming. I feel for you, I do. But I'm in a tough spot. I'm already hearing comments from some of our clients. This is hard for me to say, but I think it'd be better if you went out on top of your game."

He might as well have picked up a palette knife and jabbed it through her heart. All the blood rushed into her ears. This wasn't happening.

"I'll give you a couple more weeks to transition Justin in. He's willing to work with your schedule. Make sure your students are comfortable with a new teacher, that sort of thing." He reached over and patted her slight hand with his calloused, huge one. Noticing her stiffen and pull away, he retreated quickly and shut her door. She heard him in the hall tell a student they needed to come back by later, that she was busy.

Amber looked out over her classroom. The last thing she wanted to do was to die a bit every day for the next two weeks. And the pity. The students would all pity her—at least the ones she could explain the situation to. Tears fell unhindered from her eyes. She rose and wandered through the art stations, past paint encrusted stands and stools, past pottery wheels, past sculptures and smocks. The very smell of this room had worked its way into her lifeblood. To leave it behind seemed unthinkable.

"I'm sorry."

She glanced toward the doorway and saw Justin's shape there. The sadness in his voice told her he meant it, but it did little to calm the turmoil stirring in her heart.

"Yeah," she squeaked out as her voice cracked. Her throat strained against the coming tide of emotions. Crying alone was one thing; crying with your best friend's boyfriend was quite another.

"I want you to know this wasn't my idea. I think they should keep you." He cleared his voice. "Your paintings at the desert were the best work you've done in years. They're nuts to toss you."

If students and parents were already mentioning her performance, there wasn't anything left to say. It didn't matter what her private work looked like if she couldn't tell them what she saw in *their* work.

"It's fine."

"It's not. I think you should call Ethan and get him involved.

They work with advocacy lawyers." He moved through the doorway, coming nearer.

"The very last thing I want to do is work where I'm not wanted. I don't want them to keep me around because they feel sorry for me or because I'm threatening to sue. If Brandon wanted to, he'd work something out. As it is..." She swallowed hard, not able to continue.

"As it is, he's covering his tail." Justin's disgust fueled the feeling boiling inside her.

"Maybe so. But I certainly can't comment on the children's work, and I can't instruct them where they need help. He's right about that. I'm done." She didn't know what she'd do next, though. Amber had hoped a new plan would evolve before she had to leave. No such luck.

"This sucks." Justin nudged one of the stools with his foot, the metal legs catching on the linoleum, screeching. "I mean, really."

"Yeah." She went to the back of the room and began to empty boxes. Then she started filling them with her personal belongings. Some old canvases she could reuse. Her private brush collection. Textbooks and art manuals she'd bought with her own monies. She went around the room, examining each surface, not wanting to miss a thing—because she sure didn't want to come back. Frankly, the room would be rather barren with her things packed up. Brandon was going to have to give Justin a real budget to replace it all. As if.

"What are you doing?"

"Packing."

"You've got two weeks."

Amber looked up at him. "I won't do that." She took a deep breath. "I really *can't* do that." She moved down the shelves, plucking items here and there. Then she moved to her desk and opened all the drawers, tossing out the garbage, putting the keepers into the boxes. She rolled up gifts of students' works and put them in a mailing tube to keep them safe.

"Can I help?"

Her gut reaction was to say no. But she couldn't afford to do that anymore. "Yes, you can. Please encourage Katie. She's got such an imagination, and I'm afraid when she moves into the public school sector, not all the teachers are going to see that as an attribute."

"I get it."

"She's very good. So is Nathan. And Liam. And—" Her voice broke, so she stopped.

Justin came and put a hand on her shoulder. "Look, why don't you at least come in tomorrow and say good-bye?"

She shook her head. "This might sound selfish. I know it does. But I can't handle it right now. I'll come back for a visit. I promise."

Amber handed Justin her grade book and private client list. He put them on the desk and stacked the boxes together. Then he grabbed the handcart and motioned to her. "Lead the way."

"I don't have a car."

"Right. I do. I'll stash this stuff in my car and bring it by tonight. And Shannon."

"Thanks." She hugged him and headed toward Brandon's office. As she walked one way, and Justin walked the other, she felt the gap of who she had been widening from whom she now was. Like putty pulled out too far, stretching until the fine threads snapped, leaving two uneven lumps where one whole one had been. Both useless to make anything out of.

Amber knocked on Brandon's office door. He called for her to enter.

"I need you to cut my last check." That's not how she meant to start out, but suddenly finances were first and foremost on her mind. Her rent was paid this month, but her disability paperwork wasn't completely processed yet, and she didn't even know how much that would be at this point. Or if she started a job, could she keep getting disability? And who would hire her?

"Hang on now. We've got a couple weeks to worry about that."

"No, we really don't. I can't come in here every day for the next two weeks and leave part of my soul behind, and that's what you're asking me to do. So, I'm done. Today. Justin is ready and willing to take over, and once I'm feeling more secure, I'll come back and say good-bye to my students."

Brandon got to his feet. "I didn't mean to push you out."

"You kind of did. Let's not go there, okay? You need to respect my decision because I have to have some sense of control with this whole thing."

"Okay. I get that." He came around to her side of the desk. "I hope you know how sorry I am."

Amber met his gaze. "I can see you are, but right now, I don't care. Right now, I'm mad. And I'm leaving before I tell you how I really feel." She pulled on her coat. "I want my check mailed to me tomorrow. Are we clear?"

"Crystal. I totally get it." His laid-back attitude that she'd once found charming now annoyed her to no end.

"No, you don't." If he did, she wouldn't be in this position. At least, not yet. She made her way to the door.

"You were a great teacher, Amber. One of the students' favorites."

Her hand froze on the knob. Nothing he said would set right in her mind. Nothing at all. She opened the door and left without looking back.

●—————— • • • • ——————●

Ethan stood near her waiting for the church doors to open. It was different than her church. Older. More foreboding, especially at night. Their breath froze in the chilly night air. She tucked her hands in her jacket pockets. She was in the midst of a group that seemed to know each other. One would call out a name and another answer. Three had guide dogs. Most had canes. One had a personal guide.

Kind of like Ethan, she supposed. He was here to make introductions and then he'd leave her. On her own.

A tall, golden-haired older woman came up the street, with a cane moving back and forth. Her steps never wavered. She seemed to know where each crack in the sidewalk was, where each step led up or down, even where each person was standing outside.

"Greetings, everyone. Let me open the door, and we'll get the heat turned on and the coffee perking. Sorry I'm late." Her slight Greek accent gave her an air of mystery.

Amber frowned. The woman seemed familiar.

She leaned over toward Ethan. "Have I met her before?"

Ethan thought for a moment. "No. She does come into the office now and then, but I don't think any of your appointments have coincided. Maybe you saw her in the building?"

Another irony in her life—Amber never forgot a face. She shook her head. Maybe she lived in the same area.

He took Amber by the elbow and led her up the steps.

"I can still see, you know."

Ethan let out a sigh. "We're practicing. Remember, having what's left of your sight is a *gift*."

"Right." She nodded, trying to agree but realizing what a liar she'd become. She felt him direct her to the refreshments table.

"Coffee on your left, tea on your right, doughnuts far right." He leaned closer. "They're really good too. There's a bacon maple one near the left lower corner. I'd grab it."

She did, avoiding the raised monstrosity dipped in fruity kid's cereal. She poured herself a cup of coffee, putting her thumb inside the lip so she could feel when the liquid got to the top. Practice made perfect. She hoped. Then he led her to the desks. Having a tabletop in front of her was more comforting than she would have thought. Boundaries used to make her feel hemmed in, but not so much anymore.

"Okay, I'll come by and see you home in about two hours." He patted her back.

"I'm fine. I only live a couple blocks away."

"Right. You're fine. Got it. See you soon."

She shook her head. He was being overly protective. A woman leaned in by her.

"Ethan your guy?"

Amber looked her over. The woman was attractive, in her thirties.

"Uh, no. He's helping me get adjusted to all this." The idea of Ethan being *her* guy made her stomach wobble with uncertainty. She'd had enough of men for a while. Hopefully he wasn't getting the wrong impression. Friendship yes, relationship no.

"That's what I meant. He was my guy too. Great counselor. I don't think I would have survived that first year without him. I graduated. Don't worry, you will too."

"Oh." Amber frowned as a sudden inexplicable wave of disappointment washed over her. Before she could give that more thought, the leader stood in front of the group.

"Are you all settled?"

Everyone affirmed they'd gotten their coffee and doughnuts and were sitting down.

"Great. As most of you know, my name is Maggie Floros. Yes, I'm of Greek origins. No, I'm not connected." Everyone laughed. "I've been blind since my early twenties. I've been a counselor for the blind for over twenty years. I know from my roster we have a first timer here. Amber, would you introduce yourself to us?"

Amber felt another wave of uncertainty. She hadn't expected to be singled out.

"Amber, you here?"

The idea that she could sit very still and not have anyone know she was there was equally troubling and liberating.

"Yes, sorry. I'm Amber Kirk. I'm, uh, new."

"Welcome, Amber. Can you tell us about yourself?"

"I'm a..." What was she now? Not a teacher, maybe not even an artist. "Unemployed." Bitterness rose.

"What did you do before you lost your sight?"

Amber chewed her lip for a moment. "I haven't lost it yet." Why did she say that? "I mean, I can mostly still see." *Shut up.* She changed her tactics. "I was given notice this morning. I used to be an art teacher for grade school and high school students."

Many nodded in appreciation and made affirming noises. "That's great."

"Wow, an artist."

"Bummer." The last comment came from the older man in the upper right corner.

"Let's hear from you guys. Who's working right now?"

Everyone but the older man said they were working. She supposed the conversation was to make her feel better. It didn't. She suddenly pictured them all sitting at desks and answering phones or stuck in some other mundane job that would kill her a piece at a time.

"Don't give up yet, Amber. Okay?"

"Okay." Amber slipped down in her seat and waited for the other topics at hand to be discussed. People shared their challenges and laughed at their mishaps. Except for the man in the corner. He sat there sipping his coffee.

As the second hour came to a close, Maggie focused on the quiet, sulky man.

"Robert. We haven't heard from you tonight."

"No."

"What can we do to help you?"

"Nothing."

"That's not like you."

He stayed quiet.

"How'd your date go?"

"I don't want to talk about it."

The chorus of "ohhs" from around the room almost deafened her.

"Now, now, everyone, remember to be respectful." Maggie's voice of reason calmed them all down.

"Fine. You want to hear it? I listed that I was blind on my application for that crummy online dating site. But somehow she missed that. When I met her at the restaurant, she didn't know who I was, just struck up a conversation. Started talking about how it must be hard to be blind. When I said I was waiting for a blind date"—he laughed and the others booed— "she got real quiet and asked my name. Then she said she needed to excuse herself to the ladies' room and never came back."

"How do you know it was her?"

"No one else ever came. Had to be her."

Everyone became very somber. "That stinks, man." A younger fellow spoke up. "They shouldn't judge you like that. I mean...she doesn't know what she's missing, right?" He chuckled suggestively and several in the room guffawed and agreed. Amber felt her cheeks go hot and tried to hide it before she realized not a person in the room would even know if she wore makeup. Which she had. And a nice outfit. *Duh.*

"On behalf of womankind, I apologize to you, Robert. No one deserves to be stood up. And no, she doesn't have any idea what she's missing." There was nothing suggestive in Maggie's tone, and the atmosphere in the room shifted to one of support.

After Maggie dismissed the group, she made her way to Amber.

"I'm glad you came, Amber. I hope you'll be back next week." The woman's deep brown eyes focused slightly off her face but still gave the impression she was speaking right to her.

"I probably will. I don't have anything else to do." Amber clamped a hand over her mouth and then spoke past her fingers. "I'm sorry. It's been a really cruddy day."

Maggie's smile was contagious. Amber instantly felt important and valued. She smiled back, forgetting Maggie couldn't see her expression, but hoping she heard it in her Amber's voice. "I learned a lot."

"I'm glad. We're none of us perfect. Some a little rougher around the edges than others. But we're a cohesive, protective group. I'm sure you'll feel a part of the whole very soon."

"Thanks."

Maggie walked on, took Robert aside, and gave him a sideways hug before turning and chatting with a couple others. Amber pulled out her phone and held it up to see the time. Ethan was either very late or he'd listened to her. She hoped for the latter.

Instead of calling, she headed outside, buttoning up her trench coat, and made her way up the few blocks toward her apartment. She passed the coffee shop and moved on. As she rounded the last corner to her place, she heard footsteps behind her. She paused a minute and they stopped. She started up and they did too.

Glancing behind her, all she could see was darkness and darker shadows. The streetlight didn't make much of an impact and the headlights from passing cars only made the darkness more dramatic. She suddenly wished she'd waited. A form brushed past her, and she fell into the side of the building. The person didn't stop. Then another came up behind her. Hearing the strange gait and gasping breath, fear seized her entirely. When a hand reached out for her arm, she screamed and shoved the person away, hearing a strange clatter as something skated over the sidewalk.

"It's okay, it's me, it's me." Ethan panted, off balance, and tried to pick up his cane but was unable to get it without falling over.

"Oh no. I'm so sorry." Amber put her hand out to help him and scooped up his cane. "I could have sworn someone was following me. Are you okay?"

"I'll be fine." He rubbed a hand over his cane, inspecting it for damage. Finding none, he went back to leaning on it. "Why didn't you wait for me?"

Her regret faded quickly at his condescending tone. "I figured you finally listened to me for once and went home."

"Ouch. Not nice."

Her remorse came pouring back. At that moment, she realized she'd never apologized for being so awful to him at the hospital either.

"I'm sorry. Really." She glanced up the street. "I did feel like someone was behind me."

"Hello?" He waved at her.

"No, I mean…" She gave up, unable to explain. "Never mind. Do you want to come up for tea or anything? It's the least I can do." That would give her an opportunity to explain why she'd been so awful those weeks ago. And to thank him for the PT referral.

"No. Another time, okay? And next time, please wait." He sounded more worried than perturbed.

"Sorry, I know you're only doing your job."

Something shifted between them. "Right. Well, good night."

He waited for Amber to enter her building, and she got the sense he continued to wait until he saw her top the stairs, which took less time now she had her cane but still pained her. She was glad, because even if she couldn't see someone following her, she'd felt it. And she was sure it hadn't been Ethan.

CHAPTER 18

Amber hid a grimace of frustration as Jennifer leaned across the table and started to blot a spill from her cup. For some reason the hiss of the espresso machine, chatter of other customers, overhead music, and the overpowering aroma of coffee wasn't nearly as annoying as her mother's tendency to *mother* her.

"Mom, please." She grabbed the napkin more violently than she'd intended and made the spill worse. Sighing, she plucked several sheets from the silver canister and sopped up the mess she'd made. A baby three tables away started to scream, cutting a beeline through her nervous system. She gritted her teeth.

"I was trying to help."

"I've got to learn to do these things on my own." She took her cup from the saucer and piled the dripping napkins on it instead.

"It's like you don't need me anymore."

Amber sighed. "Mom, please. This is hard enough. You're going to have to let me find my way, okay?"

Her mother took an extended sip of her coffee and began to watch the baby. "It was just the other day you were that small."

"I was nearly four when you and Dad adopted me."

"Quit splitting straws."

They sat quietly for a few minutes, thinking about the past.

"Kyle called again."

Amber sat at attention. "What did he say?"

"That he was worried about the influence your friends have

had on you, and he felt I should intervene. He said if you wouldn't marry him and let him take care of you, then I should insist on your moving in with me."

Amber's face went hot. "Mom, Kyle isn't who he seems to be. He's kind of scary. And if it weren't for my friends, he might have hurt me the other night."

"Aren't you being dramatic?"

"No. And please make it clear you don't want to talk to him if he ever calls again. Promise me?"

Jennifer pursed her bright pink lips at Amber. "Okay. If you really think he's dangerous."

"I do."

"But he's got a point."

"What point?"

Her mother cleared her voice, a telltale sign Amber would hate whatever she would say next. "That you really can't live on your own. I think he's right. You should come home."

"No. No way. No how."

"Your job's going to end soon, and what will you do then?"

Amber started in her seat and then all her self-righteous indignation evaporated, leaving her feeling spent and exhausted.

"What?" Jennifer leaned closer. "Have they fired you?"

"They laid me off." She tried to soften the blow but it didn't work. Laid off. Let go. The end result was the same. Fired.

"But you can still see." Her mother crumpled the napkin that had been perfectly poised on her lap and tossed it on the table. "That's not fair."

"Nope, not fair." Amber looked away, wishing she was anywhere than there, trying to convince her mother how handled this whole situation was.

"Well, there's your answer."

Amber steeled herself against her mother's casting doubt. Didn't she know how hard it was for her to keep her head up against her own fears? She didn't need those closest to her giving up on her as well.

"I don't see it like that. I'm finding my way. I've been attending support meetings, getting connected to services, and I've even attended a class on prepping my apartment. I could hire someone, but they suggest doing it yourself if you can. And I can."

"I don't mean to belittle what you've done."

"Then don't. Ethan's even helped me compile a Must-See List."

Jennifer's eyebrows drew together. "What's that?"

"It's a list of things I want to see or do before I lose my sight."

"What sorts of things are on it?"

For some reason, telling her mother about the list felt like she was betraying a part of herself. "Lots of things."

"Travel?"

"Sure. Some travel."

"You don't have any money for travel."

Amber's shoulders sagged. "I can't do it all, I get that."

Instead of agreeing with her, Jennifer shook her head. "If you won't move in with me, then let me help with that."

"What do you mean?"

"You never let me help pay for school, or your car, or anything since you were sixteen years old. Let me do this."

"Mom, you can't..." Why did she have to push back so hard? Why did she keep her mother, who clearly loved her, at arm's length?

"Let me. I need to do something." Jennifer choked on her words. "You're losing your sight. But I'm your mom, watching you lose your sight. There's nothing worse than watching your child suffer. Nothing." Tears streamed down her cheeks. "Except not being able to help them or comfort them."

Shame filled Amber's being. "I'm sorry. I didn't realize."

"If you don't want me along, that's fine. But let me help you pay for it. Please. I have to be a part of this, a part of your life, somehow."

Amber went still for a minute. She'd never looked at it from her mother's perspective. She had been working so hard at keeping it together and showing how tough she was, she didn't realize she was shutting out the people she loved from helping her.

"You're right. I'm sorry."

Her mother brushed off her apology, but Amber could see the pain in the set of her shoulders, her posture, the way she cradled her cup.

"No, really. I've been stupid. And selfish."

"You'll let me help?" The hopefulness in her mother's voice heaped coals down on her head.

"I'll let you help. And I'll even invite you along here and there. There are some I need to be alone for, though."

"I understand."

"Okay." Amber wasn't sure if she'd regret her decision later, but right now the happiness she saw in her mother's eyes made it worth it. Funny how a simple thing like that grew in importance. She'd go home and write *Make Mom Happy* on her list and cross it off. Hopefully, it'd stay crossed off.

CHAPTER 19

As Amber returned to her apartment, she once again practiced taking the stairs. She could do it without peeking now and make it all the way to her door. Every now and then she'd feel edgy, but she'd suppress the feeling before panic ensued. Her knee only gave her trouble on occasion, so she'd stopped using her cane there too. In time to trade it in for a cane of another kind.

Tomorrow would be her last check up with her PT. Samantha had been a lifesaver. Amber knew she wouldn't be even half as far as she was without her. Another debt she owed Ethan.

Amber pulled her keys out and opened her door efficiently—it was easier now that the school keys and her car key were missing. And with that little cap Justin put on it. Shannon had found a gem in Justin. Mixed blessings came at her from all angles. Once she was inside, she locked the door. Glancing around at the chaos, she decided today was the day she'd get back in charge and make her place safe for a blind person. Mocha leapt at her leg and climbed up, gripping her jeans like Velcro.

"Ouch, you." She removed his paws one at a time, being careful of his tiny claws, and lifted him to her face. "Take it easy on me, okay?" He mewed at her and began to purr.

Amber tucked him under her chin as she headed into the kitchenette and gathered a couple boxes left over from unpacking her art supplies. She lined them with plastic bags and then opened the cabinet under the sink. After removing the most caustic cleaners and putting them in the box, she took inventory of what was left. For safety, the paperwork suggested only having a couple cleaners as to not confuse them. She would have to label them differently to tell them apart.

She needed to order the braille label maker. And learn braille. She'd signed up for a class, but the current one was underway, so she needed to wait a few weeks until the next one nearby started. She'd picked up a book from the library and had tried on her own, but it was like learning any language on your own—hit and miss.

She kept the powdered cleanser and dish soap. She'd heard you could use white vinegar and baking soda to clean just about anything. She'd get some bio-degradable floor solution at the market tomorrow. Amber wiped out the cabinet and put things in order. Then she closed her eyes and felt her way around the items. Garbage bags, cleaner, bucket, sponges.

Then she went through her spice cabinet and tossed out all the old stuff. She'd be able to tell most things by scent, but that'd slow cooking down considerably. Again, that label maker would come in handy. She proceeded through the kitchen, organizing pots, pans, dishware, storage containers, the works.

Hours later, she stood admiring her hard work. Her kitchen was as she'd always wanted it to be but she'd never had the time to make it. Turning around, she caught sight of all the things that needed to go and groaned.

She flipped through the phone book, tilting it first one way and then the other, but couldn't see the type. She dialed Information and asked for the local thrift store. The staff there assured her someone would be by with a truck and, for the price of gas, haul away everything. She had two hours before they'd get to her apartment.

Inspired by casting off her worldly possessions, she headed into her room and did the same with outdated clothes. She'd have to put labels in her clothes in some way that would tell her which top went well with which bottom. Shannon would say it didn't matter and to just go for it.

As she turned to her bookcase, she froze. She loved books. She loved the feel of them, the texture, the typeface, the edges of the page. The musty aroma of ink and sweet chemical odor of the glossy pages. Some books definitely smelled better than others. No more reading. At least, not that way.

Swallowing hard, she grabbed a pad of paper and began writing down the titles of the books she loved to reread. Putting aside a short stack she might want to pass on to her kids, she moved on to others she knew Shannon would enjoy. Her art books she put aside for Katie. She'd give them to Justin to pass on to her.

She loved mentoring children. Although she wasn't supposed to have favorites, she had to admit, Katie was hers. Katie had this out-of-the box imagination that would be curtailed and amputated if her teaching fell into the wrong hands. Her fanciful drawings and paintings might actually take her someplace one day. At least, Amber hoped they would. But then again, life threw curveballs when you least expected it. Or God did.

Keeping her emotions in check, Amber stacked those she'd catalogued into boxes. She pushed the boxes into the living room beside the other things. She'd make a wish list and slowly rebuild her library with braille copies—another cost not counted in the loss.

The downstairs buzzer sounded and she pushed the button, letting in the movers. A knock on her door brought her back from her dip into self-pity, and she put Mocha in the bathroom. She opened her door to two young men with handcarts. After directing them to the right piles, they removed twenty-eight years of accumulated life.

As she closed the door behind them, she heard Mocha mewing from the bathroom and let him free.

"Sorry, buddy." She gave him fresh water and food and then curled up on her bed, exhausted. The conversation with her mother replayed in her mind. She didn't know why she continued to push her mother away. The more she pushed back, the harder her mom held on. It was a no-win tug-o-war. Why was it so hard for her to let anyone get close to her?

For many years Amber chalked it up to being adopted, but then, Shannon had lived her childhood in foster care and she wasn't afraid to get close to people. Well, not to her and a select group of others. It was too simple to say she was afraid of being abandoned again.

Rain began to beat down on the window, and Amber smiled, enjoying the ticking sound of each drop as it hit, the wind flowing by, the tree branches clacking together. Storms fed a place in her soul. As the wind raged outside, she fell to sleep.

Awaking in the pitch black, Amber panicked, feeling around her bed, unable to remember where she was or how she got there. She could see nothing at all. "Not yet," she begged, "please not yet. Not yet." A sob tore at her throat as she tumbled from the bed and hit the floor, knocking the wind from her lungs. Gasping, she rolled onto her stomach. She saw a flashing blue light nearby and crawled toward the beacon. It was her phone. A message on her phone. She could see it. She pushed the message icon and heard Shannon's voice.

"Hey, you holding up okay? Power's out all over downtown. Gimme a call and let me know."

Power outage. Not blindness. Not yet.

Relief filled her but didn't quite pop the bubble of fear still harbored in her chest. It never left these days, but it hadn't gotten closer than this. As she caught her breath, she thought about what it would really be like. Pretending didn't cut it, because she could always open her eyes and still see most of the world around her—although admittedly this grew harder daily.

The phone rang and jolted her system. Ethan.

"Hello."

"You doing okay? I'm closing up early because of the power outage but wondered if you could use some extra sandwiches."

"Extra...sandwiches?" *What in the world?*

"Sorry, that was backhanded. We were having a staff meeting and lost power. With the storm ramping up faster than the weather service indicated, I've sent everyone home and have a surplus of sandwiches and salads. Are you hungry?"

Still a bit backhanded, but from her position on the floor, company and free food sounded perfect. And maybe he could give her ideas about organizing her clothes. She thought about her underwear and bras strewn around the room. *Or not.*

"Sure. My pantry is quite bare, and I really don't want to head out in this." In fact, she'd rather go hungry or maybe snack on Mocha's food.

"Great. See you in a few."

Amber headed right toward her stash of emergency candles and lit a couple around her living room. She brushed her hair and pushed the remaining boxes to the far wall. Then she used the talk command on her phone to text Justin.

"Text Justin." The phone beeped but did nothing. She sighed aloud, not giving up. "Text Justin."

"What's your message?" came the automatic response.

"I have books for Katie. Please let me know when you can pick up." She paused, waiting for the phone to get the idea.

"Message sent."

It had taken quite a lot of practice, but her Android voice app was working fairly well. Sometimes it sent erroneous messages, but for the most part, it got the meaning across. Opening e-mail was another issue altogether, though. She needed something for that. She'd ask Ethan about that too.

After taking stock and making sure everything looked presentable, she fed Mocha his dinner. He was all about the food lately, her growing kitty. She moved to the couch to sit as a knock came at her door. Strange, she hadn't heard the buzzer. Maybe he'd followed someone in. Of course, the buzzer was electronic. She peered through the peephole, not sure what she expected to see in the dark. The knock came again and startled her.

Her heart raced. She couldn't see in the hall at all. No shadow, no shape, nothing.

"Who is it?" She expected to hear Ethan's warm voice in response. Nothing came but another knock. The air whirred with tension. Another knock, louder.

"Who's there?" Fear laced her words, so she restated more forcefully. "Tell me who it is."

Nothing. She reached up and flipped two more locks, securing her door. Then she pulled out her phone, ready with "call police" on the tip of her tongue. She put her ear against the door and heard footsteps. Then a thud at the base of her door made her jump.

"Tell me who it is." Her voice shook despite her effort to sound authoritative. And taller. She hoped she sounded tall. And muscular.

"It's me. Ethan. My arms are full. Can you help a guy out?"

Amber, her heart in her throat, flipped all the latches and swung open the door. Ethan stood there laden with white deli bags and a couple cups of something in hot containers.

"Take the cocoa, take the cocoa. It burns." He laughed and she took the cups from him. He closed the door with his foot and put the food bags down on the table.

"Sorry about kicking your door. Kinda tricky maneuvering all this and my cane up your stairs."

"Oh, that's okay. Sorry it took me so long to answer." She shook her head at herself.

"What do you mean?" Ethan began unloading food onto the table.

Amber paused. "I mean you had to knock like three times to gain entry. With all those bags rustling, you must not have heard me on the other side of the door."

Ethan straightened. "I only kicked the one time."

The blood rushed through Amber's ears. "Oh. I'm sure it was someone at the wrong apartment then."

Instead of listening to her, Ethan went to the door, opened it and turned on his phone's flashlight. He flipped the beam left and right, then up the stairwell, and listened.

"No one's there now." He closed the door and locked it.

"I'm sure it's nothing." Her mouth said the words, but her heart didn't believe them. Someone had been out there. Someone angry. She didn't know how she knew it, but she did.

"Well, I'll be here for a bit, so if they come back, I'll take them to task with my walking stick." He tried joking, but it fell flat. She laughed anyway and put out dinner plates.

"Thanks for the free food."

He handed her a sandwich and a salad container. "You're the first person I thought of." He smiled and sat down.

She didn't like how glad she was he'd said that. She was his current project and a friend. She knew that. And right then it was the worst idea in the world to start a relationship. With anyone. And being blind... Her thoughts disturbed her. She moved into the living room toward one of the candles and brought it back to the table, illuminating their meal.

"This looks great."

He handed her the cranberry sauce.

"That's okay, I don't really like eating that plain."

"Who said anything about plain? Slather it on your turkey sandwich."

"Eh. No." She shook her head.

"Come on. You've never put cranberry sauce on your turkey

sam'mich? How can that be?" He opened her sandwich and put some on a small section.

"You're going to make me try it? No one makes me try anything. Seriously, ask my mom."

"Trust me, okay. Have I ever led you astray? Do it for me?" She couldn't see his eyes clearly in this light—really, she was losing that ability altogether—but his tone melted all her defenses.

"Fine. But don't tell my mom." She took a bite and tasted the tang on her tongue and the saltiness of the turkey and mayo. "Wow. Okay. That's wonderful."

"See? Told you that you could trust me."

His words carried something akin to comfort to her hurting spirit. Somehow she knew she could trust him. The same way she knew she couldn't trust Kyle. Maybe she was developing some kind of sixth sense.

They ate in silence and then her phone notification went off, alerting her to a text. And then another and then a third. She hated to interrupt their conversation, but she needed to know who was texting her. Only Shannon usually blasted her with messages like that. She hoped it wasn't personal.

"Sorry, I need to hear these."

"Oh, that's fine. I'll leave the..." He tapered off as he looked around. "I'll go in the living room and try not to listen."

Amber laughed, uncomfortable, but not sure what else to do. "I'm sure it's fine. Hang on." She pushed the tab button on her phone. "Hello, Galaxy."

The phone responded.

"Read text."

The mechanical voice started to relay the message. "From Justin. Katie will love the books. I think you should be the one to give them to her, though. Don't walk away from all of this. But take your time. No rush."

Amber felt her face go hot, but she put the phone down with nonchalance.

"Do you mind if I ask who Katie is?"

"She's one of my students. One of my best students." Amber waved toward where she knew a pile of books sat on her right, near the wall. "I was packing away my art books today, and there were several that she'd love and benefit from." That wasn't the only reason. Katie had talent and ambition. And she reminded Amber of herself at that age—desperate to share her art, to connect with someone. Anyone.

"So why are you having Justin give them to her?"

Amber swallowed a sip of cocoa that was hotter than she'd expected. It burned all the way down her throat. "I was fired. Or laid off. Whatever makes it sound nicer."

Ethan started. "But you can still see. That's discrimination."

"It is and it isn't. I can't see details all that well." She'd been hiding it from herself and from everyone else. Admitting it, though, hurt.

"I didn't realize."

"I'm running out of time. And my boss wanted me to transition Justin in. I couldn't do it. Call me selfish or whatever, I couldn't sit there and watch all my dreams get handed to someone else. As nice as Justin is, and as much as I like him, I couldn't."

"It'd make you too angry. Too jealous?"

He *did* understand. "Exactly. I'm having enough trouble with all of this. As if going blind isn't bad enough, now I get to do nothing. I certainly can't watch him doing the thing I want to be doing. That I felt called to do." She choked on her emotions. He reached over to comfort her, but she backed away from the table. "Please don't."

"Why not?"

"Because if you do, I'll probably lose it, and I don't know you well enough to bawl in front of you."

He reached over and took her hand anyway. True to form, she

began to cry. He scooted his chair nearer, and she leaned on his shoulder. He put a hand on her back, holding her.

"This is so not fair," she whimpered.

"I know it isn't. Trust me. I know. But you're going to be okay, Amber."

He didn't sound like a counselor. He sounded like her friend. And for the moment, she decided to pretend that's all he was. Because she needed it.

CHAPTER 20

She pulled back from Ethan, embarrassed to have let her guard down so fully. She never did that with anyone. Well, besides Shannon.

Instead of looking self-conscious for her, he handed her a tissue. "Better now?"

"Yes." She wiped her eyes and blew her nose.

"You can't carry all this by yourself. You need someone to lean on." He took a breath. "I'm here for you."

She tried to read the meaning in his words. Amber didn't like ambiguity. Even less so now. Everything was best out on the table so there wouldn't be any surprises. Instead of asking straight out, though, she sidled up to the question. Her courage seemed to be disappearing with her eyesight.

"You're a great counselor." She waved at the food before them. "You've gone above and beyond here."

Ethan cleared his voice as if to say something significant but instead said, "Thanks."

She wished she knew him better and could see him more clearly. The tone, the set of his posture, and shadows were all she had tonight.

"A woman in my group shared with me how supportive you were with her too."

Ethan moved back in his chair, thinking. "I guess I've counseled a handful of folks who are in that group." He cleared his throat again. "But..."

"But what?"

"I'm not friends with them."

"Like we're friends?" She bit her lip, hoping.

"Right."

Amber caught herself smiling. Her heart felt lighter than it had in a while. "I'm really glad you said that." Her stupid walls were down again, and here she was saying things she'd never dreamed she would. She hoped she didn't regret this later.

"You are?"

"Yeah, I feel the same way. I was worried I was reading more into the sandwiches and the walks home and the coffee. I'm not very good at judging people, I guess." She'd chosen so poorly in the past. Always trusting people when she shouldn't, never trusting those she should. She hoped she didn't screw it up this time.

He gave her a grin even she could see. "You're better than you know."

"Oh, trust me." She shook her head.

"I do." His words carried something to her she hadn't felt since the first time she met Shannon. A connection. An understanding. Rather than delve too deeply there, she redirected the conversation, probing a question she found herself asking everyone she got close to. "Were you adopted?"

Ethan sat back, curious. "No. Why?"

"Oh, no reason." She stopped herself that time. She didn't want to divulge too much too fast. What if he walked away from her too? Then she'd feel even more stupid.

"Were you?"

"Yes. When I was four." Her mother had taken her back to visit the home many times, so she hadn't lost her connection. When she was six, she met Shannon at the group home and found out her mother had abandoned her too, and they'd immediately connected. Although Shannon had never been placed with a permanent family, they'd bonded over that. Clearly Ethan wasn't connecting the dots like she did. "It's nothing."

They started eating again. "Do you go to church anywhere?" His question surprised her.

"I do. With my mom at the Community Revival Center. What about you?"

"I do. It started as a home church, and now we've got around thirty people coming. Some singles, some with families."

"Who leads?"

"There's an older couple, Henry and Chloe, who started it. It's within walking distance of my apartment, and they organize outreach projects for the homeless around the downtown area with other local groups. It's very hands-on. I like that."

It sounded good to her as well.

"You said you felt like you were called to teach art, so that made me wonder where you were at."

She didn't want to mislead Ethan. "Right now, God and I are on rocky ground. But we're talking again."

Ethan gave her another smile. "I've been on plenty of rocky ground with God in my life."

He understood that too.

"If you're done, I'll help you clean up." Ethan grabbed his cane and started collecting the garbage while she repacked the leftovers.

"You can take these with you when you go, but I'll stick them in the fridge for now."

"No, that's okay. Keep it. I'm well-stocked right now."

They moved to the couch, taking the candles with them. He shuffled some papers off the cushions before he sat down next to her. "'Amber's Must-See List,'" he read. "You've added some since we talked about it."

"And marked off some."

"But not whale watching?"

"No, not yet. I don't know a thing about that. Considering I've lived near the ocean my whole life, it seems silly." Amber didn't even know if she still wanted to go.

"I have a friend who worked for a place years ago. I'll call him and get the info. I know there are some seasons where it's better than others."

"It'll probably be too late." She hadn't meant to sound so despondent. She thought she was okay with doing it. Or with not doing it.

"Don't give up."

"Okay."

"Promise?"

She sighed. "Fine. Promise."

He looked at the others. He chuckled, though she didn't see anything funny about it. "*Travel to Australia.*"

"I know—adventurous, right? My mom told me she'd even pay for it, but I'm not sure I can go. I've got Mocha now."

"It feels big?" He nodded.

"Yes. So does whale watching. Everything does."

"Don't let the bigness of all this get to you." He read down her list. "*See My Mom's Face.* What's that mean?"

"My birth mom. I don't remember what she looks like. I'd like to know. I want to see her face when I tell her I have the same disease." Her tone was anything but compassionate.

"She lost her sight also?" Ethan's voice held a funny tone Amber couldn't place.

"Yes. And then she quit on me and gave me away."

"You don't know if that's the whole story, though."

"No, I guess I don't. I'll never know."

Ethan grew contemplative and kept reading down her list. "I think you should try for as many of these as you can."

"Easier said."

Instead of arguing, Ethan pulled out his own list from his wallet. It wasn't titled, like hers, and many were crossed off, but he shared it anyway.

"*Australia.*" She laughed along with him, understanding. "Haven't made it yet?"

"No." His tone changed again. If she knew him better, she'd know what that meant.

He pulled a pen from his jacket pocket and wrote *Whale Watching with Amber* on his, though, and it sent a thrill of hope through her.

"Thanks." She bumped her shoulder into his. "Why do you have a list, anyway?"

He went quiet for a minute as if looking for the right words. "Everyone should have a list. Life's too short to let it slip by."

Amber frowned at him. She was about to ask him to explain, but he bent his neck and checked his watch. "I'd better head out. I've got an early meeting." He pulled himself up on his cane and pocketed his list. "Thanks for sharing dinner with me."

Instead of letting him walk out on her again, though, she put her hand on his arm. "Hang on. There's something I need to say."

He stopped, waiting for her to continue.

"In the hospital that day." She shook her head. "I was so rude. About the cane and losing my sight, and..." She let out a breath. "I owe you a huge apology."

"It's fine."

"No, it's not."

"Well, it's fine now. I knew it was the pain talking."

"I *was* on drugs." She dismissed his excusing her but then made light of it. "Good ones, though."

"Well, then it was the drugs talking. Either way, no harm."

Amber knew he wasn't being completely honest. "I promise not to do it again."

Ethan's eyes filled with question. "Do what again?"

"Be thoughtless and take you for granted." *Whoa, where'd that come from?*

He nodded. "Thanks." His voice said he wasn't holding her to it, but she redoubled the promise in her head.

Before she realized it, he'd closed the gap between them and given her a light kiss on the cheek. "Thanks again for dinner." Instead of romance in his eyes, though, she saw instant regret.

"You're welcome." She tried to keep it light, letting him know she didn't misinterpret him. Right then she'd do whatever she could to keep his friendship.

After warning him to be careful in the dark, she watched his shadow head to the stairs and heard him limping down each one. Then she closed and locked her door, latching the chain. Mocha leapt at her from the dark, and she let out a scream of fright before chiding him.

"Bad kitty." She tucked him under her chin and blew out the candles before heading to bed.

CHAPTER 21

Amber sat in the coffee shop, adjusting to the sounds of the espresso machine's steam, elevator music streaming overhead, and chatting customers. She was doing her best to desensitize, but it wasn't working yet. She glanced down at the folded cane on the table near her. She'd picked it up the other day, and today was her inaugural walk. So far so good. It felt strange, as if she were claiming a disability before she had one. She knew that wasn't true. It was so odd losing an ability like this, at degrees. But to lose her sight gradually was a sort of blessing in itself, as Ethan kept reminding her.

A particularly sharp hiss of steam startled her. As she looked up, she saw a familiar shape.

"Sam?"

Dr. Samantha Blythe turned and waved at her. Once she'd been served, she joined Amber at her table.

"I didn't know you hung out here." Amber moved her cane and made room for Sam to put her drink down.

"I had an appointment nearby. I've come here with Ethan a couple times, so I knew it was a good spot."

At the mention of his name, Amber went silent. It'd been over a week, and he hadn't contacted her. She must have done something wrong, said something wrong.

"Everything okay?"

"Oh, sure."

Sam leaned forward. "How's the knee?"

"I'm being good and doing all my stretches." Amber saluted her with her coffee.

"Good girl." Sam's jovial mood shifted. "Have you seen Ethan lately?"

"About a week ago. Why?"

"I got the impression you were friends."

"Yes." He'd said it, and Amber hoped it was still true. "Is everything okay?"

Sam hesitated. "You might want to check in on him."

"Check in on him? Is he sick?"

Sam shrugged. "Maybe give him a call? I've got to run." Sam gathered her things. "Be sure to keep in touch and let me know how things are going."

Amber leaned back against her seat, a sinking feeling in her stomach. They'd only been official friends for a short time, but she'd already let Ethan down. Her eyes locked on her new cane, and she rubbed her fingers over the smooth shapes and sharp ends. In another life, it'd be a tent pole, but now it acted as a lifeline. She'd checked out the retracting ones too, but they'd collapsed under pressure in the store and made her feel insecure. The long poles looked like the best, but she hadn't caved in yet.

Caved in? Her thoughts betrayed the ridiculous hope she still harbored in her heart that this wasn't really happening. She needed to not only accept this, but embrace it. She didn't have the courage. Not yet. People kept telling her how brave she was. She wasn't. At all.

She heard a familiar laugh near her table. Kyle. He didn't live down here, he didn't work down here, so there was no reason for him to be in her coffee shop. Ever. She picked up her cane and flipped it open. She hoped he'd not seen her. Slipping outside the shop, she headed toward Ethan's office.

The crisp, sunny day greeted her. She closed her eyes for a

moment and let the rays soak into her deprived skin. She'd shut herself away from this, away from life, for weeks now. Her legs ached for exercise. Amber moved swiftly up the sidewalk, waving her cane back and forth as Maggie had taught her.

Listening for the change in textures, the differing sounds echoing back from the tip of her cane, she made her way up the block. People stared, some moved aside, some smiled. Some of the people she shared the sidewalk with looked her way with annoyance and sometimes with pity. It was the latter that made her wish her sight was gone altogether already. Empathy was desired, pity was not.

The clack and clatter from her cane soon became her only company as the crowds from the busy business district dissipated and she arrived at the doctor's office buildings. Most were closing for the night. She hoped Ethan was still there. Even if he'd left, the walk wasn't wasted on her. Moving and breathing in the fresh air lifted her spirits.

Once inside, Amber felt the directory with her fingers and practiced reading the braille. Then she moved to the elevator stalls and waited for one to arrive. As she rode it up, hearing the ding, the floors being called off, she felt distinctly different. She embraced the aids now, rather than feeling like they were encroaching on her freedoms. In the few months since her diagnosis, she'd gone from feeling threatened to slightly empowered. The doors opened and she headed into the office, a chime signaling her arrival. The receptionist called out to her past closed glass doors.

"Sorry, we're closing. Did you have an appointment?"

"No, it's me, Amber Kirk. Is Ethan around?"

"Uh, let me check." Cheryl picked up the phone and spoke quietly into it. She opened the glass but never looked straight at her. "He said you can go in."

Amber approached Ethan's office and knocked.

"Come in."

She opened the door and went inside. Ethan sat behind a huge stack of files. There were several discarded coffee cups nearby surrounded by piles of discarded papers. She'd never known him to keep an untidy office.

"You must be busy lately." She motioned to his desk and the file boxes hedging him in like the walls of a haphazard castle.

His face looked haggard. "Yeah, I'm up against a big deadline." He ran his hands over his eyes. "How are you?"

She held up her cane. "Maggie got me started with this. I'm signed up for a braille class that starts next month. Christmas is two weeks away, and I'm done with shopping. All in all, it's going well." She gave him a huge grin, but he didn't respond in kind. She kept babbling, filling in the gaps, hoping he'd interrupt at any moment. "You've never mentioned any family. I was thinking, if you didn't have other plans, you could join my mom, me, and Shannon for Christmas. Justin's got loads of family in town."

"It depends. Can I let you know?"

She had asked him impulsively, but even so, she felt the sting of disappointment in his lack of enthusiasm.

"No rush. Maybe you could let me know by the twenty-third?"

Instead of answering, Ethan picked up several papers and slid them into the recycling bin. He tossed the coffee cups away and threw a crumpled candy bar wrapper after them.

"Maybe I should go."

He glanced at her. "No, sorry. I'm distracted with everything. Thanks for asking."

"Sure."

His hand reached out toward hers and he held it. "That didn't sound sincere, but it is. It means a lot to me that you'd ask."

"Are you hungry?" He looked like he hadn't eaten properly in a long time. There was a gray pall around his already gray eyes, making them look sunken.

"Actually, not so much."

"Okay. Well, I'd better get out there and practice." She waved her cane again.

"You go." He gave her the thumbs-up and a half-hearted smile.

Amber moved to leave but stopped, looking behind her. "Everything okay with you?"

"As good as can be expected. I'll call you about Christmas."

So much for their open friendship. Whatever Amber had felt last week had been whisked away by something else.

She waved at him and left the office, moved past the closed reception area where Cheryl sat sniffling. Colds were going around.

Maybe it was her new sixth sense, but something seemed wrong. Really amiss. If only someone would tell her what it was.

CHAPTER 22

When Amber arrived home, she found Shannon sitting on the bench outside her apartment, reading a book.

"Hey, you're all caned up?" Shannon poked at her stick.

"It's a practice one. There were so many models, I went for cheap at first." *Lies.*

"Sure you did. So, next week you and I are going to hit that store in Salem I heard about that has all those tools for the blind. I've looked up the label maker and the better canes. You need something stylish. If they don't have one, then we need to come out with a line. That's all there is to that." She reached up and untied the multicolored scarf from around her neck and wrapped it around Amber's cane.

"It looks cool, I'll admit, but it changes the sounds."

Shannon bit her lip. "Whatever. I thought I knew you. Choosing practicality over design. Seriously?"

"I'll get over it."

Amber opened her door, and Shannon walked with her to the mailbox. Amber kept her eyes closed, found her name, and took her mail. After tucking it into her bag, she headed up the stairs, never missing a beat.

"That was awesome." Shannon patted her back encouragingly, but her voice said something different.

"I know, right? Every time it gets easier. I hope I can figure out a way to pay for this place. I don't want to move just as I start to manage things."

The fear she'd soon be homeless niggled in the back of her mind. It was unreasonable and stupid. She could live with Shannon or her mom. She knew that. But she wanted her independence. Shoot, she *needed* her independence.

After entering her apartment, she turned on the kettle for some tea and started going through her mail. She sat at the table and reached for a magnifying glass, reading the addresses and scanning them quickly. She heard Shannon gasp.

"Oh my God." When Shannon said God, she was really calling on Him, not saying it as some vague interjection.

"You okay?" Amber searched her friend's face.

Horror filled Shannon's eyes. "This is real, isn't it? I mean, I knew it. But seeing you with your cane outside and now barely able to read your mail..." Shannon started to cry. "I'm sorry. Some support system I am."

Amber reached over and took her friend's hand. "It's okay. I'm living with this daily, and every now and then it hits me like that. This is real, this is serious, this is life-changing. But I'm going to be okay. Somehow."

"God's got this."

"One way or another," they said together.

"Worst thing?" Shannon started on their familiar game, but Amber wasn't playing. Instead, her eyes were riveted to the magnifying glass and the letter underneath. This was why he'd looked so overworked. This was why Cheryl was sniffling. Why didn't Ethan tell her?

"This. This is the worst thing." She held it out.

Shannon scanned it quickly and then reread it. "Oh no."

Ethan was stepping down at Tapestry for the time being due to illness. He hoped to return, but there wasn't any guarantee at this time. They'd find her another counselor to fill in during his absence.

She didn't want another counselor. She needed Ethan.

"Why didn't he tell me?"

"Maybe it's no big deal. Or maybe he thought he had told you. Maybe he's trying to spare your feelings. Why did you wait to tell your mom about your blindness? You wanted to spare her."

Amber stared openly at Shannon. "Seriously?"

"Okay, you wanted to avoid drama."

"Understatement. Use a different word."

"Hysterics?"

"Better." Amber reread the letter and then began to pace in her apartment. "What do you think it is?" Mocha chased behind her after a string on the cuff of her pants. At one point, his teeth bit her ankle. She brushed him off.

"Why don't you call him?"

"It must not be that bad if he's returning. Maybe he needs surgery or something." Her mind whirled. "I bet it has to do with his leg. He's been leaning heavier on his cane."

"How can you tell?"

"The sound of it's different. I can't explain it. It sounds more like a thud than a clunk."

"O...kay." Shannon frowned.

"And Sam saw him this afternoon."

"Your physical therapist?"

"Right. She told me to check in with him. She couldn't say why." This was it—it had to be.

"She can't share all that doctor patient stuff but figured sending you would be safe. Well, you gave him the chance. You can't be friends with someone that doesn't reach back. It sucks but it's true."

Amber twirled her hair around her fingers, thinking. "I guess you're right. Something feels..."

"Do you know where he lives?"

Amber looked up. "No, actually I don't."

"Well, if he's going to disappear on you like that, you'd better at least get his address so you can send him a card or something."

"I invited him to Christmas."

Shannon stared at her, mouth agape.

"What?" Amber dropped eye contact.

"You don't invite people to Christmas or anything else. You only invite me because I'm practically family."

"So?"

"You never invited Kyle to any holidays."

Amber picked up Mocha and sank down on the couch, ignoring the implications.

"When your mom tries to add her friends to the celebration, you have a fit."

Amber kept scratching Mocha behind the ears.

"I see." Shannon began humming to herself, something she only did when she had one-upped someone in an argument.

"What?"

"You know what." She opened a furnishings style magazine. "I think the change to neutrals is going to help artists in a huge way. No more being commissioned to match someone's latest flashy sofa or area rug. Paint something bold and brash, they'll work around it."

"Not furnishings, the Ethan thing."

"Oh, the Ethan thing." Shannon put air quotes around her words. "I didn't know you were a thing."

Amber closed her eyes and flopped back against the sofa. "Stop, okay? You're going to make me all self-conscious the next time I'm around him. I'm in no position to dive into a relationship right now, and I'm certainly not thinking about that. We're friends."

"Friends. Got it." Shannon tossed down the magazine. "If that's true, then a friend would call another friend if they were worried about them. Period."

"You're right." Amber fished her phone from her pocket. "Call Ethan's cell."

Her phone chirped back. "Calling Ethan." Amber put the receiver up to her ear and Shannon excused herself to the bathroom.

"Hello?"

"This is Amber."

"Everything okay?"

"That's what I was going to ask you. I got this letter today..." Amber stopped, hoping he'd fill in the blanks.

"Right. Don't worry, I've got a plan. In fact, I've been talking to Maggie about taking you on as a personal client."

That familiar sense of abandonment filled her, and she closed her eyes against the emptiness soon to follow. Her first instinct was to hang up the phone and let him fade out of her life. But anger overloaded her best intentions. Again.

"Friends are supposed to be there for each other."

"True." His tone was non-committal.

"You said that's what we were. Change your mind much?"

"Amber, listen—"

"That's cool. I'm sure Maggie can help me out in these last days. I'm dealing fine with this anyway. I don't need anyone to walk me through. Let's call this good then. No harm, no foul."

"Amber..." He sounded exasperated.

"I should go." Run, get out of there before they leave you. A motto to live by. At least, that was the one she'd lived by for a long time. Racing away alleviated that sense of impending doom and panic. It made her feel in control.

"What about Christmas?" His voice sounded weak, exhausted.

"What?"

"Can I come for Christmas?"

What for? She didn't understand him one bit. "Okay."

"Thanks. We'll talk again, okay? I need to go." He hung up without saying good-bye.

Shannon came out of the bathroom, drying her hands on her pants. "There are no towels in there, or in the cabinet or the clean pile. Where are you hiding them?"

"They're in that other clean pile." She motioned toward a mound on the floor near the end of the couch.

"What's the verdict?" Shannon stood with her hands out, air drying.

"I don't know, really. But I think I've been a grade-A jerk. I can't figure out how that came about."

"Is he coming for Christmas?"

"He said he would."

"Well, in a couple days, call him again and give him your mom's address." She could always count on Shannon to be practical.

Nodding, Amber reached over through the pile of towels and tossed one at Shannon. She caught it and dried her hands the rest of the way.

"I've got to go. You going to be okay?"

"Yeah. I'll be fine."

After locking the door behind Shannon, she sat down and read the letter once again. This time she noticed a second folded sheet, written in braille, inside the envelope. She ran her fingers over the letters and wished could she read already.

The phone rang.

"Hello?"

"Amber? This is Maggie Floros." Her warm, accented voice reached through the phone, offering an instant connection.

"Hi, Maggie."

"Listen, I just got off the phone with Ethan. He explained everything and recommended I take you on as a client as he'll not be able to continue with you."

"That's what he's told me." Amber couldn't apologize for the cold tone of her voice. This didn't make her happy at all.

"I'm very sorry this happened. We can't count on life being calm and calculated, can we? Always a curved ball tossed at us, yes?"

Amber laughed but didn't mean it. God was pitching again. "Curve ball. Right."

"So, we make the best. How's your cane?"

Amber flipped open the folded cane. "Good. I"—she paused—"think I need something more serious."

"Cast iron?"

"Exactly."

Maggie laughed and Amber instantly warmed to her. "I'll have some samples at the next group meeting, and you can do a survey and ask the others what they prefer and why. That's the best way."

"Sounds fine to me."

"Have there been any changes?"

The light mood shifted. "Yes. I'm worse."

"Have you told anyone?"

"No."

"Okay. Then I won't speak of it. But keep in mind, you're not saving anyone any pain except yourself. And all you're doing is prolonging the inevitable."

"Who are you to tell me what to do?" Amber's face went hot, and she broke out in a prickly sweat all over her body.

"I'm no one. No one at all." She chuckled. "But I'm blind. I was once sighted, and now I'm not. I tried to hide it from those I loved most. In the end, I was only hiding it from myself. It's best not to do that. Fewer regrets all around."

Amber clenched her teeth and eyes, doing her best not to scream.

"I can hear that, you know? Grinding is bad for the teeth. Listen to me, okay? This won't stop. It's like a fast-moving train coming at you full force. Instead of letting it hit you, why not jump on and ride?"

The visual became very clear in her head. "I'll try," she managed to squeak out.

"Good girl. See you next Tuesday at group. Plan to be early and we'll go over some things and visit. I'll bring extra doughnuts."

"What could be better?"

"Exactly." She laughed again.

When the call ended, Mocha jumped on the table, startling her, bumping his kitten head against her forehead. "Well, I guess Maggie's our buddy now." *Like it or not.*

CHAPTER 23

The sunrise broke into Amber's apartment, filling it with a golden-red light matching her hair color. Amber recorded it in her memory, painted it in her mind, and quickly transferred it to canvas. The light splashed across the wooden framed windows, through the warbled glass, over her couch, and finally settled on the round splotch of sleeping brown kitten.

Amber's brush moved fast to capture it all before the memory faded from her mind. She'd paint a second and third to imprint the vision. She needed to store all these things up for later. And not much later, she feared.

It'd been nearly two weeks since she'd heard from Ethan. Maggie proved to be a competent replacement, but she wasn't the friend Amber had discovered she'd needed. She'd spent her life focused on art and hanging out with Shannon, and that had been enough. She'd never been one to build auxiliary relationships. She had people she knew at work, Shannon, and her mom. Her mom had more friends than she could count, often blurring the line between business and personal. Amber often wondered at her mom's ability to keep them all satisfied and connected. Not that her mother lacked sincerity—it just didn't seem possible to be friends with that many people without losing yourself. Or letting someone else down.

Shannon seemed to have a good many friends but kept her personal confidences for Amber and now Justin. Justin better not hurt Shannon, or he'd wish he'd never crossed Amber's path. She couldn't tolerate betrayal.

Three hours and four cups of coffee later, three canvases leaned against the wall. Mocha walked up to them, sniffed, approved, and moved on. He'd never tried to rub against them—thankfully, Amber didn't have to worry about inventing a new, unwanted kind of kitty art. For all his curiosity, he didn't seem that interested in her painting, except to draw her away from it to play.

Instead of heading right to the shower, Amber decided to take a walk with her new, more substantial cane. She pulled on a sweatshirt, gloves, and a knitted beanie before heading out the door. She'd begun to walk with her eyes clenched closed at the start, but now she could leave them relaxed and only felt the temptation to peek once in a while.

There were so many things unsettled still. But she'd been reading in her Bible more, jotting down verses she wanted to find in her braille Bible or listen to on her Bible app. Yesterday's verse of the day had been Psalm 46:10. *Be still, and know that I am God; I will be exalted among the nations, I will be exalted in the earth.*

The portion about being still really settled into her. She'd been madly—no, that wasn't the word. Desperately. No. *Frantically.* She'd been frantically trying to mark off bucket list items and prepare for the worst. Funny how she used to worry about so many things. All those what ifs of the past seemed meaningless in the face of her losing her sight.

She moved out of the building and down the street, the crisp December air nearly stealing her breath. The temperature had dropped into the twenties, and the rain had dried up, leaving brittle leaves and crunching grass in their wake. She wished for snow. One last big snow storm for her to paint into her memory.

Looking up at the blue, cloudless sky, she could tell it wouldn't be today. As she headed down the streets she knew by heart and into a block she was less familiar with, she slowed and listened, taking stock of her surroundings. Traffic picked up, rushing by, exhaust filling her sinuses. In the distance, she heard a squirrel yelling at the birds stealing his stash. The park was a block away. And two blocks past that, Powell's City of Books—her safe haven on rainy days.

Amber headed past the park and up another block to the store. As she entered, she could almost smell the book ink floating off the pages as they aged. Many people pushed past her as if she didn't exist, but that had nothing to do with her disability. They had a goal in mind.

What was her goal, though? She opened her eyes and found the help desk.

"Yes?" A woman with an air of busyness and distraction turned her way, still clicking on the keys on the computer in front of her.

"Do you have any books in braille?"

"Louis Braille would be in biographies."

"No, not books *on* Braille, books *in* braille."

Her eyebrows furrowed and she tapped her computer. "I'm afraid not. Most of the customers with sight challenges order audio books. We do have those."

Audio books were a good solution, but they didn't offer the tactile experience she wanted.

"Sorry. You might be able to find stores online. I could look some up for you."

Amber shook her head. "Thanks anyway." She moved away, frustrated. The bumping bodies that had previously felt like camaraderie now felt like shunning. She walked up the ramp and through the doorway, ignoring excited exclamations by children, and headed past the park, past her coffee shop, and back to her apartment.

Instead of that feeling of adventure and taking life once again by the reigns, she felt defeated. As she opened the door, she heard the gruff call of her landlord from his apartment door.

"Sorry to bug you there. I wanted to know your move out day."

Amber frowned and moved over by him. "I'm not moving out."

He looked away. "I heard you lost your job. And then the other day your boyfriend told me you were getting married. I have a prospective tenant."

"I'm not leaving. I don't have a boyfriend. In fact, if you see him, call the cops. He's harassing me."

"I don't want to get in the middle of a fight or nothing."

"Tell your prospective tenant they're out of luck. Besides, I have a lease."

"You can buy your way out of that. Or..." He cleared his throat. "You know, if you can't pay the rent."

"I can pay."

Amber stomped up the stairs and was inside her apartment before she realized she hadn't counted steps or felt the wall. He'd made her break training. Kyle had to stop.

Her cell rang, startling her. "Justin calling."

"Answer." She waited a second for it to obey. "Hi, Justin."

"Hey, are we on for this afternoon?"

Searching her mind, she came up empty. "I'm sorry?"

"You were coming by to say good-bye to the students. They've been asking about you. Especially Katie."

She sighed. "I forgot." More like blocked it. Could she even manage this today? Being shut out of her favorite bookstore, being practically kicked out of her apartment, and facing a room of her students might prove too much for her. "I don't know, Justin."

"Please come. Shannon's on her way over to pick you up."

She sighed again. Trapped.

"Come on, Amber. Please?"

"Okay. How long do I have?"

"Fifteen?"

"Of course. Why would I need more? See you."

She hung up and raced into the shower. As she climbed out, she heard knocking on her door. After wrapping up in a robe, she headed to the door and peeked through the hole and groaned at her silliness. As if. She hadn't been able to see out that thing for a week.

"Who is it?"

"Shannon."

"How did you get in? I didn't buzz."

"The door wasn't closed all the way."

She'd talk to the landlord, but he'd probably ignore her and start talking about the rent again. Once the door was unlocked, she moved aside to let Shannon in and raced back to her bedroom.

"You forgot."

Calling out to her, Amber tried to hide her discomfiture. "No, I'm running late."

"Liar."

She towel-dried her hair and braided it before pulling on a sweater and jeans. Then she put on a light coat of lipstick and raced out.

"See? Ready."

"Uh huh." Shannon put Mocha down, and they headed out to the car. Once inside and on the road, the stereo blasting, the implications of the day weighed her down.

"You okay?" Shannon shot her a look, but she ignored it.

"Feels odd not riding the bus. I'm kind of getting used to it." She still needed to sell her car. Once she did, the parking space rental alone would pay half her rent—not to mention any money she got for the car. Amber reached out and turned down the radio.

"Sound thing still getting to you?"

"Yes. Which sucks because between the two of us, I liked the louder music." She never had.

"You're nuts." Shannon laughed. "At least you've got your sense of humor."

"If nothing else."

Shannon punched her.

"Ouch."

"Well shut up."

"I was joking." Amber rubbed her arm. After that exchange, they stayed quiet, each to their own thoughts.

Shannon pulled into the parking lot of the school, found a spot, and turned off the engine. They both stared at the one story, faded-yellow stucco building framed in tall pines and oaks. Everything about the outside said "institutional," but inside were minds that understood and appreciated the freedom of expression and creativity so many others never would.

"You ready?" Shannon's voice broke the quiet.

"No." Tears streamed against her will, and Amber wiped at them with furious swipes of her shaking fingertips. She gave up and used her sweater.

"You want to pray?"

Amber knew what that cost her friend to offer. Though she loved Jesus, Shannon held her faith in private.

"No." Amber shook her head as Shannon held out her hand.

"Then that means we really need to." Shannon bowed her head and started. "Father, Amber's about to face her biggest fear. In the midst of it all, she's got to say good-bye to her dream of teaching art. She loved this dream. We don't know why you let this happen, but we trust you to make something out of it. Something amazing." Shannon sniffed. "Please give her the courage she needs to say good-bye to this and hello to something new. Amen."

Amber kept her eyes closed. She listened to Shannon blow her nose and unhook her seatbelt.

"Hey, you know I'm with you."

Three words. *I'm with you.* Simple. They meant everything. Shannon took Amber's hand. "You've got this."

She didn't. There was no way she could do this. But somehow she exited the car, walked across the parking lot, her arm linked with Shannon's, and entered the building. The familiar smells of turpentine, paint, and clay met her at the door. This had been her world, her second home, her refuge on bad days—and the place that drove her the craziest in life.

They walked down the hall together, and already the hushed tones and whispers alerted her that something was going on. Her legs stiffened in protest.

"Please don't." They'd planned a party. How could she ever face them?

"They need it as much as you do."

Maybe they did. It didn't mean she had to do it, though. She felt her body backing up. If she could run safely, she would. Something bumped her from behind. The cold, hard, metallic shape chilled her back. She turned to see the pay phone.

"Figures it'd be you." Amber wanted to knock it from the wall and stomp on it till all its coins spilled like silver blood across the mottled carpet. "Traitor."

Shannon took her hand and led her up the rest of the way until they stood outside the door. She leaned over and whispered, "It's now or never."

The phrase burned itself into her psyche. She wanted to scream *never.* Instead she nodded, took a deep breath and said, "Hey, where is everyone? It's so quiet." Her superpower hearing picked up snickering and giggles. She smiled. Not a big smile, but a real smile nonetheless. Shannon led her by her arm, encouraging Amber through the touch.

"Let's do this."

CHAPTER 24

A s they entered her old classroom, cheers and clapping filled the room. Her students and their parents sat around on stools and chairs, and along the walls many of her pieces were hanging. It wasn't just *her*, but also her art, on display. The latter was more personal.

Childish arms hugged her about the waist, and Amber looked down into Katie's face, beaming with excitement and love.

"I'm glad you're here. I've missed you." Her saucer-sized blue eyes penetrated through the pain and insecurity building inside Amber. Instead of crying, she smiled.

"Thanks, kiddo. Did you get the books?"

She nodded. "My parents were really grateful." Katie looked to the side toward where her folks stood. They came forward, hands out.

"Thanks for all you've done for Katie."

"My pleasure." It really had been.

"You'll stop by and see us now and then, won't you? I want to show you how I'm doing."

Amber didn't know what to say. Hadn't her students been told why she'd left?

Before she could stumble out an excuse, Katie's mom offered an apology. At least, she probably thought it was one. "Katie, remember your teacher is losing her sight. She won't be able to see your work any longer." She pulled her back, embarrassed. "I'm sorry, she didn't think."

Instead of being contrite, Katie said something that warmed her to the core. "I know that, but I can tell her about it and she can feel it."

"It's true," she said. Amber looked down and gave Katie a grateful look. "I can see it in my mind. Here, let me show you." She pulled Katie's parents toward a display of her latest work, still confused as to how they were taken from her apartment without her knowledge but knowing Shannon and Justin had everything to do with it. Had Ethan known? She glanced around, realizing that Ethan wasn't there. She wished he was. Silly of her.

Instead of dwelling on disappointment, she turned to the matter at hand and began to show Katie her paintings. They were all there—the river studies, the sunrises and sunsets over Portland, the tree and the desert. All of them. She began to explain her method and how she painted them with her eyes closed, memorizing her pallet, and remembering the emotion. "The beauty of God is all around us, and when we take it in, we can keep parts of it with us forever in our memory. In Psalm 4 it says the heavens declare the glory of God. He shows us He's faithful and powerful and beautiful. It's all there for us."

She hadn't realized it until she'd said it that it was true. Her whole life, she'd known it was true. She began pacing and speaking the thoughts she'd stored up in her heart.

"In Romans, Paul reminds us that since the creation of the world, Jesus's eternal power and divine nature, invisible though they are, have been understood and seen through the things He has made." All these verses she'd memorized as a child came flooding back. "In the beginning was the Word, and the Word was with God and was God, and through Him all things were made." Her voice rang out clear and full of a confidence she hadn't known she possessed. She knew her school wasn't affiliated with any church, but the freedom she felt in expressing her emotions, along with a sudden newness of gratefulness growing in her heart, took the fear of condemnation away.

When she stopped talking and looked up, she realized the room had gone quiet, and all eyes and ears were tuned to her. Those closest smiled in appreciation. Her peripheral picked up movement toward her, and her mother came into focus, eyes full of tears, wrapping her arms around Amber.

"I'm so proud of you." Jennifer sniffed and pulled out a floral embroidered handkerchief to dab at her cheeks.

"Thanks, Mom." Her mother had never told her that, though she sensed it. It meant the world to hear it. Before she could thank her, though, a deep male voice interrupted them.

"Miss Kirk, can I have a moment of your time?"

Amber turned to find a tall, older man in a dark gray suit behind her. His silver hair and otherwise severe style might have thrown others off, but she heard the pleasure in his tone.

"Yes?"

"Your employer, Mr. Glass, asked me here tonight. I'm Rafe Applegate. I own an art house and small café in the Pearl district. I'd love for you do to a showing. What do you think about that?"

Amber had heard of Rafe Applegate. If he said he liked an artist, that garnered loads of positive attention from the local scene.

"I'm not sure what to say." She was taken aback first by the party, then by her courage to speak her heart, and now a possible showing? Why couldn't she have gotten a showing before? She'd applied many times to multiple places and festivals. The competition in the area was especially tough. Everyone thought they were an artist. It was hip. And there were a ton of great ones.

"Say yes. If your showing is successful, you can be sure I'll sponsor you for the next Rose City Arts Alive. You'll get the exposure you deserve there."

Her spirit cried yes, but her head had a question. "Why now?"

"I'm not sure what you mean." He sounded confused.

"I've tried to get exposure before. Why now?"

"Sometimes it's who you know, Miss Kirk. Sometimes it's timing. Sometimes it's pure talent."

She put her hand up to stop him. "And sometimes it's because she's blind."

"Amber!" Her mother's horrified exclamation stopped all the near activity and drew attention to what was being said.

Rafe leaned over, his voice serious and reprimanding. "I can assure you, Miss Kirk, this isn't a pity play."

"But there's marketing potential."

"You say that like it's a bad thing. You have amazing talent, or I wouldn't have agreed to come tonight. While you do have a hook, it's not pity motivating me, nor money, Miss Kirk—it's potential. You've got it." He pulled out his card and handed it to her. "If you want to see where that potential could take you, then call. Otherwise, we won't waste each other's time, and I wish you the best." He began to move away.

"Wait, I'm sorry." Amber recovered from her shock and perceived insult. "I would like to hear more."

"Then call me and we'll have a meeting." His friendly tone now carried hesitation. She'd blown it. Oh, she'd call, but he'd be busy.

Stupid. Stupid. Why do you ruin everything?

Rafe moved off through the crowd, heading toward the door. Something stirred her to follow. She excused herself and moved passed Shannon and her encouraging looks. By the time she caught up to Rafe, he was nearly at the outer door to the parking lot. Amber raced past the pay phone, giving it a wide berth and trying not to notice its mocking face.

"Mr. Applegate?" She was breathless and desperate sounding, but she didn't care. He turned.

"Yes?"

"I really am very sorry."

He waited.

"I didn't mean to insult you. I've had a lot of trouble coming to terms with all these changes, and tonight..." She paused, reigning in her emotions but doing a poor job of it. "Tonight was unexpected. This surprise party, my students saying good-bye, my art on display, you. It was all too much."

"I see."

"Is it okay if I call you?"

She could sense him sizing her up. "Let's plan on that showing. A month from today sound all right? I'd like to have the desert scenes, the cityscapes, and a few more river studies. Have you thought of the ocean?"

"That's next on my list."

"Excellent. Is a month too soon?"

Maybe. It might be. But she wouldn't say so. "No. It's fine." She'd get Shannon or Justin to drive her. *Or Ethan.* She hadn't a clue where she and Ethan sat, but surely he could be counted on to drive her to the ocean. Whale watching was on his bucket list too.

"Good. Call that number and make arrangements to have your work delivered. I'll let you know the set-up date, and you can give me your opinions on layout." He chuckled. "I make no promises on listening to you, however."

Amber wasn't sure how to take that, so she laughed along.

He gave her a nod. "Congratulations, Miss Kirk. Your life is about to change." He said it as if change were a good thing.

Her smile faltered and she steadied herself against the doorframe as he made his way to his car. Shannon came up behind her.

"Looked like you worked it all out. Everyone's waiting. Are you ready?"

Amber didn't dare trust her voice, so she nodded. Ready or not.

CHAPTER 25

Ethan hadn't answered the last three phone calls, so Amber took it upon herself to contact his receptionist and get his address. Strangely enough, she gave it to her.

Now, though, standing on the front steps of his home, she wondered if she was intruding. Maybe he didn't want anything to do with her. She had probably misread his interest, his friendship, and there was nothing between them but a professional relationship.

The cold breeze whipped around her, and she shivered. Ethan's place was part of an old Victorian cut in half to make a duplex. The dormant rose bushes by the stoop rattled and scraped against the building, their thorns catching on one another in the wind.

Before she lost courage, she knocked. No one answered. As she was about to make her escape, she heard him call from inside.

"Hang on."

His voice sounded strained. She shouldn't have come. Her first thought was to run and hide behind the fence in front of his house. Knowing how well she did maneuvering steps in a hurry, she decided against it. Instead, she braced herself for an uncomfortable meeting.

The door opened, revealing a pale but otherwise healthy-looking Ethan, leaning heavily on his cane.

"Amber?" He sounded surprised, but happily so. *Good so far.*

"You weren't answering your messages, and I needed to ask you something. Hope you don't mind me stopping by." Her mouth rushed ahead of her thoughts.

"No. Sorry I haven't called you. I've been really tied up." He kept the door open just far enough for him to see her. He looked behind him. "I'd invite you in, but my place is a wreck."

"I don't mind. I can't see it if you keep the lights down low." Her repertoire of self-deprecating blind jokes was increasing. See, she was growing, accepting it.

"Can you give me a sec?"

"Sure."

He closed the door, and she heard shuffling and a thump. A couple minutes later, he opened the door again and ushered her inside. The lights were bright now, but she didn't notice anything too awful, besides a huge pile of dirty dishes at the sink.

"Can I help you with those?" She moved toward his kitchen. "I know how hard it is to keep up with stuff when you're not feeling well."

"I'm not feeling too bad, really."

She furrowed her brows at him. "What's that supposed to mean?"

"I mean, I'll probably feel worse before I feel better. You know how that goes." He didn't explain.

Instead of following that confounding line of questioning, she turned toward the dishes and began to run a sink full of suds. "I wanted to ask a favor."

"Oh?" He limped into the kitchen and picked up a towel to dry.

"No, just let them air dry. Don't wear yourself out." She waved him off. If she hadn't known better, she would have thought he'd scowled at her. He tossed the towel into a heap on the counter.

"Right. Well, what then?"

She ignored his growing grumpy state. "It's about our bucket lists. You know, where they crossed over? Whale watching—not Australia. I need to go within a month."

"I don't know." He sank down on a kitchen chair.

"It's probably rushing things, but I really need some ocean studies, and there's no time like the present."

"I see." He grew thoughtful and then pulled a stack of loose papers closer to him and began flipping through, reading. "Don't you think it's too cold to be out on the ocean at this time of year?"

"I can dress warmly."

"Kind of hard to paint with all those rolling waves."

"I need to do quick studies. I'll set up my easel on the shore afterward with all my notes." She tapped the side of her head.

He glanced up into her face, and for a moment she thought he looked worn and haggard, but then his eyes crinkled and his voice changed. "You know what? Now's a great time. The schedule says the day after Christmas is perfect. Our next opportunity wouldn't be until March, and that'd be too late."

"The whales run during Christmas break? I was thinking more after the first of the year." That'd be enough time to get them done.

"I don't think the whales know it's Christmas." He snickered.

"Right." She was being a dope. As she stacked the last plate, a stinging sensation ran through her hand. "Ouch." She pulled it back to see bright red blood dripping down the side.

"Oh, shoot." Ethan moved toward her, grabbing the towel. "I should have warned you there was a knife."

"I can't believe I didn't..." Didn't *see it.*

"Have you been back to see Dr. Birkman?" The pressure he applied to her hand made it hurt worse.

"No." She winced, unable to keep playing it cool.

"You should."

Everyone lived to give her advice. "I'll know when I need to. Besides, what can he do for me but confirm it?"

"Look, I get this is hard, but avoiding a professional opinion isn't going to make it disappear. You need his letter of recommendation, anyway, for your disability hearing."

"I don't know if I need to go on disability."

"What's that supposed to mean?"

"I've got an art showing lined up."

"So, Rafe liked your work?"

"Who told you?" She hadn't mentioned Rafe's name.

He pulled back the towel to see if the bleeding had stopped, then he led her to a chair and took out a first aid kit from the cabinet near the sink and started to fix her up.

"You won't need stitches. When was your last tetanus shot?"

"Two years ago. I jabbed my hand on a nail while reusing a donated canvas." She watched him work on her hand, noticing how comfortable she was having him doctor her. If he'd been anyone else, she would have done it herself, and not nearly so well. "Hey, don't go changing the subject. Who told you?"

"Shannon told me Rafe Applegate was coming."

"When?" She turned over her hand, checking his work. Very professional. Ethan had an excellent bedside manner and skill.

"Make sure to keep an eye on that." He cleaned up the table, tossing the bloody towel in the sink and throwing the crunchy bandage wrappers into the garbage.

"When?" she persisted.

"When she invited me to the party."

He hadn't come. He'd known but chosen not to attend.

"You weren't well?" Her tone, no matter how nonchalant she tried to be, revealed her disappointment. She hated feeling like that. She only needed two people in her life—her mom and Shannon. And not too much of her mom at any one time. It didn't matter that he hadn't come. At least, that's what her head said. Her mouth said, "I missed seeing you there." *Oh. My. Word.*

"With everything going on..." He shrugged. "I heard it was great."

From who? Again, no elaboration. At least he could have made up a reason, anything. Anger got the better of her.

"I'd better go." She gathered her things together, fumbling with her coat. "I guess I'll make that appointment on the whaler and check off my own list." Bitterness built in her throat, but it appeared to go unnoticed by Ethan, who was laughing.

"What's funny?" She set her jaw, ready for an argument.

"It's not a whaler. That kind of defeats the purpose."

Her cheeks went hot. "Right. Whatever it's called, I'll go on my own. Sorry to bother you. Get some rest." As she moved past him, he held her arm.

"I thought I was coming?"

"I didn't want to overburden you."

"You're not." He sighed. "Do you want me to call?"

She did. For some reason the last thing she wanted to do was set this up. Or go alone. But going alone was ten times better than forcing your company on someone. Or appearing desperate.

"Look, I'll call and let you know what they say. We'll firm up plans on Christmas."

Her head shot up. "Christmas?"

"Yeah, I'm still invited, aren't I?" He actually sounded hurt. He was the hardest person ever to read.

"Sure." She began scribbling on a loose scrap of paper on the table. "Here's my mom's address. Come over around four. Shannon will be there. She always spends Christmas with us."

"How long has she been doing that?"

"Since grade school. My mom would volunteer at an after-school program as a way of thanking the organizers and keeping me involved and connected with where I came from. It was sponsored by the same agency my mom found me through. I'd go along to play with the kids." There'd been a handful of friends she'd gotten to know, and one by one they were all placed—all except one.

"Doesn't Shannon have her own family?"

"No. She grew up in foster care. Several homes, actually. She never got that forever family." Instead, she got a lot of horrid ones.

"But you did?"

"Yes." Her voice faltered.

"No reason to feel guilty about that."

Well, *he* seemed to read *her* without any problems. She picked at the bandage on her hand.

"I'm not guilty. I wish my parents would have adopted Shannon too. My dad wouldn't go for it, so she became like part of the family—but not." Her dad hadn't wanted to adopt someone that didn't look like them, and Shannon's Asian heritage didn't fit that bill.

"You're sisters of a kind. Must be nice."

"No brothers or sisters for you?"

"I'm an only child and my parents live back east. We're not close." His words were weighted with hidden meaning. When he didn't continue, she decided that was her cue to leave.

Underneath all her banter, worry simmered. She was intruding into his private life and didn't know if she should be. If they were friends, then all was well. But where they stood, only one of them knew, and it wasn't her. As Amber turned around to say good-bye, she saw, once again, his fatigued expression.

"Are you okay? I mean, I know you left work because of illness, but..." She paused, hoping he'd fill in the blanks.

"I'm tired. Lots to do. You'd think stepping away from a job would give me more time."

"If you weren't so good at your job, then maybe it would be."

He sidestepped her compliment. If she only knew him better. At least as well as he apparently knew her. This whole friendship thing seemed more of an enigma than ever. She'd been terrible at it her whole life. Her longest and best friendship was with Shannon, and maybe that was because she grew up with her. Making friends as an adult seemed so much harder.

She moved through the door, dying to know why he'd really taken time off but afraid to ask. Afraid he'd tell her it was none of her business after all.

"See you at Christmas."

"I'll text you with the info on the whale-watching expedition." He followed her to the door and closed it behind her.

The chill outside ushered her all the way home.

CHAPTER 26

"Where are the napkins?" Jennifer raced around the house, tucking loose hair back into her bun as she got the table ready for Christmas dinner. Cold dishes were set out, tall red tapers lit, and twinkling garland framed the dining room window. Amber watched, amazed at her otherwise organized mother whirling in panic. She glanced at Shannon, who lifted her hands in question.

Instead of offering to help for the tenth time, they moved into the living room and sat in the armchairs flanking the fireplace. The Christmas tree sat opposite them in the front window, alit with white lights and surrounded by a display of blue and green foil-wrapped gifts. Outside, the bushes and trim mirrored the twinkling golden hue, and rare stray flakes of snow wisped down. Amber couldn't see them, but Shannon described them for her.

"Think of the lightest, whitest snow you can, then add a slight breeze. Every time the air shifts, so do they, dancing and falling in a rhythm all their own."

"Are they sticking?" Amber wanted so badly to see snow one more time.

"Let's go look." Shannon started toward the door and Amber followed. They forwent coats but grabbed scarves. When the door opened, they heard Jennifer gasp from the kitchen.

"Don't tell me he's early?"

"No, he's not. We're going outside to see the snow." Amber grabbed gloves as well, tucking them in her pockets.

Jennifer muttered something relieved, and they shut the door behind them.

"Make sure you use the rail. It's slippery out here. Don't want to break anything." Shannon's singsong tone and subsequent giggle rang in her ears.

"Yeah, yeah." Amber could foresee many years of stair jokes and jabs in her future.

Once down, she sat on the bottom step and looked up at the darkening sky. It was only three thirty but the cloud coverage thickened, blocking out the sun. The white flakes blended in with the sky, making it near impossible for her to see it, but she could feel the tickle on her face and the tiny sting of cold against her skin as the flakes melted.

The smell of pine and a crisp-cleanness in the air cut through her senses, and she closed her eyes, imagining.

"What do you see?"

"I'm not seeing, I'm feeling." She opened her eyes and breathed out a puff of steamy air. "Remember when we'd sit on the porch with cut straws in our hands and pretend we were smoking to freak out the moms in the neighborhood?"

"Remember the trouble we both got into when your dad came home early and your nosey neighbor, Mrs. Grimes, raced out to tell him what we'd been up to?"

Laughter bubbled up out of Amber. "You took the blame."

"Of course I did." She sat down on the steps next to Amber, bumping her shoulder.

"You never told me why."

"Why do you think? You worshipped your dad."

Amber's brows knit together. "You did that for me?"

"And I'd do it again in a second."

Moisture gathered in her eyes. "You've always been there for me."

"And vice-versa." Shannon lifted her hand palm up to catch errant flakes.

Normally, Shannon had tried to be as perfect as she could around Amber's dad. They'd held out hope and planned that someday her father would relent and discover he needed a second daughter after all. He never had. After his death, Shannon went to the local beauty-supply store and bought hair dye. She stood at his graveside with iridescent blue hair, crying along with Amber. Shannon never pretended to be anything she wasn't after that.

If only Amber could be so brave.

The snow started to fall in earnest, growing into big, fluffy, misshapen clumps. Within minutes the mottled grass had gone white.

"Oh." Amber patted her pockets for a pen and pad she kept there and started making hurried sketches.

"I'll get your easel. Grab a coat."

They headed inside, and moments later, Amber was set up on the porch, facing out, taking in the scene. With the snow fell a silent shroud, blocking out the city sounds, replacing it with an ethereal peace. Her brush scratched the rough canvas as she plastered white paint all over it and cut in pink hues from the street lamps and yellow-gold glows from the lights in the bushes and along the sidewalk. Soon those were gone too, and the cars in the driveways were masked entirely.

She pulled another canvas out and headed down the steps to face her childhood home. Snow fell like rain, fast and hard, and still she painted. The edge of the roof, the gabled windows, the Victorian eves. Scalloped shingles framed glowing windows, and splashes of light emanated from where the tree stood in the living room window. Instead of more bright white, she replaced the bulbs with the colors she'd always wanted it to have. They seemed to twinkle back at her. She grabbed another frame, pushing the previous one at Shannon, and closed her eyes, feeling the surface with her hands, smile blazing, face aglow with love and the enjoyment of capturing it how she always had it in her mind.

She prayed. She prayed and praised and thanked. She would have this memory forever.

"Oh my." A masculine voice came from behind. She opened her eyes to see that Shannon had covered both her and her canvas with a large golfing umbrella, most likely found in her mother's front closet, and on the other side of her stood Ethan, enraptured.

"That's amazing." His voice, gravelly with emotion, echoed in the otherwise quiet evening.

Amber gave him a huge grin. An artist liked nothing more than knowing she'd achieved her goal of touching another.

"Thank you."

"I've never seen anything like it. It's incredible." He reached out to touch it and pulled back, realizing what he was doing. Instead, he gave her shoulder a gentle touch. "I'm so glad I got to see this."

Shannon cleared her voice and they jumped. "Do you want to do another?"

"Yes. But you need to move the umbrella." Amber lifted the last frame to the easel. She tipped her head up, staring into the ever-darkening sky, watching the flakes fall with the 3-D effect that used to make her blink. Now she braced her eyes wide, taking it all in, the light-gray, dark-gray and floating masses of white, sinking down, falling on her face, hitting her eyes. Opening her mouth, she let several land and melt on her tongue, tasting the essence of Christmas, the newness of life, and crispness of beginnings. She laughed.

Clenching her eyes closed then, she felt her way around the flat spaces, marking it with her thumbnail, counting the staples on the back so she knew her world perfectly. Then, taking up a brush of teal and aquamarine, of white and gray, of night and light, she worked out the scene as she always felt it would be. She thanked God once again for these last looks at the beauty and majesty only He could design, shared with her in a way for only her to see.

Her arms moved with rapid fluidity, her breaths came in starts and stops as she felt her way around the edges and slathered color and brilliance and muted serenity. In another part of her mind she heard the crunch of dress shoes and the murmurs of those around her—but that seemed a world away, another lifetime. Light and movement danced in perfect harmony. There was this, and this was all that mattered.

Once done, the cold that numbed her fingers and turned them and her nose bright red penetrated her senses and brought her back to the now around her. She turned and caught her mother's face, gloved hand pressed to her lips stifling her sobs. Shannon, eyes shining and proud, rubbed her back. Ethan, glowing with an aura she'd never noticed about him before, smiling at her like he'd never seen her until now.

It was his face out of them all she committed to memory.

After she caught her breath, they cleaned up and moved inside, thawing their frozen fingers around cups of buttered rum at the table.

Dinner rushed by in a wave of deliciousness. Ethan's tired expression took a break for the evening, and he charmed them all with stories from his childhood. It certainly didn't sound as if he and his parents weren't close. He spoke of his mother's traditional cooking, of his father's relentless pursuit of the perfect antique to add to his collection.

"Then, Ethan, you're Cuban?" Jennifer, who must have been feeling her tongue loosening after a glass of wine, thought the evening had turned no-holds-barred. Everyone went still at the table, waiting to see Ethan's reaction.

"My mother was from Cuba, but my father is an all-American

mutt." He gave them an easy grin and carried the turkey to the kitchen.

"Mom," Amber hissed, "seriously."

"He's the one that brought it up." She gave them both a scowl. "What's the big deal?"

Ethan wandered back in, taking up her mother's cause. "It's okay. Lots of people wonder why my last name's Griffith if I'm Cuban. I've had to explain more than once that it's just my mom's side."

That did it. Jennifer loved him. Amber saw the immediate connection, and her mother gave her a nod of approval not even Kyle had the honor of gaining.

Amber shot Shannon an *uh-oh* look and Shannon broke the tension. "Presents anyone?"

They moved into the living room to find a few more had joined the base of the tree. Ethan excused himself to his car and came back in carrying several sacks, each one holding a gift. He shook his head, and snow flew from it.

"Oh, sorry about that. It's really coming down."

Her mother grabbed a towel she'd brought from the scrap bucket for that purpose and opened it over the entryway floor.

"There we go." Again, she beamed at Ethan.

Warning alarms went off in Amber's head, and she saw Shannon hadn't missed the exchange—but she was giggling, not worried. She gave Amber a wink. Amber frowned and shook her head. This wasn't what she'd planned. Friendship. That's what she was after—and her mother was about to ruin it if she wasn't careful. Poor guy.

But the poor guy didn't seem to mind the glances or implications of her mother's hints.

"Amber doesn't date often. She's not seeing anyone right now."

Amber waited for the deer-in-the-headlights look in Ethan's eyes, but it never happened. "Me either." His tone carried something she began to recognize as teasing. At one point, she leaned near him.

"I'm so sorry about my mom and all this dating stuff."

He shrugged. "You've never seen the like of it until you meet my mom. No worries. I won't take it seriously." He gave her a comforting smile, but she suddenly had trouble returning it.

"Well, that's good." She moved uneasily back to her seat and opened a sweater and scarf set, three pairs of woolen socks, a gift card, and e-reader.

"Wow, Mom, thanks." She held up the e-reader, wondering what her mom had in mind.

"You can download all sorts of audio books and listen to them on your device. You can even get voice command software for it. I know how much you love reading."

"Neat." She showed Ethan and Shannon, who were busily opening their own gifts.

"I didn't expect anything. This is great." Ethan held up a scarf and gloves set.

Jennifer's face broke into a pleased grin.

Shannon leaned closer to Amber, whispering with an exaggerated English accent. "Fifty more points to *Ethan-dor.*"

"Shut up." Amber knocked her shoulder.

Ethan chose that moment to pass Amber, Shannon, and her mother their presents. Jennifer received the latest Greene & Greene architectural coffee table book. Shannon opened a gift card to a specialty jewelry store in the Pearl—a place she frequented quite often.

"That's so cool. I know exactly what I'll get. Thanks."

For Amber, though, a book of a different sort. As she flipped it open, she found some famous works of art reconstructed through embossing in a new tactile design to be touched and experienced. She closed her eyes, feeling the raised edges and shapes of modern art, classical design, art deco, and her favorite, art nouveau.

"This is unbelievable." Ideas for improving her own art to make it visual for other sight-impaired people sparked in her mind. "Seriously. I couldn't think of a better gift." Amber hadn't meant to be so gushy and felt her cheeks go warm with embarrassment.

Ethan took it in stride. "I'm glad you like it."

After dessert, they broke up and each got ready to go their own way.

As Amber pulled on her coat, her mother tried to convince her to stay. "It's so dangerous out there. Your room is ready. Shannon, you can stay too. Ethan—" Jennifer stopped, not sure if she should invite him to stay as well.

"I've got to go, Mom. Mocha needs to be fed. Plus, he's probably cold." She buttoned her coat up. "I didn't know the sky would open up like this."

"Well at least let me drive you. I don't want you taking the bus. You know they practically only have one plow for this whole city."

"As if you can drive better than a trained bus driver? No offense, Mom, but no. I'll be fine. Really."

"Let me drive you. I grew up on the east coast." Ethan shrugged into his jacket. "This is nothing. I can take you home too, Shannon."

"Thanks, but Justin's picking me up." As if on cue, a horn honked outside. "There's my ride. Thanks for everything, Jennifer. Merry Christmas!" She shook Ethan's hand and then pulled Amber close, singing softly in her ear. "You're just too good to be true." She jabbed Amber in the ribs and left before Amber could retaliate.

Ethan finished buttoning up his coat and reached for his cane. "Ready?"

"Thanks for taking her home, Ethan. Call me when you're settled in, okay?" She gave Amber a warm kiss on the cheek and a hug. "Thanks for a lovely Christmas, sweetie." Jennifer's voice filled with emotion that Amber didn't want to deal with right then. Her mother's next sentence would have something to do with it being their last sighted Christmas together. There were continual "lasts" with her mother lately. She wanted this whole day to be special and beautiful, with nothing to mar it.

"Thanks so much, Mom." She gathered her things together. "I'll get my paintings in a week when I'm sure they'll be safe to move. You might want to air out my bedroom tomorrow, though." Her mother hated the smell of oil paints and the way the off-gasses permeated everything around them. On the other hand, if Amber cut open a vein, she'd leak linseed oil.

Ethan limped down the stairs on his cane, she gripped the rail, watching every footfall with care. The crunch of the snow under her shoes stirred a childish joy in her heart. She laughed and ran past Ethan, falling to the ground to make a snow angel. He put their things in the car and moved to stand over the top of her.

"Nice."

"Take a picture." She moved her arms up and down, feeling the snow sneaking its way under her collar and down the neck of her jacket.

Ethan pulled out his cellphone and snapped some shots. Then he tossed his cane down and joined her, laughing with exuberance, shifting his arms up and down in the snow.

"Is this on your bucket list?" Amber turned her head toward him.

"Totally will be now. I never took the time to do this as a kid."

"I know, right? Going home tonight and putting it on there just to cross it off." She sat up, the snow sticking to her hair in clumps, hanging from the red-golden strands like crystal ornaments. Ethan sat up and brushed himself off, and then reached over and tried to ruffle the sticky clumps, getting his fingers entangled in her hair.

"Oh, sorry." He tried to extricate himself but failed miserably.

Amber reached up to still his hand and got it loose, holding it a second too long. She dropped it as the heat in his grasp made its way to her bloodstream.

"I'm going to soak your car." She climbed to her feet, wincing as her knee protested.

"Are you sure you should be off your crutches?"

"I'm normally okay. It's not every day I toss myself into the snow, you know."

"I suppose not." He pulled his cane nearer and used it to get up. As he caught her watching, the joy faded from his eyes. "We'd better get moving." His tone went as cold as the air around them.

CHAPTER 27

The drive on the way to her apartment was strained and silent. Ethan's car slid every now and then as it broke through piles of snowdrifts on the move.

"You got this okay?" The urge to ask overrode her concern for his ego. If that was something he suffered from, she couldn't tell.

Instead of being insulted, he gave her a reassuring smile. "Yes, this is nothing. We'll be fine. We're almost there."

"Oh, good." The world around them swirled white with dashes of blackness, bright street lights, and oncoming traffic. She breathed a sigh of relief when he pulled to a stop outside her apartment.

"I'll walk you up." He climbed out and opened the car door for her.

He helped her carry things inside, and their snow encrusted shoes slipped their way up the stairs to her place. She unlocked the door without looking at her keys and moved around inside, turning on the lights so her whole place blazed. Mocha stretched on the couch and jumped down to meet her at his food dish. She complied, leaving him noisily noshing away at his meal.

"He's got you trained."

"Oh yeah. Since day one. This is nothing. You should see him when I forget to take care of the kitty box."

"Not a pretty sight?"

"It's the fit he pitches. Moans and cries like I've broken his heart." She chuckled. "Then again, I wouldn't want to use a dirty porta-potty all of my days, so he *does* have a point."

"I never thought of it that way."

"I have lots of time for such deep thoughts." She took off her coat, hanging it over the chair. "Can I get you a cup of coffee or cocoa?"

He glanced out the windows. "Rain check? I'm not so worried about me, but the other drivers out there scare me to death."

"Right. Forgot about the snow." Strange. She really had.

He moved toward her and gave her a gentle hug. "Thanks for making this a great Christmas." The musky scent of his cologne swirled around her, once again reminding her of safety and comfort. Something else hung in the air between them, something left unsaid, but he moved away before she could ask.

"Thanks for my book."

His eyes sparkled at her. "I'm really glad you liked it."

"Do you want your present?"

"You gave me gloves."

"My mom gave you gloves."

"She signed it from the both of you."

Amber smiled. "She would." Moving toward the living room wall, she returned with a wrapped package. After tearing off the paper, he held it out, blinking in appreciation. In his hands was one of her river studies. The very place he mentioned to her that he liked to go and think.

The cool colors of the sky and river, the warmth of the green trees and grass, and the blaze of the sun and floating clouds came alive in the room under his gaze.

"I don't know what to say." His eyes filled with unshed tears.

"Surprised?" Her heart swelled at the connection she'd made with him. Plus, making anyone cry with happiness with one of her pictures brought a whole new level in the pleasure of giving.

"You don't know—" He choked. "This place." He couldn't continue. "Thank you." He pulled her into a tight embrace, and she'd realized she'd hit more nerves than intended. She felt him shake in her arms.

"Ethan? What is it?"

He pulled back, shamefaced, wiping at his eyes. "I'm sorry. I'm not usually like this."

"It kinda looks like you are. It's okay. Christmas can get to folks. Plus, you're away from your family. That's hard."

Holding the picture away again, staring at it, his walls came down. "This is the place I went when I first had..." He cleared his throat. "Had surgery on my leg. It quickly became the place I went to be alone with God. I had to walk a set distance every day from my apartment, and this was my go-to spot." He cleared his voice. "At first, it was the place I went to sit angrily. Then it became the place I'd go and rage at God. And finally, the place I made peace."

Amber remembered her time in the desert. "I get that."

"He took so much." His voice cracked.

"I get that too." She took his hand. "Are you okay?"

He made eye contact with her, and she could see the question in his eyes. Could she see him? She nodded.

"For now, I can still see you."

"I wanted this to be so different."

Amber's brows knit. "This?"

He moved a hand back and forth between them. "This. I don't make friends easily. I know lots of people, and I'm well-connected in the community, but not people I hang out with."

"I think that's hard for most guys." She remembered her dad saying something similar one day after a company trip to a soccer game. He said that they could drink and scream and cheer with one another, but counting on another guy to listen and be there for the hard times wasn't something he'd ever found.

"Maybe so." He sighed as if looking for the right words. "No matter what happens, I'm really grateful for your friendship."

"Well, I don't like the sound of that." Really, she didn't. She'd started to think maybe there was a chance for them to be something more. Regret from letting down her guard washed over her. Would she never learn?

"I meant I'm glad we're getting to know one another."

Oh. Again, something more floated between them, but she got the impression that if she pushed, he'd withdraw all the way.

"Is this something to do with why you left your job?"

"Took a leave. Sort of." He moved away. "I have to have surgery again on my leg."

"I'm so sorry. Everything will be okay, though, right?"

"Right."

"I'll come visit you in the hospital and bring you home-cooked meals." She grinned. "I start my cooking for the visually impaired class next week. You're the victim I was looking for."

He laughed. "Great. I'm sure it'll be better than hospital food. And before you know it, you'll be the cook you once were."

"I hope not."

"Why?"

"I haven't ever been able to cook."

That garnered a guffaw. "Super. Thanks. I'm sure that it'll make it a memorable experience." He moved toward the door, carrying his painting.

"Thanks again for this. God knew I needed it, especially when I'll be laid up." He hugged her again. "Merry Christmas."

"Wait, when's your surgery?"

"Next week."

"When, exactly?"

Ethan hedged. "I'll have to check."

"Seriously?"

"Fine. Thursday at six a.m."

"That's only a few days from now! Plus there's our whale

expedition tomorrow. Are you sure you're up to it?" Had she pushed him into this?

"Absolutely. And I'll pick you up at five a.m."

"Great...wait...what? Five a.m.?"

"Whales wait for no man. Or woman."

"Super. You bring the coffee." This idea sounded less fun by the minute. Freezing cold, rocking on a ship out in the ocean at five in the morning. *Yay, fun.*

"Whose idea was this again?"

"If I can do it, so can you." He opened the door and gave her the thumbs-up signal.

She chewed on her lip and gave him a look that made him laugh down the hall, down the stairs, and out the front door.

CHAPTER 28

Ethan directed her up the dock toward a rocking skiff tied off and ready for boarding. He hung back, gathering his gear. Amber took a deep breath, smelling the salt and something else like a promise. Excitement vibrated through her. The snow had melted enough for safe travel, and here at the coast was non-existent. By the time they were done, no trace would remain. Yesterday had been such a gift. Maybe today would be too?

Amber slung her backpack, holding her oil pastels, paper and, most importantly, travel mug of coffee, over her shoulder. The sign over the entryway read WHALE RIDER OCEAN EXCURSIONS. *Creative.* She moved along with a growing crowd of feet-sliding zombies up the gangplank. A bearded man at the head of the boat motioned for them to gather closer.

"If you're here for the last orca sightings of the year, then you're at the right spot. If you're not sure what an orca is, or what that big blue expanse is out there, then you've got bigger problems than I can fix." His practiced speech earned a few chuckles.

"The weather is stirred up, so things could get rocky out there. If that's the case, we'll come back in. Bobby will hand out the life vests. You will wear a life vest at all times until we are safely back at the docks. If you, for any reason, remove your life vest, you'll have to answer to me. And you really don't want to do that." More chuckles. He handed around a contract releasing the company from being sued should anyone do something foolish like leap into a whale's mouth. Bobby, his right-hand man, came around with some scruffy-looking orange life jackets. She slipped hers over her head.

"Attractive." Ethan came up behind her already wearing his. But his was much cooler and more modern than hers. His lay flat and was more like foam with a zipper than ratty stained cloth.

"Why do you rate the stylish jacket?"

"It's all in who you know."

The boat started up, and they moved out into the bay and then made for the ocean. The wind picked up significantly away from shore. Amber caught herself gripping the inner railing.

"You okay there?" Ethan motioned toward her white knuckles.

"Sure." She loosened her grip until he looked away, and then her grasp doubled in strength as the boat rocked and shifted with one wave after another. Maybe this wasn't the best idea after all.

Ethan reached into her pack and offered her the travel mug. "Drink."

"Um...uh-uh." She moved her face away.

"Drink. It'll settle your stomach."

She groaned but submitted. After twenty minutes, they still hadn't seen anything, and the wind now carried the bite of rain. It was cold. Despite the nausea, she was hungry.

"How long is this trip?"

"About two hours. You hanging in there?"

It was all she could do to nod. She leaned over, resting her forehead against her arms, and stared at the bottom of the boat. It lifted and fell, rocked and shifted. Her head began to loll.

"Look up."

"No way."

"Amber, listen to me. Look up."

When she was a kid there was nothing she wanted to do more than ride a rollercoaster. All the other kids did, and they loved it—they screamed in laughter and it looked like the best thing in the world. She waited in the long line at the amusement park and finally got into her seat. As soon as they went over the first loop, though, she knew she was in trouble. Where the others laughed and screamed, all she could do was put her head down and grit her teeth together to hold back the vomit.

"You're nuts."

He leaned down next to her, speaking calmly into her ear, his warm timbre reverberating throughout her. "If you look up and keep your eyes on the horizon, you'll adjust faster and it'll help with the nausea. You'll get your sea legs."

"Never," she grunted as her stomach roiled. Stupid girl. Stupid, stupid. Never again. What was she thinking? She had no business being out on the ocean looking at large, meat-eating mammals. The first thing on her bucket list should be to stay alive. This was definitely the opposite of staying alive. *Oh, please, make it stop.*

"Amber." Ethan's tone told her she'd better listen or else.

Amber forced her head up, pushing past her straining neck muscles, and tried to make eye contact. Try as she might, it didn't work—they kept lolling closed. She felt his hand under her chin, warm and comforting.

"Come on. Look at me."

She cracked her eyes open a tiny bit and found his, sweet and worried, peering back into hers. He really did have a nice smile and kind eyes. The kindest eyes.

"Okay, now keep looking." He moved her head ever so slowly so she could see out over the side of the boat and off toward the horizon. For some reason, she'd expected it to be going up and down with the boat, like in the movies, but the ocean wasn't really rolling all that badly. The world began to level out, and her nausea subsided. It didn't go away but it improved.

Amber took a breath, not realizing she hadn't been breathing at all. How she'd stayed conscious, she hadn't a clue.

"That a girl." Had anyone else said that to her, she would have clobbered them for being condescending. But when Ethan said it, it carried a different feel altogether. "You've got this."

She nodded ever so slightly but kept her eyes riveted on the horizon. Before she knew it, she was seeing more than the gray of the sea, the sky, the boat. Colors began to emerge. The sun materialized, drawing out the teal and aquamarine, the foamy loam. She kept one arm braced on the inner rail and found a seat. Then she pulled out her notebook and began to sketch with her pastels, blocking in what she saw with what she felt.

Her first drawings had an undertone of Pepto-Bismol, but as she gained her sea legs, the chalky pink faded while and bright blues and flashes of black and white appeared. At first, Ethan didn't seem to get it, and then he said, "Hey...hey...whales!" He looked to the edge where she'd been sketching and saw the pod. The boat shifted as people crowded over to see, blocking her view, but that was okay. She had it in her head.

"Can you move? She's trying to capture the scene."

A ginormous man turned to scowl, but then he caught sight of Amber's cane.

"What for? She can't see anyway."

The energy, the very air around Ethan shifted. "Apologize."

"Why should I? If she's blind, I'm not blocking her view."

Ethan began to move at the man who outweighed him by at least sixty pounds. She pulled him back.

"I'm not blind completely. I'm here trying to see things on my bucket list. Whales are one of the things I wanted to make sure I saw. What would be on your list?"

The man frowned. "I guess I never thought about it. Yellowstone. Yeah. That'd be on my list, I've always wanted to go to Yellowstone."

A slender woman with short-cropped hair piped up. "I love

waterfalls. Big or little. The rainbows they make in the mist remind me of the first rainbow in the Bible. I love that story."

Murmurs shifted throughout the boat.

"I'd love to see my children's faces one last time." This other woman began to cry. "I wish they'd come home."

"I want to travel through all the sites of the major historical monuments across the country." Bobby sniffed. "I've always loved history."

And the wishes went on and on.

"I want to see London." A slight woman spoke with such wistfulness, Amber prayed she'd get to go soon.

Before she knew it, they were no longer looking at the whales, who seemed to notice their absence and moved even closer to the boat like a group of kids having been ignored too long. Instead, the group turned introspective and began talking about the things they missed in life, and the things they hoped for still. It wasn't until a huge splash washed over the deck they turned to see the pod closer than ever, one whale in particular.

The leader lifted up, and Amber could have sworn it made eye contact with her. Her heart leapt into her throat and her spirit lightened. What an amazing creature. So beautiful, so graceful, so powerful and in control in this great expanse that no one could tame. No person. Save one.

Amber pictured Jesus walking out on the water, calming the seas, and Peter striking out of the ship, braving the waves to get to his Lord. Did he fear the big fish, the sharks, the creatures of the deep? Was it only the storm Peter had trusted the Lord to calm or was it every aspect of his life?

"Don't take your eyes off of His, or you'll sink."

"What?" Ethan looked down at her. "What did you say?"

"Jesus. Don't take your eyes off of Him, like Peter did, or you'll sink."

Ethan took the seat next to her. "You're right."

She gave him a sideways smile. "When I first got my diagnosis, I thought life was going to end and I'd spend the rest of my days trapped in my apartment. But you showed me another door, another path. I don't think I ever thanked you for that." She took his hand. "Next to Shannon, you're my closest friend. I'm not sure what I would have done without you."

Ethan paled. She'd overstepped. She had to say something to save this. Why was she always saying things too fast, too soon? She'd never learn. Being too open scared people away.

"I've got to tell you something." Ethan swallowed hard.

"Don't mind me, please. I'm being silly."

"No, you're not. You're right. These past few months, although miserable for you, have been a real blessing to me. I've gotten to know you and Shannon. And Justin." He looked out at the sea and the retreating whales. People had moved away, but some were still talking about what they'd want to see. "I've kept to myself these past few years. I can't say, before we met, that there was anyone in Oregon I could have called who I could count on."

"Dr. Blythe cares about you. And so does Maggie. Oh, and that gal in my group—she kinda likes you a lot." She nudged him, trying to lighten the mood.

"It's different knowing people and feeling connected to people."

"I can see that. I'm like that too."

He nodded. "I know. Maybe that's why we get along so well. Why you and Shannon and I all get along so well. We know what it's like."

"What it's like?"

"To be abandoned. To be forgotten."

"Your folks?"

He pursed his lips. "They loved me, but when I had my first problem with my knee, they tried to make me quit my job and move back into their house. I was offered this job out here, and I took it because I had to try to be on my own. They were so angry. My mom had this girl picked out for me to marry."

At the mention of the word "marry," Amber's stomach clenched.

"Did you like her?"

"We'd known each other for years, grew up together, but I didn't think our relationship had anything romantic to it. Apparently, she did. I wasn't exactly unhappy to move to the other side of the country... but my family thought it was the end of the world. They told me when I was ready to be part of the family again, to move home. Until then..." He slouched down in his chair.

"You've got to face surgery all on your own? Do they even know?"

"They don't answer my calls, and I'm not about to leave a message about it."

Amber frowned. "It's knee surgery. I had it too. It's a drag, but you heal."

He sighed. Again.

"It's not just knee surgery." Instead of answering the questioning look in her eye, he pulled up his pant leg.

All the blood drained from her extremities as her eyes locked on his leg. Amber couldn't believe he'd been hiding this from her.

CHAPTER 29

Seething. Angry. He'd totally screwed up her day. And was their entire friendship one complete lie after another? For him to hide this from her was unforgiveable. She stomped down the pier to the car and tossed her backpack inside. She'd ripped the keys from his hands. It gave her cause to pause. Looking down, she checked to see if there were any of his fingers in the rings. All clear.

After unpacking the trunk, she dragged her gear over to the flat spot she found earlier that day. The weather had cleared, but it could mist up again at any moment. She needed to hold the memory picture in her head and get it down fast.

She set up and started to paint, but her emotion got in the way. She cared about Ethan much more than she'd realized. What he showed her frightened her. And to think he was going to go through the next week without saying a thing to anyone.

Amber looked at the canvas, seeing a mass of disconnection and raw emotion. She growled, tossing it aside. She set up another, and began slashing colors, but they all turned out red and harsh.

"Not going so well?" Ethan's voice carried a timidity she'd never heard before.

"No. Not going so well. This day is really screwed."

"Hang on. This is happening to me, not you." He tried to sound angry, but all she heard was quiet desperation.

"Stop it. You're not John Wayne in *The Quiet Man*. You're a—"

"A liar?" He plopped down on a rock next to her. "Go ahead. Say it."

She turned on him. "You're missing the entire lower half of your leg."

"Right."

"All this time you've been wearing a prosthetic leg, and you never told me? Even when I made a complete fool out of myself at the hospital over the cane comment."

"Yep."

"And you're having more removed and weren't going to say a thing?"

"Yes."

"I'm waiting to hear the good reason behind this." She picked up a stone from the shore and chucked it at the sea. *Take that.*

"Because I had this girlfriend once. Well, not a girlfriend. She was this woman I took out a couple times. Actually, she was the third woman." He stopped. "Geez, Amber. They all ended the same, so it's no wonder they mash together in my mind. We have a great time, they share some background stuff, I show them my leg, and they turn all white and claim a headache's come on and leave. I never hear from them again. End of story."

"Well, then. They. Are. Idiots."

"Maybe so. But evidence says otherwise."

"If I say they're idiots, then they are idiots. End of story."

"Fine." He put a hand up in front of his mouth. She could tell he was trying to hide a smile.

"This isn't funny."

His eyes narrowed at her. "No kidding."

"When were you going to tell me?"

"I figured it'd come up in the hospital."

"And then I'd go all wishy-washy and become the shallowest person you know and leave you?"

"Something like that." He lowered his head across his arms, resting on his knees.

"You sure don't think much of me."

His head snapped up. "That's not true."

She waved her paintbrush at him. "Then give me a little credit, okay?"

"Okay."

Amber moved back to her painting and tried a third time. She could still feel the betrayal, sadness, and disappointment. The fear. Her anger ebbed along with the tide. This time the colors were gray and bland with the tiniest bit of green escaping into the scene. She closed her eyes and dug deep. White caps. Fluffy clouds. Black-eyed whale. Her shoulders relaxed, and the brush moved easier now.

She didn't open her eyes but kept painting. "Friends count on each other no matter what. If we're going to stay friends, you've got to give and take, sharing both joys and hardships. Or there's no point to it."

"Hardships wear people out. They get tired of it. Too much pressure. They can't fix it, so they feel helpless and walk away because it's too hard to see their loved ones suffer."

"Wimps." Amber sniffed. She hated to admit it, but she'd heard one story after another like that in group. What was wrong with people? Couldn't anyone be counted on anymore? *I have to leave because I can't watch you suffer.* It all seemed so selfish and self-serving. Didn't they know what their leaving did to the one they left?

Devastation. Complete and utter. Like death. Like when her dad died. Or when her birth mom walked out on her. She wasn't better off without her birth mom. She loved Jennifer, sure. Jennifer chose her, and Amber would be forever grateful for that. Being chosen made her feel valuable again. But it didn't take away that empty feeling inside that couldn't be filled by anyone here on earth.

Maybe it wasn't supposed to be. No matter how much she wished it was true. Only God could begin to fill that void in her life—and Jesus was holding the shovel.

Still, it didn't mean she couldn't stand by Ethan or anyone else and keep pointing them in the right direction. She wouldn't be that person. Christians were supposed to be Jesus's hands and feet and love others for Him. You couldn't do that very well if you walked out on the people that needed you most because *you* couldn't handle it. No one could handle all of it. That's where God came in. His strength, His peace. All of it. Everyone got tired now and then. But leaving? No. *That* wasn't in her vocabulary.

Amber turned to Ethan and pushed back on his forehead so he'd look at her. His eyes questioned and she nodded again. She could see him.

"I'm not that person, okay? I can be counted on. I'm not going to run away because you're missing part of your leg."

He looked deeply into her eyes, penetrating through all her defenses, measuring her.

"Even if it's my whole leg?"

She gulped. *Oh, Ethan.* "Even if it's your whole leg."

He measured her some more.

"Even if it's cancer. And surgery might not get it all. And chemo takes my hair, maybe my teeth?" She could hear the silent cry: *Even if I die?*

Oh, God no. Please no. "Even then." A horrible shudder worked through her body. She fell to her knees in front of him, rocks and sand digging in through her jeans, tracing his tears with her fingers. "Even then." She moved into his embrace as he moved into hers, and they mourned in their fear and grief together.

CHAPTER 30

Once it's said and done, all that's left in this life is love and relationship. Amber woke up sure of it. Mocha leapt on her chest and chased his toy mouse. She scrubbed the back of his neck and tossed his toy across the room, watching his shadowy form chase it with abandon. She said a prayer of thanks for her mother, Shannon, Justin, and Ethan.

Ethan's surgery was tomorrow.

Her heart was heavy. She'd prayed and prayed for God to have mercy on Ethan. Today she'd haul over to his place the meals she'd learned how to make in cooking class. As she'd practiced, she made two apiece and stuck one in the freezer. Tonight, she'd go to her support group.

If ever Ethan needed support, it was now.

He'd sworn her to secrecy. Except to Shannon. He knew she'd tell Shannon anyway. But why he didn't want anyone else to know, to be praying for him, she couldn't figure.

"It's my choice." His voice had been firm and intimidating. He'd meant it. For sure. The last thing she wanted to do was break confidence with him when they were starting to trust each other.

Maggie knew, though. He'd told her as a professional courtesy. Last week at group, she sensed Maggie had inside knowledge when someone asked her where Ethan had gone to and she'd hedged. Now, from Ethan's words, she knew Maggie understood the implications of this surgery—if not the overall physical dangers. She might not know the details, but she knew enough.

As much as Amber resented being tossed into Maggie's lap, she had to admit she liked the woman. Because Maggie shared her blindness too, it created a connection on another level. Besides, she was likeable.

Amber showered and dressed. She packed the frozen meals in heat-safe containers and loaded them into vinyl grocery bags. Not for the first time did she wish her apartment had an elevator. But the building's super had suggested she lock up a portable cart under the stairs on the bicycle rack. That thing was a Godsend.

She loaded her wares into the cart and headed out the door, walking the ten blocks toward Ethan's house. She stopped by the newspaper stand. She couldn't read the print any longer, but the worker knew her.

"Hey, Jimmy. I need a handful of puzzle magazines and some of those gossipy rags. The more outlandish the better."

Jimmy handed them over, and she paid him before tucking them inside the bags. She'd stick them near Ethan's recovery bed at the hospital and leave a couple at home for him. It'd give them something to laugh about. And if they needed anything, it was laughter.

Amber unbuttoned her coat, letting in a cool breeze. The temperature had risen to an uncommon fifty degrees. Sunshine beat down on the top of her head, and she sighed. She had her cane out, swinging and counting corners of buildings and listening to sounds. She kept her eyes closed during her walks, now, because counting on her failing sight had started to throw her off. She moved up, past block nine and then ten. She turned the corner and felt her way up the street, past the fence to the path of the entry to his duplex.

"Okay. Here I go." This whole situation had her freaked, even more so than losing her sight, if that could be believed. That had happened to her. This was happening to Ethan. She had to admit to herself she needed him in her life, in any form, as long as they were friends.

She knocked on the door and waited. Nothing.

Amber's knuckles rapped again on the wooden door. She leaned closer. Still nothing. Hadn't she told him she was coming?

She called to him through the door. "Ethan, it's Amber. I've got your food. Yes, that's a threat." It really was. Her meals would keep him sustained with nutrients—but not much else. She waited. Nothing.

Reaching out, she put her hand on the doorknob, not sure if she was overstepping her bounds. She didn't want to intrude. The doorknob didn't budge. A gnawing worry in the pit of her stomach built. Something was wrong.

She stepped down and began to search under rocks and pots by the front door. A dragonfly statue under the rosebush caught her attention. She flipped it and underneath, surrounded by a curly worm, some roly-poly bugs, and mud sat a key. After wiping it off on her jeans, she fitted it into the lock. It worked.

Inside the house felt still. Overly so. The lights were off.

"Ethan? It's Amber." She moved through the darkness with her cane, ears straining for signs of life. Maybe he really wasn't home. She would have to explain the mud she was inadvertently tracking through his place.

A strange sound filtered through to her ears. Breathing. But not normal breaths. Pants. She rushed toward the sound and opened Ethan's bedroom door.

"Ethan?"

She heard shuddering breathing now, and moved closer, to the bathroom. An awful aroma of excrement and sick met her. Ethan lay on the floor, one leg twisted under him, his shortened leg uncovered. Actually, all of him was uncovered. She closed her eyes to give him privacy.

"Oh no. Ethan." She moved to her knees. "Ethan, can you hear me?" She felt his torso and neck to see if she could find any sign of injury.

His skin was cold and clammy, and he shivered despite the temperature in the apartment. She fumbled with her cell phone and called emergency services. Then she pulled towels down and began to clean him up. In other circumstances, she wouldn't have dared touch any of the mess or be so intimate with a man. But this was Ethan, and he needed her.

She tossed the soiled towels into the tub and pulled the comforter off his bed, then tucked a pillow under his head, feeling a large lump. Moments later, the EMTs opened the door.

"Hello?"

She'd forgotten they'd be in the dark. "Back here. I'm a friend. I'm blind." She'd been told to be clear with people in case of emergency. "I found him about twenty minutes ago."

"Do you know his health history?"

"I know he's scheduled for surgery tomorrow for cancer on his bad leg." She moved back, out of their way.

"Do you know how long he's been unconscious?"

"No. I found him like this, in his own mess. I suspect he took a shower and fell. He could have been here all night. I felt a knot on his head."

The EMTSs began to take Ethan's vitals, hooked up a saline IV, and got him on the gurney. They wrapped pre-heated blankets around him, and his shivers subsided.

"Do you know which hospital his surgery is scheduled at?"

"Legacy, here downtown."

"That's where we're taking him." They moved him out after getting her contact info. It'd only taken minutes for them to arrive and leave. The front door stood open, the breeze blowing outside, and the only sign of anything amiss the retreating sounds of the ambulance in the distance.

She called Shannon and told her what happened. Then she turned on all the lights, doing her best to see. After putting the towels in his washer, she moved over the floor with cleaning wipes and scrubbed it clean. She proceeded to clean the rest of the bathroom too. Then she moved the towels to the dryer and tossed his bedding into the wash. While the different loads ran, she went through his desk, searching for his address book. She didn't find it but found his cell phone under some loose papers on top.

Ethan's phone was different than hers. She prayed he had voice commands installed and didn't have a password on it. She fiddled with some buttons. Double tapping until she heard a familiar chirp.

"Call Mom."

The phone beeped. Amber prayed. The voice command answered, "Calling Mom." *Yes! Now, please answer.*

The number rang. Rang again. "Hello? Ethan?"

"Hi. My name is Amber. I'm a friend of Ethan's. Is this his mother?"

The heavily accented woman answered. "Yes. Is my Ethan okay?" Amber was encouraged by the fear she heard in his mother's voice.

"I'm not sure. I came to visit him and found him unconscious. He's been taken by ambulance to the hospital. I'm going to add your phone number to my phone, and I'll call you again when I know anything."

She could hear crying. "No. Ethan. My baby."

A voice in the background called to her, a man. "What's happened?"

"Ethan is sick. He's in the hospital."

She couldn't hear the response. Then the woman came back on the phone with her.

"What is your name, please?"

"Amber. I'm a good friend."

"Amber, please call us again soon. What is your number?"

Amber dictated her number to Ethan's mom. "I'm heading to the hospital now. When I know anything at all, I'll call you."

His mother's voice was small. Distant. "Please. Yes."

Amber said good-bye, feeling helpless. She wished she could say something to encourage his parents. She didn't understand the intricacies of their separation, but she needed to respect Ethan's decision to cut them out of his life. She hoped she hadn't overstepped. But like the homeless girl on the street that day, Ethan had parents and they deserved to know if he was sick or injured. Or worse.

Amber headed into his room and went through his laundry, packing fresh clothes in a bag. She grabbed his toothbrush and hairbrush, his razor. She moved by his bed and saw a book he'd been reading and his Bible. She packed those too.

She stowed all the meals she'd prepared in his freezer and checked his fridge for other foods he'd need. All she found was old milk and bagels and crusty, out-of-date cream cheese. He didn't eat much better than she did. Maybe the food she made *would* be a blessing.

She heard the door open and Shannon's voice call, "Amber?"

"Yes, I'm here. Thanks for coming." Amber grabbed her cane and the bag she'd packed, then turned off all the lights in his house. Dark once again, they headed out. Amber locked the deadbolt and tucked the key in her pocket, along with the set of his keys she'd found on the desk.

They drove in silence up to the hospital. When they got there, no one would tell them anything except where to wait. And wait they did.

Two hours later, Justin showed up with sandwiches. They sat and ate together.

"Wasn't he coming in for surgery tomorrow?" Justin took a sip of his Jolt.

Amber nodded.

"Freaky. I hope he's okay."

She did too.

They waited. Sat. Waited some more. The sun set and still they waited. Amber found herself jealous of those in the waiting room who could read the magazines. She closed her eyes and tried to sleep.

"Amber?"

She looked up and squinted, trying to see who it was.

"It's me, Samantha Blythe."

"Hi, Sam."

"Is everything okay?"

She related how she'd found Ethan. All but the naked, messy part. "I'm so worried."

"I'll see what I can find out, okay? He'd hate it if he knew you were out here worrying. He thinks so much of you."

Did he? That simple sentiment made it all worth it. She hoped he knew how important he was to her, as well.

Her phone rang and called out, "Maggie Floros."

"Hi, Maggie. Sorry, I know I'm late. I hadn't realized the time. Ethan's in the hospital. I found him passed out earlier today."

"Oh no. What is wrong with Ethan?"

"I don't know. My PT therapist came by a while ago and said she'd see if she could find out. I'm afraid I won't be at our meeting or group tonight."

"No worries. Give me a call later, okay? Let Ethan know we're all thinking of him."

"I will."

Amber tucked her phone back in her pocket. Again, that feeling of familiarity struck her with Maggie. It was probably that whole teacher/blindness thing they had in common.

"I know a little about what's going on." Sam came back in and pulled a chair over by Amber. Her face was void of her familiar smile, and the tone sent fear throughout Amber's body.

"Tell me."

"He did fall, and got quite a bad knock on his head. He's got a concussion."

"Okay." Concussions happened. "What aren't you saying?"

"The reason for his fall." Sam took a deep breath. "How much do you know?"

Amber looked sideways at Shannon. "I told Justin."

Okay. Well, there you go. Hard to keep a secret when it was about someone you cared for. "We know he lost his leg to cancer and that they were going to have to do more surgery, that the cancer came back."

"Okay. Then I'm not breaking confidences. The cancer is back, and not only in his bad leg. It's in the bone in the other leg. It broke, and that's why he fell."

"Oh, God." Amber looked up at the ceiling as if He resided there. Why?

"They are taking him into surgery early. It's bad."

"He's going to lose his other leg?"

"I can't say much more. I've probably said too much already. Do you have a relationship with God?"

"Yes."

"Then tap it. Pray." She squeezed Amber's good knee and moved to leave. "He'll be in surgery until late. I'd suggest going home to rest and coming back in the morning. It's going to be a long one."

It was one of those moments when her own horrible circumstance, like blindness, suddenly became irrelevant in light of someone else's predicament. She hadn't felt sorry for herself once that day.

"We'll drop you off at your place and pick you up again in the morning." Shannon stretched her back, and Justin began to clean up their food garbage.

"No. That's okay. I'm staying." She couldn't even think of going home.

"Amber," Shannon started. But seeing the expression on Amber's face, she stopped. "Fine. Look, let's go to your place. You can grab a shower, change of clothes, your e-reader and some headphones. We'll feed Mocha and pick up takeout and come back. You'll be gone all of a couple hours. Okay?"

Amber pondered the situation. "Okay. And could you stop by in the morning and feed Mocha before coming over here?"

"Absolutely. I've got my little kitty-nephew covered."

Amber pulled out her phone and Ethan's. "Can you put his mom's number into my phone and name it 'Ethan's Mom'?"

Shannon nodded and took care of it. Then Justin drove her to her apartment and said he'd be back in an hour. He and Shannon went to get dinner, and she went inside. As she showered, she couldn't get the image of Ethan, splayed out on the floor, in pain and suffering, out of her mind. She let herself have a good cry as she prayed. Then she dressed and fed Mocha. She gathered her things and packed her charger cords and e-reader in her pack. She stowed her digital pad too. After she was all the way ready, she called Ethan's mom to give her the latest. She let her draw her own conclusions as to what the doctors might be doing to Ethan in surgery.

Amber found she couldn't say it aloud.

CHAPTER 31

Ethan lay asleep in his hospital room. Amber kept the blinds closed, knowing he needed to rest. The sounds of the equipment monitoring his vital signs comforted her. The nurses came in and out, and the doctor stopped by to check his bandages. All in all, uneventful.

After pulling out her earphones, she stowed her things on the table and used his bathroom. She came back out, glanced at his bed, smiled at him, and sat back down. It was then she realized his eyes were open. And he wasn't a happy camper.

"Pain," he gritted out.

Amber hit the call button, and a team raced in. They asked her to step out and paged the doctor. As she stood in the hall, relief filled her that they would be the ones to tell him. It wasn't on her anymore.

"God," she whispered, "help me to be the best friend I can for him. Help me to have the right words." Or no words. She'd discovered that with her blindness—sometimes no words were the best ones.

The nurses and doctor left, and she went back inside. Ethan lay looking out the now-opened window. She sat down in the chair nearest his bed. He didn't say a word, but he moved his arm.

"My hand," he whispered, "is open."

Amber didn't need a second invitation. She moved closer and took his hand in hers. They sat there like that for a long time. Nurses came and went, and still she held his hand. He drifted to sleep, and still she held his hand. At one point, she too, fell asleep, but when she woke, they were still holding hands.

The sun drifted across the sky, shifting the shadows in the hospital room, covering it with lines of differing angles. Shannon and Justin stopped by, leaving flowers. Lunch came and went. He didn't eat.

When the nurse asked him to try to eliminate, she left the room until he was done. Then she came back in and took his hand again.

He cleared his voice, found it raspy, and she brought him a glass with ice water. He sipped past the straw, not making eye contact. She fumbled and water spilled. Grabbing a towel, she sopped it up.

"Sorry, I'm such a klutz." She looked up at him, embarrassed. He reached out and stilled her arm, taking the towel from her, his face going red, his eyes narrowing.

"You found me." His voice accused, not thanked, her.

"Yes." She didn't say anything else. In his shock-induced state, she was surprised he remember anything at all, let alone that.

He shook his head slightly and looked away, disgust in his eyes. But not at her.

"It's no big deal." She tried to comfort him. It didn't work. "I didn't see anything. I closed my eyes."

"It's a huge deal. How long have you been here?" Anger laced every word.

"Since it happened. Well, best as I could. I left to shower last night and came back right away." From the look in his eyes, she could tell that wasn't what he'd meant.

"Well, you've done your part. Go home." Oh. He hadn't wanted to be comforted with the thought she'd never left him alone. Hardly. Now that the medication had worked through his system, he didn't want her there. He *wanted* to be alone.

Too bad. Been there, done that.

"I'm going to go grab dinner. What sounds good?"

"Go away, Amber." He closed his eyes.

"Chinese? Sounds good to me too." She pulled out her stick and pushed her things to the table. "Be back in a few." She put on her lightest, most carefree voice and walked out of his room. Once in the hall, though, she leaned against the doorframe, trying to get her bearings. From inside his room she heard heartbreaking sobs as reality crashed down. She wept with him.

She moved down the hall and out of the hospital. She went four blocks over and ordered Chinese takeout, all the extras, and two drinks. Then she tapped her way back, holding their food in one hand, her cane in the other. The food smelled good, and she hoped it triggered his appetite.

Once on his floor, she heard yells and knew it was him.

"Get out. Get out." Rage and harsh words filled her ears. This wasn't like Ethan. She moved to go past the nurse.

"You might want to give him a moment."

"Why?"

"It's finally hitting him."

Amber waited. She took stock of her own feelings. She prayed. Taking a deep breath to steel her reserve, she knocked on the door and pushed it open.

"Henry's Chinese Palace delivers." She put the food and containers onto the sink counter and pulled the table over his bed.

"I told you to leave."

"And I did. Now I'm back." She remembered how spiteful she'd been to him, to Shannon, to her mother after her knee surgery. Her tiny, insignificant, nothing surgery. She sure felt sorry for herself then. Now, all she felt was foolish.

"The kung pao chicken is spicy, but you like the spicy stuff, right?" She put out a plate with a small amount of everything on it. "That nasty anesthesia is well out of your system by now. You must be starving." She dipped an eggroll into the sweet-and-sour sauce and held it up for him to take a bite. "Go on."

He didn't move, so she put it nearer his nose. The aroma worked its magic, and he took a bite. It was well over twenty-four hours since he'd eaten. She had no idea still how long he'd been out on the floor.

She fed him a few more bites until he decided he could feed himself. He pushed himself up in the bed and grimaced. His eyes locked onto his legs. Or what used to be his legs.

Amber talked and talked. She told him stories about Mocha, and ate, and told him about her mother's latest house sale. He picked at his food. After an hour, satisfied he'd eaten enough, she packed it away and then stowed it in the fridge in the break room around the corner with Ethan's name on it. She grabbed a juice box for the two of them and went back inside.

Moving closer to his bed, she handed him his juice. Ethan was staring out the window, desolation on his face. His color was better.

"Want to hear a book? I've gotten a couple good mysteries and one sappy romance. Or you can try a Sudoku puzzle. You won't get much help from me, I'm afraid."

He didn't speak. He didn't look at her. She rambled. Half an hour later, Samantha Blythe came in in full PT mode. The pressure to be his sole source of entertainment evaporated. The relief was palpable.

"Well, now. Here we are again." She walked closer to his bed. "Your doctor said you and I are going to be spending a lot of quality time together, which, as you know, is my favorite kind of time."

Samantha lifted the blankets to check his legs. Ethan grabbed her hand.

"I don't want *her* to see." He spat in Amber's direction.

Amber's face went ashen.

"I think it's too late for that, pal, don't you?" Sam ignored him and took some measurements. "I'll have some temporary prosthetics made for you by tomorrow, and we'll get the good ones ordered up.

A lot has improved in the past few years. You'll be amazed. For now, start doing bed pushups. You remember what I mean?"

Ethan nodded.

"Great. See you bright and early. Keep up your protein levels and drink lots of fluids. It'll help you heal." She waved at Amber and as she left, gave her a thumbs-up of encouragement. Amber didn't see it. But Ethan did.

"She forgets you're blind. She gave you the thumbs-up sign."

Harsh. She thickened her skin. "Great. Thanks for translating."

"Sorry. Look, it's best you go. Really."

"I'm not going to. Remember? No wishy-washy friends need apply."

Ethan groaned and lay back against the bed, defeated.

"I will be sleeping at home tonight, though. These chairs are the pits."

Her phone rang. "Ethan's mom is calling," came the automated voice.

"Oh, crud." She fumbled it, trying to silence the ring.

Ethan looked at her. No, he seethed at her. Yeah. Better word. *Seethed.* She answered even though he waved at her, pleaded with her, begged her.

"This is Amber." She looked away from Ethan, who'd begun cussing under his breath.

"I don't know if he'd want that right now. Would you like to speak to him?" She shuffled to his bed and handed him her phone. He didn't lift his hand. She did it for him and forced it in his palm. The nasty looks continued as he lifted the phone. At least he didn't sound angry with his mother.

"Mama? I'm okay, Mama."

Amber heard a string of Cuban words, panic and love pouring forth. Forgiveness. Ethan held her phone to his ear and sank back against his pillow. After he said good-bye, he held out the phone to her. She slid it back in her pocket.

"Is there anything else I need to know?"

Amber pretended to not hear the accusation in his voice. She might as well get it over with. "I stocked your fridge, did your laundry, and cleaned your house."

"Great."

"I also contacted a company to line up some disabled services. They're going to drop off a few things at your apartment tomorrow. A rail on your bed. A shower chair."

"How do you know I don't have a chair already?" he demanded, but then his face went pink when he realized she'd seen everything in his bathroom. *Everything.*

"I know I'm overstepping, but I also know you want to get out of here as fast as you can, right?"

"Right."

"And they're not going to let you go if you're not ready at home. So I'm getting you ready."

She didn't tell him the rest yet. She'd wait for that.

"What else?"

"I'm not sure what you mean." She fiddled with her cane.

"You're hedging. I can always tell when you start chewing your lip."

"Not fair. I can't see your tells."

His tone lowered. "Your eyes, they're worse?"

"Much worse." She moved her hands as if to say no big deal.

"But we haven't finished your bucket list."

"My mom still intends to take me to the Australian outback and get us lost." She didn't know how important that was now. Life had taken another sharp turn when she least expected it.

"You have to go. Make plans to leave tomorrow. You'll never

feel the heat and see the colors like you need to." His voice held an edge of urgency to it.

"I'll call the nurse."

"How'd you know?"

"I can hear your pain." She hit the call button. The nurse responded fast. "He's hurting."

Once she'd administered his pain meds, she turned down the lights. "He's going to need to rest some more."

"Thanks. I was heading out in a minute." *Taking the hint.*

"Amber...are you there?" His words swam in his mouth.

"I'm here." She shuffled over to his bedside.

"You need to see it. See it all. Please?"

She felt like she was missing something. "I'll try."

"For me. Do it for me. My bucket list." He squeezed her hand tightly, and then his grasp relaxed as the pain meds took over and he dropped off to sleep.

He couldn't have meant without him. Could he?

CHAPTER 32

The church felt empty as she entered, and the aroma of burnt coffee and day-old doughnuts was missing. Maggie must have been arriving late. Amber moved through the building with her cane, making out corners and the entry to the main meeting room. She'd never been inside the sanctuary; the doors had been closed on her first visit. In fact, she'd stopped thinking of their meeting site as a church at all. She'd never turned on the lights, and couldn't make them out in the semi-darkness. No matter—the darkness was beginning to be a friend now, or at least an acquaintance. She moved ahead, not giving it another thought.

Once in the meeting room, she heard the front doors slide open and close. Amber waited but no one entered the room, so she figured she'd imagined it. Instead of sitting still, she started shifting chairs here and there and cleaned the main table of previous inhabitants' garbage.

A sliding sound caught her attention. "Hey, Maggie. I'm the first one here, so do I get my choice of doughnuts?"

No one answered. The hair stood up on the back of her neck, and all her senses heightened. If it'd been any of the group, they would have shouted out—she knew this from past experience and from being chided for not doing so at her second meeting.

She flipped her cane open and held it tightly. Maggie had showed her how to use it to subdue an attacker. At the time, she balked at the idea. Who'd attack a blind girl? Now, she wasn't so sure. Her eyes strained in the darkness, giving her an instant stress headache. Or maybe it was the fear. Her pulse thudded in her neck, and she listened for any movement.

A chair slid. Then a desk shifted.

She backed up and felt the table behind her, all the time acting as if she weren't afraid or alerted while her heart beat so hard it might have choked her.

A voice from the foyer met her ears. "Amber, you here? I'm glad you could get in. I thought you'd be standing out in the cold." She heard lights being switched on and the heating system turning over with a mechanical clunk. A shadow shifted in her peripheral.

"I'm here, Maggie. Someone else is here too, but I don't know them."

She wasn't sure she hadn't imagined it all. Maybe she was being paranoid? At that, a chair clanked against metal and the shadow moved, startling her.

"Help!"

"Hey," Maggie yelled. "Who are you?"

The only answer was a thump.

"Maggie, are you okay?" She raced to where she imagined her to be and found Maggie in a heap on the floor. She started to sit up.

"Oh my gosh. Are you all right?" She helped Maggie off the floor.

"I don't know who that was, but he certainly wasn't blind." Maggie took Amber's arm, and they headed into the kitchen area to make coffee.

"Do you think we should call someone?"

"They're long gone now, but I think I'll inform the church. It was probably a transient hoping for a place to stay. Probably more scared of us than we were." She tried laughing, but Amber could hear the unsettledness in her voice.

After they got the coffee perking, they moved into the classroom. "How's your week going?"

Amber wasn't sure where to start. "Ethan's in the hospital. They've..." She'd yet to say it aloud. Shannon and Justin knew because they'd seen him. She took a deep breath and mustered on. "They've taken his other leg."

"Oh no." Maggie sat down. "Will they do chemo and radiation?"

"I'm not sure. I'm guessing yes, since the cancer spread so badly. He won't talk to me about it. He isn't talking much at all." Not a word all day. "He's retreating inside himself."

"I know how that can be. So hard. Such a shame. He's well-liked by everyone. He does such good work."

"Don't count him out yet." Amber felt her ire rise in his defense.

"Please. I'd never." Maggie clucked her tongue, and once again Amber felt a familiarity. She wished she knew who Maggie reminded her of.

"How's your braille class going?"

"Do I really need to learn braille? I've been listening to books on tape."

"And even the sighted do that. There are things you're going to want braille for. You didn't go?"

"This whole thing happened with Ethan, and it fell by the wayside."

"You waited for that class for three weeks. Maybe the teacher will excuse the absence and give you a chance to get caught up. I know—get your assignment and I can help you."

"Why can't you teach me altogether?" Amber held out hope. She'd been dreading going. What if she couldn't do it?

"I'm no teacher. At least not that kind."

"Teachers come in all shapes." Her voice lowered. "I sure miss my students."

"But soon you'll have an art show and become famous." Maggie patted Amber's arm. "I can say I know a famous blind artist, painting her way around the country."

Amber scowled. "I don't want to be a *blind* artist. I want to be an artist."

"Don't shun the special for the commonplace." She clucked again.

"What's that supposed to mean?"

"To see without eyes is a much greater gift than seeing with."

Amber knew what she was saying, but the words grated on her. "Still."

"Still." Maggie laughed and her stomach growled. "I'm beginning to regret having Sherri pick up the doughnuts tonight. I didn't get dinner."

"I ate with Ethan."

Maggie let that settle and asked the question Amber could feel building.

"He's important to you, yes?"

"He's my friend."

Maggie smiled. "I see, I see." She patted Amber's hand. "The heart is tricky."

At that moment, the door opened and the others trickled in. Sherri unloaded the doughnuts, and Amber took two. She chalked that up to a benefit of hanging out with other blind people. She could eat junk food and not feel guilty. She frowned at her own thoughts.

People shared but all Amber could do was think of Ethan, lying alone in the hospital room. She wouldn't be by to see him tomorrow because she had to set up for her show with Rafe. What held such excitement and promise a week ago now seemed fruitless. Sherri's question interrupted Amber's thoughts.

"When did you lose your sight, Maggie?"

"It was a long time ago. Not long after I came to this country, actually. I followed my husband here. I knew I wasn't seeing like I should, but I put off going to the doctor because we were so poor. It wouldn't have done any good, as it turns out." The room went quiet. "So that is that."

Amber got the idea there was much more to Maggie's story, but she didn't ask and neither did anyone else. One of the rules was not to pressure anyone—and she figured Maggie counted.

The clock in the hall chimed eight. "That's our cue. Thanks, everyone, for coming. I have a request. There was a transient here earlier. Let's leave together and make sure no one is on their own, okay?"

The men mumbled about protecting all the women, and Sherri took offense and said she could take them all. This started an entirely different and colorful conversation. Amber grinned and realized it was the first time in a long time she'd had anything to smile about.

She heard Maggie and Sherri talking about children. She'd never pictured Sherri with kids, but she had two. Maybe it could be done after all? A renewed bitterness filled her at the thought of her birth mother giving her up.

"I admire what you're doing," Maggie said to Sherri. "To raise a child is very hard. It's good you have your husband."

"Even if you didn't have your husband, could you imagine giving up your child?" Amber didn't realize she'd spoken until she heard them both go still.

"Perhaps it's easy to pass judgment when you don't have the experience of another?" Maggie's voice trembled.

"I really don't know what I'd do without my husband." Sherri spoke with conviction and a hint of jealousy. "I couldn't imagine taking them to the store, or school, or any of those things without him."

"You'd be surprised what you can do if you have to." Amber didn't let up, her anger intensifying. "One day they'll be helping you at the store, or driving you places. People that give up their kids because they can't handle life have no idea what they've done to those they've dumped."

"I think it's time we left. We'll leave this for another time."

Maggie's tone belied controlled anger and sadness. She headed to the door with the others, leaving Amber and Sherri to come up behind.

"Do you have children, Amber?" Sherri asked her pointedly.

"No."

"Then you don't know what it's like or how I feel. Or how anyone else feels. I'd suggest you follow the rules and give me the benefit of the doubt. Once you've faced my challenges, then we'll talk." She shifted past Amber, leaving her only heated words and self-doubt.

I know how I feel. It wasn't about them. What about their kids? The damage leaving did to them. Why did everyone leave?

The others filtered out to the bus stop as Maggie locked the door. She moved alongside Amber.

"Do you see anyone about?"

Amber strained her eyes. "It's hard to tell, but I don't think so." The hope of completing her bucket list was fading along with her eyesight.

"Good." She moved toward the others, and Amber followed behind the group, standing apart. She'd been in the wrong. Stepping forward, she approached Maggie.

"Maggie?" She had no excuse that'd be worthwhile. No matter who she wanted to be, her anger always followed and still got the better of her.

"Yes?"

"I'm sorry. I think I have a lot to work through. I keep thinking I'm done with it all, but then it creeps back in."

"Someone left you?"

"I'm adopted."

Amber heard Maggie draw a quick breath. "Ethan did not tell me."

"It's not his story to tell. And besides, it's ancient history. I'll apologize to Sherri next week, but for now, please accept my apology."

"Of course. I must go." Maggie rushed off, leaving Amber behind with her broken emotions. Would she ever be able to forgive her mother for leaving her? Or at least let the feelings go?

CHAPTER 33

Rafe swept through his café, giving clear and concise instructions to his staff as to where to hang every painting. He looked as comfortable in his suit today as he had the other night. She couldn't ever imagine him wearing jeans and a ratty T-shirt. Now and then he'd ask Amber if she agreed with his design—but she could tell he didn't really want her opinion. That was okay. She was more than willing to bend to his knowledge and experience.

Amber stood by the window, watching the wind whip the last few remaining leaves into a dance to the music of the traffic going by. She heard rap and pop coming from car stereos, mixing with something classical next door.

"We're not going to make it to Butchart Gardens, are we?" Shannon came up and put her arm around Amber's shoulder.

All Amber could do was shake her head. She'd known it for a while now. She'd probably not even make it to the Portland Rose Garden. Spring blooms were months away. "I'll have to use my imagination."

"I hate this."

Emotions threatened to overtake her, but she fought them off. This wasn't the time. "We'll find other things closer by. What about Silver Falls?"

"I don't want you hiking on those paths in this weather. Too slippery."

Amber pondered that. "Crater Lake?"

"There's quite a lot of snow. I'm not sure I can drive that. But Justin could."

Ethan had Crater Lake on his list. And several other things she'd added to her own. In fact, her own seemed much less important now. Even the one about seeing her birth mother's face. Her outburst of vindictive anger tempered her desire for revenge. Since that day with Maggie, she'd felt little but regret. And sorrow.

They moved in unison toward the close wall and looked at the whale studies and ocean studies and her final paintings. The ones she did after she and Ethan poured their hearts out. Where she promised him that she'd be there for him no matter what. That he could count on her.

"I feel so rotten."

"You wish Ethan were here. You must be worried about him."

"That. Yes. But also, I feel rotten for me. I really wanted him here. And at my teaching retirement party. Why didn't he come?"

"He never said. I think it was right after he got the initial news from his doctors about his leg. He probably didn't want to be a downer."

Ethan had tossed her from his rehab room yesterday. Or he would have if he hadn't been so weak. Nearly a month on chemo. He'd shaved his head. She'd offered to do the same. That didn't go over too well. Thus, her eviction.

"It's understandable, you wanting him." Amber heard the double meaning but ignored it.

"He's really miserable in rehab."

"I'd be too. As soon as this round of chemo is over, he can move back into his place, can't he?"

"Yes. I had a hospital bed moved in and all the disabled access stuff installed. Justin built the ramp in front, and I got the building manager to open the cabinet below the sink and wrap all the pipes to keep him from hitting something and burning himself."

"You've got everything handled for Ethan."

Amber nodded, going down mental lists.

"What about you, sweetie?"

Amber frowned. "What about me?"

Shannon waited.

"I'm fine." Amber waved her off. Losing her eyesight was nothing compared to losing Ethan. *Losing Ethan.* The thought reverberated through her. He'd come to mean so much to her. He was her counselor, her friend. Next to Shannon, he was in line as her best friend.

"Have you told Maggie how bad your sight's gotten?"

"No. Maggie and I aren't seeing eye to eye."

"Ha-ha."

"Yeah, gotta come up with some new phrases. It's stupid, but I keep hoping Ethan will take over my counseling again."

"Even if he was back at work, I think you're long past his being able to counsel you dispassionately."

She sighed. Shannon was right.

"What happened with Maggie?"

"It's a long story. I kind of passed judgment aloud on people that abandon their kids because *they're* disabled."

"You mean blind."

"Yeah. Anyway, she's canceled our last three meetings. I've decided to believe it's because I'm ready to move ahead." She shifted her gaze away, acting indifferent and feeling anything but. Maggie hadn't arrived early enough for them to meet last week, and the two previous weeks she'd simply sent a text.

"My anger's better. I've been feeling sorry for her."

"Maggie?"

"No. Little Amber. Sounds dumb, right?"

Shannon shook her head. "I spent well over a year mourning for little Shannon. You wonder what you might have been. I did. What would I have been if I'd had parents that loved me instead of being tossed around in the foster system?"

"Your dad loved you, Shannon."

"In his own insane way."

"He did his best." Bipolar was complicated and tricky, even more so when you didn't have a support system.

They both went quiet thinking of parents who did their best but their best wasn't anywhere close to where it needed to be. Amber added in the weaknesses of her own adoptive father, who'd kept Shannon from joining their family formally.

In her heart, though, Shannon would always be her sister. No matter what.

"Well, you two, what do you think?" Rafe came up behind them, waving his arm toward her work and its layout.

Amber widened her eyes to try and take in the details of her first showing. This was something she wanted to remember. She walked past nested tables and cozy wood booths draped in cloth. Twinkle lights adorned each booth and up and around the potted plants in the corners, lighting the dark places. Overhead, Rafe hung old-fashioned incandescent bulbs with golden burning filaments. The cedar beams crossing the ceiling were also wrapped in white lights.

She drew closer to the walls, seeing each of her paintings set off by a spotlight. She waved her hand in front of the light.

"Good, not too warm."

Rafe put a hand over his heart. "Heavens no. I had quite a bad experience when I first opened and showed a creative 3D artist. The heat from the lamps activated the glue holding his works together and pieces began to fall off during the first showing." He shivered. "Horrible. The poor man. Not to mention poor me," he guffawed.

"Glue sticks are very unreliable." Amber nodded to Shannon, who agreed.

"Dangerously so. I like nails."

"Indeed."

"Well, now that's settled, let's move on. The event will be catered. We'll have coffee and wine from local vintners, local chocolatiers, and local cheesemakers." He gave a last cursory look around. "Tell me, does it meet with your approval?"

"Yes." She wished she could be more excited. This was her big chance.

"Anything amiss?"

Shannon stepped in. "No. It's all great. Amber's feeling under the weather today." She took Amber by the arm. "I'm actually going to take her home."

"Of course. Be here tomorrow at five. Wear something stunning—but nothing that isn't you. Be authentic."

"Got it. Stunning and authentic. With bells on." Amber gave him a thumbs-up. As they left the café, she leaned toward Shannon. "Did I just give him the thumbs-up and say with bells on?"

"Yeah. You need a nap."

"Could we go see Ethan first?"

Shannon went quiet. "You've got a lot to process and so does he. On a lot of levels. Maybe you should let him have a day alone." She heard the implication that maybe *she* should take a day off from caring for Ethan.

"You're probably right."

Shannon dropped her off at her building, and she went upstairs. Instead of resting, though, she pulled her easel into the light and let the sunshine warm her back. She grabbed her pastels and closed her eyes, seeing the gallery and café in her mind, and recreated her event. Hours later, she put it aside.

Tomorrow she'd show it to Ethan.

CHAPTER 34

Tomorrow arrived. Amber didn't go see Ethan. Her insecurity at being shut out kept her from trying. Instead, she got her hair cut and went into her favorite second-hand store and bought a knockout dress—a blue velvet number. She dug through her closet and found some silver-strapped high heels and a flashy clutch.

Sitting there, looking up at all her clothes, now mostly organized by color, she realized she still didn't have a great system. When her eyes went completely, she wouldn't know one from the next. She'd fit right in with the art set.

Her cell rang.

"Shannon calling."

"Yep?"

"Hey, you. Ready to go? We're downstairs in the car."

"Oh, shoot. Already?"

"Got'cha." Shannon chuckled. "Be about an hour. Okay?"

"Not cool." Amber climbed up from her closet floor and fell over the pile she'd made behind her and forgotten about. "Oomph."

"You okay? Amber?"

Amber extracted a sock from her mouth. At least it was clean. She dug around, listening for Shannon's voice and found her phone.

"Yeah. I fell over my clothes."

"You really have to do something about that."

"I'll get right on that." Amber hung up. She had to admit, staring at the ever-growing clean pile of clothes, something must be done. Mocha leapt through and bounded at her chest.

"You like the pile, don't you, buddy?" She ruffled his fur and teased him with one of her knee-highs. After playing for a few minutes, she started to sort things and quickly got frustrated. It was too dark in her apartment to see anything.

She got up and did her makeup, leaning as close to the mirror as she could. Then she fed Mocha, pulled on her coat, and waited until Shannon texted her they were downstairs.

Justin and Shannon chatted and teased, and she carried on with them until they pulled into the parking garage. Then, the idea she would be on display as well as her work sank in and began to twist in her chest. All the clever things she wanted to say disappeared. All her courage hid.

They climbed out of the car into the echo-filled cement building. Car tires squealed as they rounded corners on all five floors looking for the best spots. The smell of automobile oil and damp pavement filled her senses. Her heels clicked, and the sound ricocheted off the hard surfaces, like they were chasing them to the elevator.

A group of teens climbed in with them, chuckling and nudging each other. Her fist tightened around her cane. As they exited the car, they jostled and bumped her aside. Justin caught her as she tipped sideways and snagged her heel in the space between the elevator and the floor. It snapped off.

"That did not happen." She hobbled out of the elevator, nearly tripping again.

"Let me see it." Justin motioned for her to take off her shoe. "I have some Rhinokind glue back at my place. Do you want me to take them home and fix them?"

"That wouldn't work very well. It won't dry until tomorrow."

"Maybe that cute little shoe place down the street from the café will be open."

She held out hope. It wasn't.

The three of them stood staring at the door's closed sign.

"Now what?"

"I bet Rafe has something we can use. Let's sneak into the back, and I'll get his attention."

They rounded the corner and went down the back alley. Amber hit every puddle, splashing mud and oil up on her tights. Shannon tried to steer her away, but she kept listing to one side, off balance, and seemed to have perfect aim. The garbage bins outside brought a new meaning to the idea of rank-smelling in her mind.

By the time they arrived at the back door, her spirits had sunk to a new low.

"I'm going home. Tell them I was sick."

"No way." Shannon pulled out some handy wipes and attacked her legs until the spots looked more like freckles than oil. Then she took off her own flashy black spikes and held them out. Amber shook her head.

"Yes." Shannon moved closer.

"You're two sizes bigger than me. The next thing you know I'll be dumping my drink into someone's lap."

Shannon pulled tissues out of her purse, stuffed the toes of the shoes, and held them out again. "There. Okay?"

"You know how I hate to have my toes cramped."

"Or rumpled socks or seam lines. I'm surprised you wear shoes at all. Put them on." Amber could almost hear her friend's eyes roll.

"Fine." She slipped them on and cringed at the cramped, ruffled spaces. "I can't do this. I'll be biting my lip all night to keep from screaming."

"You can scream afterward. Get in there." Shannon gave her a gentle push in the direction of the gallery.

Meanwhile, Justin had disappeared inside and alerted Rafe they'd arrived. Rafe came through the back, chastisement in his tone until Amber moved into the light.

"Oh my. Aren't you beautiful. Perfect." He held out his hand, motioning in a circle, having her turn. "Splendid. They are going to love you." He took her coat from her, hung it up, and encircled her arm with his. "Shall we?"

"Sure." *No. Get me out of here.*

They moved through the back door, her being led around and introduced to the guests. She shook hands, nodded, and laughed at all the appropriate moments. The nerves she had all day faded away, and suddenly she was in her element. She'd never been one for small talk, but now she found herself chatting with buyers, with prospective artists, with people who were inspired by her. *By her.*

"Let me introduce you to a great patron of the arts, Wilshire Heart, and his lovely wife, Matilde."

Amber didn't miss the careful stress on the word patron. She put her hand out and took his wife's hand first, then his. She complimented Mrs. Heart on her perfume and answered Mr. Heart's question about her inspiration.

"I want to remember it all, and the best way to do that is to re-experience it over and over again in my mind and put it to paper or canvas, or whatever is at hand. The more I do that, the clearer it becomes."

"But each one changes." Matilde Heart's voice lilted with a dream-like quality.

"Yes. It changes in my mind too. Each one becomes more beautiful to me every time I paint it, every time I look at it from a new angle. It's not only an expression of appreciation in my mind, but in my soul."

"Ah. Now that's lovely." She turned to her husband. "Wilshire, I want to support this young woman. You need to buy her paintings. I want three for our beach house and one for the Old Portland." She reached over and pressed Amber's hand between hers, leaning closer. "And when you've got something new, you let us know right away. I can't wait to tell my friends I have a Kirk on my walls."

For some reason, the way Mrs. Heart said *Kirk*, it sounded more like, "I've got a moose," or "I've got a bear on my wall." She shivered.

Rafe whispered in her ear. "You are doing wonderful. The tally is now at ten."

"Ten what?"

"Pieces, my dear. And the Hearts will get the word out in no time. You've done it. Congratulations." He excused himself, leaving her alone in a crowd of people, swelling with the noise of conversation and the aroma of food. A woman backed into her, and she knocked into a table, spilling someone's drink.

"I'm very sorry."

The man at the table excused her and cleaned it up. "No worries."

As she turned around, she saw a familiar face nearby. Who she was with surprised her even more.

"Mom." She greeted Jennifer and looked to her companion. "Kyle."

"Look who I met on the way here from the parking garage." She heard the tension in her mother's voice.

"I didn't know about your showing. You must be thrilled." His words said congratulations, but his voice told another story.

"Yes, it's going very well, thanks."

"I wasn't invited. Do you think it's okay if I'm here?"

Not at all. "I didn't know you were interested in art."

"More the artist than the work," he said, obviously trying to be clever.

Shannon and Justin appeared at her side. Shannon handed her mom a glass of cider. "Jennifer, here you go."

"Thanks." Jennifer tossed it back and asked for another. Shannon went to fetch it.

Justin stood tall next to Amber in full-protection mode. "Thought we'd seen the last of you, Kyle. This isn't your neighborhood, is it?"

"I was here on business."

Amber squinted at his clothes. There was something familiar about them. The color maybe.

"Want me to step closer for inspection?" His voice was suggestive. She moved back. "I'm going to take a look around. Good to see you all." He slipped through the crowd, and Amber lost sight of him.

"I can't believe his nerve." Justin's anger radiated as heat.

"Thanks for coming to my rescue."

"Any time. Seriously. If you see him anywhere in your vicinity, you should call the cops. I don't trust him."

In the past, Amber might have made an excuse for Kyle. But never again.

Rafe interrupted them. "You've sold every piece."

Shannon, Amber, and Justin all stood stunned, mouths agape.

"You heard me. I'm going to have prints made before they're delivered. It will delay things, but it'll be well worth it. I'm working on setting up a line of greeting cards as well. I thought you could go on a Must-See painting tour. You'd paint things you had to see before your sight is lost forever. It's got great play."

Amber's head swam.

"All expenses paid once you've signed a contract with me."

"A contract?"

"Yes. You've really got something here, Amber, and I think we'll work very well together. I'll act as your agent and organizer."

"This is the answer to our prayers." Jennifer hugged a numb Amber to her chest. "You've done it, sweetie. It's what you've always wanted."

Or was it? Something was missing. Or...someone.

CHAPTER 35

Creeping quietly into Ethan's room, Amber saw he was asleep, so she decided to grab lunch and come back. He'd love Mexican. She headed out again and hit the local taco shop, returning with enough to feed four.

Amber spoke to the nurse out front. Today's PT had been very rough. His parents had come and gone in the past week. It'd been best that she'd stayed away then—out of their way. She hadn't been able to face him. She called Monday, but he didn't say much, so she hadn't called again, sure he was tired of her. Finally, her distress of losing their friendship altogether overrode her fear of rejection.

As she came back in, he turned toward her.

"I'm awake." Somehow, without her saying anything, he knew how quickly her sight was dimming.

"I can tell from your talking. I'm quick that way. Brought you Mexican."

"Wonderful. All I've eaten all week was Cuban. My mother made all my favorite dishes and stocked my freezer at home." He took a crunchy bite of taco, and all she could hear was their chewing. "She was sorry not to meet you."

Amber looked down at her food. "Things have been kind of nuts."

"And you didn't know if I ever wanted to see you again."

She looked up at him, not sure what to say.

"I've been a real idiot."

Amber wiped a tear from her cheek. "No. I've been so pushy."

"My mom told me all you'd done in my apartment. I wish you'd said something."

She'd tried but he wouldn't hear it. "I wanted you to be able to come home."

"My last chemo is tomorrow."

"Your last?" Amber's heart soared.

"For now. This round. Then we'll wait while I recover and do some blood work. We'll pray a lot." She could tell by the tilt of his head he was smiling at her. She could hear it in his voice.

"An awful lot."

They ate more. The atmosphere lightened with what she prayed wasn't false hope.

"I'm sorry I missed your showing." He wiped his mouth and put down the remainder of the single taco he'd been working on before laying back, spent.

"Yeah. It went really well."

"How well?"

"They all sold. All of them. I've got regular clients lining up. Rafe wants to..." She stopped.

"Rafe wants what?" Something odd entered his voice. A new strain.

"He wants to send me around the country to see everything on my Must-See List. At least what's in the U.S."

"How generous of him."

"He wants to be my agent. He's organizing prints of my work, a line of stationery, all of that. It's rather overwhelming."

He nodded. "When do you leave?"

"I haven't decided. It's a huge commitment. I feel odd going without you." Somehow, their bucket lists had combined in her mind as one.

"I'm not taking world tours anytime soon." His voice said *if ever*. She didn't like hearing that.

"Well, there's no rush." Liar. The sun might be out in full force, but her vision grew grayer by the day. The fog would soon roll in permanently.

"And you'll be going with him?"

"I'm not sure. Like I said, the details need to be ironed out."

He closed his eyes, effectively shutting her out. She didn't let him. She needed to know his thoughts. She'd stay for him. There wasn't much she wouldn't do for him.

"What do you think I should do?"

He didn't speak for a while. She thought he was pondering his advice, but she couldn't have been more wrong.

"My opinion can't count for much. I don't know anything about the art world."

"But you know me, and I care about what you think."

He shifted in his bed, his head turned toward the window.

"My parents want me to move home with them."

"But your apartment is all ready for you, remember? Once you're clear of the cancer, and back on your feet, it'll all be okay." She hadn't meant to say *back on your feet*. She mentally slugged herself. No more using the words *see* or *feet*.

"They've got a point, you know? It's going to be a while before I'm strong enough for the prosthetics. Sam said there are some great PT people in Boston."

"But..." She stopped before *what about me* came out.

"They said I'll be strong enough in a week to go. I'm going to have my place packed up. My folks are going to drive me home—I can't imagine flying in this condition, you know? I'm sorry for all the effort you put into everything."

Sorry?

"You've already decided, then?" The shift of gravity was almost too much to bear. Her world had flipped on its axis. The sun cut through the room and she shut her eyes against the light.

"It's for the best. I'll keep in touch."

Keep in touch?

She couldn't swallow the emotion building. He still hadn't looked at her.

"Maybe in your travels you could stop by and say hi. That'd be nice."

Nice. The foundations of her world were falling apart. As much as she'd leaned on her cane for help, she'd emotionally been counting on Ethan. Huge mistake. All her life she'd never needed anyone but her mother and Shannon. And God. She shouldn't have let her guard down. *You deserve this. You're an idiot. You should have known better.*

"Could you call the nurse?"

His words brought her back, and she started moving toward him. "Are you okay?"

He still didn't look at her. "I have to use the bathroom." His words were detached. Heavy.

She left the room and made her way to the nurse's station, alerting them to his need. When the nurse came out a while later, she sounded flustered. "Man."

"Everything okay?"

"He's in a bad place today." She looked apologetic. "He's asked not to have any more visitors."

"Oh." Amber moved to his room's door and stopped short, effectively feeling it slammed in her face. She'd left her coat inside. Nothing could make her go back in. Not now. It was stupid to feel so hurt considering what he was going through. But it had taken everything she could muster to come there today. To open up to him. And he'd shut her out again. Probably permanently this time.

Maybe she wasn't up to this after all. She couldn't make him want to stay friends, to rely on her. Could she really be a shifting reed on the wind? Only there for the good times. When the bad came, she cut and ran like everyone else. She reached out to knock on the door but drew back. Instead, she turned to the nurse.

"Would you retrieve my coat and my cane?"

"Oh, of course."

The nurse went in and came out, handing them to her, along with the rest of the tacos in the sack. "I'm sorry about this."

"It's fine." What else could she say? She wandered away in a daze, floating down the hall, out onto the sidewalk, past his room window—but she didn't look. Two could play that game. Besides, she couldn't have seen him anyway. She went on, and on, past her bus stop. She handed the remaining tacos to a homeless man on the corner and then kept walking, numb.

She went home, not even sure how she'd made it the ten blocks without one stumble or bump. Once inside, she moved aimlessly. Shannon texted her, but she didn't answer. Rafe texted her. She ignored him too. Maggie texted her, asking to meet that evening at the church.

She might as well. Another good-bye. Because she certainly wasn't going to keep using Tapestry or meeting with Maggie. The memories were too painful. She texted back YES.

Mocha slept in a sunny puddle on the couch. If she hadn't known better, she'd have thought he was her dark brown sweater, but her sweater didn't purr.

Amber sat down at her table and drank a cold cup of jasmine tea, comforted by the sweet floral overtones. Where was God in all this? It wasn't right for her to blame Him, but He seemed the most likely suspect. Or herself. Trust was a weakness. She'd learned that at a young age. Every time she thought she was over it, it came rolling downhill at her, all pointy edges and ramming her off the path.

The light streamed past the couch, onto the floor, and lit a pile of paintings growing by her wall. She'd done a larger, second study of Ethan's place by the river after he'd shared what it meant to him.

And she'd never shown him the gallery opening. Before she could change her mind, feeling a burning desire for closure, she grabbed them and her cane. She tucked Ethan's house key in her pocket and headed for his place.

If she'd ever dreamed of walking death row, this mirrored it. No one she passed showed signs of recognizing her distress. No matter. This was the right thing to do.

She stared at his apartment. She'd spent a lot of time there lately, obviously letting the familiarity of Ethan's place warp into some kind of intimacy with him. She unlocked the door and leaned the paintings up against the far wall where he'd see them when he came in. He'd have his spot with him forever. And part of her. Maybe one day that'd mean something. All she knew was that she didn't want any reminders of him.

Amber locked up on the way out and then looked around. She hoped there wasn't anyone in the area. She pretended to lean down and tie her shoe, and then tucked the key back under the ceramic dragonfly by the rose bush.

Satisfied, she moved away, not looking back.

CHAPTER 36

While she was on her way to the church, Rafe texted again. She stopped walking—it was no safer to walk and talk on the phone for her than it was to drive and talk. Both were detrimental to her health and those around her. She leaned against a cold brick wall and stayed out of the flow of foot traffic.

"Rafe?"

"Amber. Wonderful. I have the contract ready. Have you found a lawyer to look it over?"

She had yet to talk this out with her mother, but she was certain her mom could look it over for her. Contracts and indelible ink were her lifeblood. Traveling the states without her probably wasn't going to go over very well. She'd tackle the problem when she got there, though.

"Yeah, I've got that handled."

"Super. I'm making plans for us to leave in two weeks."

"Can't be soon enough for me. Can Mocha come with me?"

"Your cat?"

"You know how some people don't have kids, they have pets?"

"Sure." He waited.

"Mocha."

"Got it. I'll see what we can arrange. You'll be traveling by train in private compartments. I've checked over your bucket list, and I think we can accommodate most of them. I'll be going with you at the start."

"I'll need to get you an updated list." She didn't want to go anywhere that Ethan wanted to go anymore, on the off chance he might be there. And she certainly didn't want to paint with all that emotional baggage in her way.

"Sure thing. I'm having a web page designed too, so your fans can follow you on your travels and show up to see you paint."

"Oh." Being a spectacle wasn't part of her plan. "Really?"

"The public loves the idea of being in touch with their heroes. And you, dear girl, are a hero to many."

Amber didn't feel like a hero. She felt like a coward. Who was she to be admired? She kept her thoughts to herself, though, and agreed to meet Rafe in a couple days to finalize everything.

Having committed to his plans, she continued to the church. She'd wrap up things with Maggie tonight. The doors were unlocked, but once again, no one was inside. She felt for the lights and flipped them on. She tripped over a Bible left on the floor and picked it up. As she entered the meeting room, she realized she didn't want to wait there for Maggie. In fact, she didn't want to meet with Maggie at all. Tonight would be good-bye. No more crutches in her life.

The room was cold and unnerving without anyone else there. It brought back memories of that day the transient had been hiding there. Deciding against waiting much longer, she headed up the hall and pushed on the heavy oak sanctuary doors. Before she washed her hands of this place, she wanted to experience the whole thing. The aroma of lemon oil, old hymnals, and incense met her. She could imagine the banners hanging on the high walls, and the candles burning at the ends of the altar. She moved up the carpeted aisle and slid into the wooden pew, letting her gaze shift upward with the architecture. The dim lighting and her lack of clarity restricted her from enjoying the carved details of the beams and moldings, but she knew from seeing other old churches they were there.

She tried to relax and let the burdens of her day go. What had one of Ethan's get-well cards said? Concentrate on happy thoughts and wellness would follow. Unfortunately, all that positive thinking mumbo-jumbo had never brought her much comfort. It wasn't even biblical.

Like people quoting that verse about God not giving you more than you can handle. Complete rubbish. God had given her way more than she or Ethan could handle. Could Jesus handle being abandoned and sacrificed? Could the apostles handle being martyred? The false teachings and catchy phrases on placards did more harm than good. People ended up feeling ignored by God or let down by their own failings.

The air around her shifted, and she figured Maggie had arrived. As she was about to turn and face her, she heard a familiar voice. It wasn't Maggie. It wasn't anyone she ever wanted to talk to again.

"I didn't think you had a group support meeting tonight."

"Kyle?"

She heard him coming closer. Chills ran down Amber's back. She edged away from the side of the pew and moved over, trying to keep space between them.

"What are you doing here?"

"I'm looking out for you. Have been. For a long time."

Her sense of being followed, of being watched all those times. She should have paid attention to it.

"In my apartment building during that storm?"

Silence.

"Was it you here last month? You could have really hurt Maggie. What were you thinking?" And how many other times? Her mind started to search, feeling naked and exposed.

"I'm keeping you safe. Someone had to. Your mom certainly wasn't going to do it." His voice moved closer, and she could hear the ragged emotion in his breathing. She slid farther down the bench, the rough upholstery dragging against her slacks.

"Kyle, whatever we had, it's over."

"God told me differently. He said I needed to stick by you."

"The God I pray to didn't tell you that."

"Your God isn't my God, Amber. He's weak. He's invented. If He wasn't, He'd heal you. God wants you healthy and whole. You need to turn back to Him."

"Kyle, my relationship with God might not be perfect, but we're on a good standing."

Father, help me.

She shifted away again, but he came down one section and up on the other side. His form was a dark shadow, blending in, morphing into the dark areas playing at the edge of her vision.

"Let's go get a cup of coffee." She needed to get out of there, quickly. Her mind scrambled to find an excuse he'd believe.

"I knew when you came in here that you'd returned to Him. To me. It's a sign."

"Sure. How about tea, then?" She started to move, but he raced toward her, his hands coming down on her shoulders, shoving her. "Ouch. Kyle, you're hurting me."

"I saw you with him. All those times. And going into his house. Are you moving in together? You'll never be healed like that, Amber. You have to turn from your sin."

"I'm not—"

He clamped a sweaty hand over her mouth. "Shh. Don't lie. I know you left me for him. He got what was coming to him though, didn't he? Lost both legs. I prayed God would stop him. That's his punishment."

Rage, disgust, and fear pumped throughout her veins. Before she could pull away, he wrapped his other arm around her neck, pushing his mouth against her ear. "If you come with me, all will be well."

Amber didn't know what happened next—the order in her head was mixed. Someone screamed. Maybe it was her. Then someone yelled. Kyle? She felt herself being crushed, and then shoved against the hard floor, her head knocking the ground, hands around her throat. The blackness came on her harder than ever. Another yell kept her on the edge of consciousness.

"Get away from my daughter!" A hard thud, a sickening crack against wood, and a scream of rage filled her ears.

The next thing she knew, sirens approached, a cold cloth blanketed her eyes, and ice chilled her forehead. She was lifted and loaded onto a stretcher. And then nothing.

Amber opened her eyes, gasping—all was light and sounds and smells of cleanser and alcohol. Her mother raced to her side.

"You're okay. You're in the hospital. You've got a concussion, but otherwise all is well."

"Kyle." Her heart pounded up into her throat.

"He's been arrested. You're safe."

"Oh, thank God." Amber lay back down, her head pounding. "If you hadn't come, I don't think I'd be here. How did you know I'd be at the church?"

Jennifer didn't speak right away. She stood near Amber, hesitant.

"Mom?"

"I wasn't there."

"I don't get it. Then who clobbered Kyle?"

"Maggie. From what I understand, she hit him with her cane. More than once. She's one tough lady." Something lingered in her mom's words.

"Weird. I thought I heard her yell something about her daughter. That's why I thought it was you."

Again, Jennifer went quiet.

"Mom?" Amber squinted and searched her mother's face, wishing she could make out her eyes. "What's going on?"

"We need to talk."

"Can I rest a while?" Her eyes dropped closed of their own volition.

"We need to talk now."

Amber blinked, trying to stay alert. "Okay. What's up?"

"There's no easy way to say this." Jennifer took a deep breath. "Maggie is your mother."

"Ha-ha. Really, I'm not up for this right now."

The silence in the room spoke volumes to her.

"You're serious." *No.*

"Yes. We adopted you in Seattle and then moved to Portland. I guess Maggie did too."

Maggie. Her mother.

"How did she know?"

"She started putting things together a couple weeks ago. Your name, and being adopted, and losing your sight the same way she did. She was awfully torn up."

"Poor her." All the anger and bitterness she'd compacted in a secret corner of her heart came bubbling to the surface.

"Amber Kirk," her mother reproached, but Amber ignored her.

"No, Mom. I don't need her and I don't want her. Her life turned out fine, didn't it? She gave me up for nothing. Nothing."

"Your life turned out good too." Jennifer's voice was even, void of emotion.

"Yeah, but..." She stopped. The secret in her heart, the secret she'd hidden from herself and Jennifer, nearly came out.

"But if she'd kept you, you would have been better off." Jennifer sniffed and she began to dab at her face with a tissue.

"That's not what I meant to say."

"It's how you've always felt. I've tried. I really have. I'll never be her, will I? No matter what I do." Jennifer's voice barely squeaked out past her sobs.

"Mom. I'm sorry." Her head pounded. Could this day get any

worse? "I guess every adopted kid thinks that, even past all reason. It's stupid. She couldn't have done better than you. I couldn't have done better than you."

At the moment, nothing Amber said would make this any better. She'd held her mother at a distance her whole life because she was afraid of getting close to someone who'd leave her, and at the same time she'd hoped her birth mom would return for her.

Her selfishness and stupidity had reached the maximum for the day. She wished someone would knock her unconscious again. Her world for a nice hard brick.

"She's outside." Jennifer found her voice, although it was still shaky.

"No. I can't."

"She's so worried. You don't know what she's been through."

The child inside Amber wanted to counter her mother's words, but she held her tongue. It was definitely a skill she needed to improve on.

"Okay." She said it, but she didn't mean it. She'd manage this somehow. As her mother left, she prayed. "God, if ever I needed you, I need you now."

There was a knock on her door. She heard her own voice betray her. "Come in."

Maggie felt her way inside, using a broken cane to guide her. She felt the end of the bed and then guided herself up near Amber's head, running her hands up the side of her covers, stopping to grasp Amber's hand.

"Thank God you're okay."

Amber gulped. "I guess I have you to thank for that."

"I'm so sorry I was late." Maggie's voice shook.

Amber pushed the button, sitting the bed up so she could get a clearer look at Maggie. Her hair was dyed, but Amber could see at her roots, they shared their coloring. She leaned closer, only inches away. Maggie's eyes were the same shape as hers.

"Who do I look like more?"

Maggie smiled softly and reached out to caress Amber's hair. "You have my hair and eyes and your daddy's smile." Her lip quivered from held back emotion.

Amber felt every grieving emotion mix and well inside her. Her eyes filled and spilled over. "You remember my smile?"

"Oh, baby, I've committed your face to memory. I even have this." Maggie held up a photo of Amber as a child, smiling. It'd been copied into relief and was gray with years of fingerprints. "I look at it often."

Amber took it from her with shaky fingers. "When was this taken?"

"The day before..." Maggie stopped. "The day before I left you."

"We went to the zoo."

"And the museum. You loved all the colors."

"Still do."

"Yes." More weeping. "I'm so proud of who you've become."

Smarmy words rushed to Amber's lips, but she bit them back. "Why did you give me up?" She didn't say *leave me*. She couldn't have held it together if she had.

"I've thought about answering that question your whole life. When your dad passed, we lost his income. My eyesight was nearly gone and disability wouldn't cover all our bills. I kept hoping things would get better. I got an office job, but they said I couldn't keep up. I decided to go back to school, taking night courses, but I couldn't pay to have anyone watch you. We didn't know a soul in the city. I would try and take you with me..." She shook her head. "Keeping a toddler still in a college classroom isn't an easy thing. You were adventurous. Most teachers were understanding. Some of the students weren't. Twice you escaped."

"I ran off?"

"I had never been so scared in my life. Help for the blind wasn't then what it is now. People were judgmental. The first time, you were in the foyer of the building. The second time, though, you'd made it to the middle of the street. A car narrowly missed you. I was reported to CPS."

"Oh, no." Amber couldn't imagine it.

"They tried to give me solutions. Their favorite one was giving you up to a sighted family that could care for you better." Maggie took a shuddering breath. "I came up with all the reasons I should keep you, but their list got longer. And the more and more trouble I had paying bills and keeping you safe, the less confident I felt."

Amber could see it all happening. Maggie wasn't any slouch when it came to self-empowerment. Knowing she felt helpless against the odds made it seem all the more horrible.

"So you chose to leave me." There, she'd said it.

"I did. I found good parents who wanted you desperately. They loved you so. My only condition was they keep your name."

Amber's eyes locked on her mother's face. "You named me Amber?" She'd never thought of it, never thought to ask.

"Yes."

"Can you say why?" Her demands turned to cautionary inquiries.

"Your father was a geologist. Did you know this?"

"No, I never knew anything about him."

"Yes. Very smart. He loved the rocks and things of the earth. Petrified wood." She laughed. "He liked the trees better when they were dead and replaced by minerals. I never understood that, but something about the grain of wood, preserved for all time, connected to him. He also had a large piece of amber in a case. He let it sit in the window, and the sun would catch it and send a lovely golden hue all over the living room." She reached forward, finding Amber's face. "The same color as your hair when you were born. So beautiful."

"It's still that color."

Tears dripped down Maggie's cheeks.

Her mother had been on her Must-See List from day one. Her revenge, seeing the pain in her birth-mother's eyes, knowing she passed the gene onto her, knowing she'd abandoned her, and discovering how much better off she'd been without her.

This wasn't what she had planned. This was better. Amber leaned her head into Maggie's hand. Maggie gasped and leaned forward, hugging her gently.

"I prayed for you, dear one. Every day."

"Thank you." Amber meant it. Sherri had been right. She hadn't walked the path Maggie had. She hoped she never had to. The ache of life's circumstances bore into her until she didn't think she could stand the pain anymore. And then, as she heard Maggie's voice murmuring words of praise and thanksgiving, it lifted and evaporated.

CHAPTER 37

Amber shifted one pile after another to her bed, trying to decide what to pack. Shannon would be here soon. She could always count on her friend to be pragmatic—she'd help her and tell her what to do. And now was a time for pragmatism if ever there was one. Rafe had been very understanding, postponing this trip for two weeks while she recovered from her attack. But it was go time. Lifting her itinerary to the lamp, she narrowed her eyes and tipped her head, trying to read it.

She stared down at the piles of clothes and art supplies as they shifted in and out of her vision. Her eyes were tired. After a good night's rest, they'd be ready and so would she. She reached over to turn on the lamp near her bed and discovered it was already lit. Her heart thrummed warning in her chest, but she dismissed it. She went to flip the switch on the wall for the overhead lamp. It was on as well. Turning to the curtains to pull them back, she realized they were open. The day was cloudy. Everything was cloudy. Mottled shapes swum into her vision. She tried to blink them away, but with each blink they seemed to grow thicker. She moved to the living room and tripped over a cord, whipping the lamp to the floor with a crash.

Mocha hissed and approached, but she picked him up and placed him on the chair to keep him safe. Heading to the kitchen, she hunted under the cabinet for the dust broom. She reached inside the darkened cabinet, searching for them by touch. Then she moved back to where she figured the lamp lay in ruins and stepped on a broken shard, cutting her foot.

"Ouch. Oh, great." Perfect timing for her trip. She hopped into the bathroom and searched for the first aid box, but it wasn't where she remembered it being. The pain shot up her leg. Acting on instinct, she pulled the piece free, but when she removed it, a gush of warmth followed, wetting her jeans and the floor. She pressed against it, feeling the stickiness, as the metallic aroma filled her nostrils. She pushed a towel against the wound and then bound it with packaging tape. She moved with extra caution now and tried to sweep up the mess. The last thing she needed was to do in her other foot. She could only imagine the trail of blood behind her, like a snail's trail, marking her erratic path.

Amber's eyes strained as she tried to find all the shards. But she saw none. In fact, she didn't see the lamp mess at all. But she could feel it.

A wave of cold washed over her. No. She squinted and got closer to the floor, but all she could make out were light and dark splotches. And then only dark. She reached out and brushed her hand carefully over the carpet and found piece after piece. She swept with the hand broom and could hear that she missed by the skittering of the pieces bouncing over the edge of the dustpan. Hoping she'd found all the pieces, she waved her hand one more time—this time it caught the live wires of a broken bulb, sending a jolt of heat and pain up her arm, jarring her teeth.

She screamed and realized she'd not unplugged the lamp. The whole lamp. How could she not see the lamp? Terror filled her. She had to protect Mocha. She squeezed her eyes closed and opened them wide, willing them to work. Fog, dark and dense, filled in her vision. It reminded her of the time she'd been teaching air-brushing and one of her students accidentally turned their sprayer on her, covering her safety goggles. She pushed around with the broom, tapping, until she found the bottom of the lamp. Her fingers reached out gingerly, and she sighed aloud when she felt the base and the cord. She yanked hard and felt it pop from the wall socket.

Mocha climbed into her lap, and she pulled him into her arms. She lifted him to see his cute fuzzy face and golden eyes. Her breath caught. Nothing. The shadows she'd considered wavering enemies had come to stay. She blinked rapidly, then scrunched her eyes closed.

"No." Amber opened them wide, wider than she'd ever tried before, and the strain sent waves of pain through them. "Please. Please, no. Everything is starting to work out again. This can't be. Not yet. I'm not ready." She gripped Mocha to her chest and tried to find where she was in her apartment, but each bump of furniture, each knock of her knee terrified her.

The door buzzer went off. Someone was here. She tried to find where the door was. She fell, landing on her bad knee. Now she suffered in pain from both sides. Instead of trying to walk, she crawled toward the sound, inch by inch, feeling out in front of her with her waving hand. Her breath came in gasps and gulps. Panic crushed her.

Mocha jumped at her feet, but she ignored him. Desperation and sweat broke out all over her body. The buzzer sounded again, tapping into the nerves already set off by her brush with electrocution.

She reached the door, felt for the door button to let whoever it was into the building and pushed the button over and over again.

"Someone help. Someone come." Her shaky fingers found the locks, flipped them open and wrenched the doorknob, before she crumpled sideways into the hall.

"Please. Help me. Help me!" Gone, all gone. Everything was gone.

"Amber?" Shannon yelled to her, all the while thumping up the stairs.

"Shannon. Help me! It's gone. It's gone. Help me."

Shannon's footfalls came hard and fast up the hallway. She gathered Amber in her arms. "It's okay. I'm here. I'm here." She rocked her. "You're bleeding."

"The lamp broke. Then everything went dark. I was so afraid. I'm so scared." Amber clung to Shannon, her fingers gripping her shirt. Small. Helpless. Alone.

"Oh, sweetie. I'm so sorry. I'm so sorry."

"I thought I was ready," she cried. "I was only playing at it." She dragged the air into her lungs like a swimmer breaking the surface of the pool after being under too long. She couldn't get enough air. "I'm suffo...cating."

"You're going to be okay, you hear me?" Shannon laid her on the ground and came back with a paper sack, placing it over her nose and mouth. The brown-bag smell gagged her.

"In and out, slowly. Slow. Slower."

Amber took direction, and her breathing improved.

"Are you okay?"

Amber could only shake her head. It was so much worse than she expected. To have it fading and shift was something she'd grown accustomed to. Keeping her eyes closed as she practiced? No big deal.

Not this.

This was forever. She'd be in the dark now, forever.

After a while, her sobs quieted and understanding settled in over the terror, dampening its effects. She released her grip on Shannon and moved away, crawling to the wall and sitting against it.

"Want to go inside and sit down?"

"Soon." She leaned her head back, feeling the cold seep through her hair, the hardness and solidity of the building. She ran her fingers over the low-pile cut carpet under her. She listened. Cars passed by outside. A police car raced in the distance. A dog upstairs barked. Something climbed into her lap and walked in a circle before sitting down to purr. She ran her fingers over Mocha's back, feeling the fur and fuzz, the rumble of contentedness, his poky spine and curling tail.

Shannon went inside. Amber heard her surprise at the mess and the clanking sounds of broken ceramics. She moved by again, the shifting and rattling of the garbage bag being taken down and out. Then she thumped back up the stairs and ran the vacuum cleaner. Amber put a calming hand on Mocha.

"It's all okay. Everything's going to be okay." She wasn't sure if she was telling the cat or herself. Or if she believed it at all.

Shannon stuck her head out her doorway. "It's all safe. I got the blood off the carpet. The lamp was a total loss, but it was ugly anyway."

"You made that lamp."

"Meh. I've made more. I'll bring one over."

"Surprise me with the color."

They went quiet.

"Want to come in?"

Amber nodded and hoisted Mocha to her chest, rising by leaning against the wall and limping inside.

"Let me take a look at your foot." She started to lead Amber to the couch, but Amber waved her off.

"I'm okay." She'd done this routine a hundred times. Maybe more. But this time, her eyes were opened. She moved from the doorway, walked around the coffee table, and took a seat on the couch, putting her foot on the table. She saw it all in her head. Her sense of security rose an inch.

Shannon peeled back the bandage. "It's not bad. I'll get some disinfectant and see if we can't tape it closed and avoid a trip to the E.R." She moved through the bedroom and came back. Amber expected a lecture on the piles and the dangers of leaving stuff laying around. She didn't get one.

"Do you want me to call Rafe?"

"Yes. I want to act like everyone knows. So if you could alert the world, that'd be great. Maybe a bulletin on the news? An ad in the paper? I know...sky writer."

"Your sarcasm is alive and well. Good job."

"I've heard that my other skills will be enhanced now. Just you wait."

Shannon chuckled and finished first aid on the wound. "You need to feel it for heat and infection in a couple days." Shannon pushed once more on her foot. "Scratch that—I'll come by for the next few days and help you keep an eye on it."

"Thank you." What would she do without Shannon? She pulled her leg up and tucked it under her. "Can you see my cell?"

"Hold your hand out." Amber reached for her phone and took it, hitting the button. "Call Rafe."

"Calling Rafe."

"Hello?"

"This is Amber. I'm afraid our trip is postponed for the indefinite future. Well, probably forever." The words cut like the broken vase, but if anyone noticed, they never said.

CHAPTER 38

After Amber spoke to Rafe, Shannon perked up. "Well, how are we going to commemorate the day?"

"You're nuts." Amber looked up at the ceiling, or where she imagined the ceiling must be. No matter what happened, good or bad, if it was momentous, they always marked the day. But this time, it felt wrong. All she wanted to do was climb in bed.

"Nuts sound good and I hate nuts, therefore we need food." She heard her shuffling around and popping open a can of kitty food for Mocha.

"I can do that."

"I know it, but he tricked me. Besides, you should stay off your foot. Maybe you could give someone a call?"

"I should probably call my mom. But that's a conversation for another day when I can take the hysterics. Not now."

"What about Maggie?"

"Maybe."

"Ethan?"

"Not on your life. He's got his own baggage, obviously superior and more important than my own. I can't carry two suitcases right now." She'd quit on Ethan. Or he'd quit on her. Either way, she didn't have the energy to fight. She'd fight for him, she'd fight for their friendship. But she wasn't going to fight to convince him they should be friends in the first place. That was pointless and dumb.

And gutless. She may be many things, but gutless was not one of them.

"Maggie wins. Call her. I'll be back soon with commemoration food."

Amber heard the door close. She rolled her phone from hand to hand before she found the words she needed. "Call Maggie."

"Calling Maggie."

Amber waited. The blind needed longer to answer. "Amber?"

"Maggie," her voice cracked. She'd held it together until she heard Maggie's concern and now the floodgates opened. She started to cry. "It's gone," she sputtered. "Everything's dark."

"I don't know where you live." She heard the desperation in Maggie's voice and knew her mom would feel the same.

Amber calmed down. "I thought you'd want to know."

"You're right. Are you alone, dear one?"

"Shannon went to get dinner."

"Good. Food is good. Do you need me?"

Amber went still. She did. She needed both her moms. It seemed wrong to see Maggie first. Maggie gave her birth, but Jennifer had raised her.

"Can I call you back?"

"Yes. I'll be here."

Amber hung up. "Call Mom."

"Amber sweetie. Are you all done packing?"

Again, the emotions welled. "It's over, Mom. My sight. It's gone." She choked on a wail.

She heard her mother start to cry. "What do you need me to do?"

"Can you come? I need you." No one was more surprised than she.

"I'll be right there."

Amber hung up and then made one more decision.

"Text Shannon."

"Texting Shannon."

"Bring more food for Mom."

"Sending."

Not that she needed to. Shannon probably ordered three extra entrees and two more extra desserts than necessary anyway. Leftovers were queen. But this also gave her a heads up. She put her cell on the coffee table, glad to be done making decisions and choices. Done hoping. Hoping and waiting had worn her thin. So thin. Now it was here, and she didn't need to worry *how* she'd cope—she'd go do it.

Twenty minutes later, the door buzzed. She knew it'd be her mom. Amber imagined the furniture right where it was, saw it in her mind, and walked to the door. She reached up and hit the buzzer. "Yes?"

"It's Mom."

She buzzed her in and unlocked the door, opened it and waited. She listened to her mother's stilettos on the tile floor and her hop step on the stairs. The back of her shoes slapped against her feet as she walked up the hall. She'd know her mother's walk anywhere. She moved inside her apartment, and her mother closed the door and scooped her into a hug, tucking Amber's face under her chin, and whispered to her.

"I'm here. I'm here." She rubbed tiny circles across her back like she did when Amber was little and upset or injured. They lulled her emotions to a calm.

"Thank you, Mom." She hugged her tightly.

"I've been so afraid."

"Me too."

"Is Maggie coming?"

"No. Right now I just need my mom."

That did it. Jennifer's walls crumbled, and her words stuttered out in between sobs. After a while, she let go of Amber and found the tissues.

"I thought you'd probably have more in common with Maggie. I mean, you and I have always been more like oil and water."

"Mom..." Amber started.

"Don't try and say any different, sweetie. I know it's true. I love to shop, you love to have someone shop for you. I love crowds and people, and you love watching the action at a distance. I can't wait to try the latest cuisine, and you like takeout."

"By the way, Shannon's bringing something home."

"I should hope so." She sniffed. "You like reading books, and I love seeing plays live."

"I get it. It's okay. We're different. But the thing is, no matter what her reasons, no matter how reasonable and justified they were, she left me. And you chose me. I'll always be grateful. I wouldn't be the person I am without you, Mom. Never forget that."

Amber held out the tissue box in the direction of the blubbering.

"You don't know how long I've waited to hear that."

"I know I'm not good at saying stuff, and I'll forget again. I want you to know how grateful I am you're in my life. I love you. And I'll always need you."

"Are you sure? I've been so worried."

"I'm sure. I want Maggie in my life—but I *need* you." Once again, Niagara Falls. More tissues.

"Thanks for telling me, sweetheart. You don't know what this means to me." They moved to the couch in time for Shannon to arrive with dinner. It smelled wonderful.

"What did you bring us?" Jennifer sounded hopeful and more at ease than she had in a long time.

"Tacos."

Amber's shoulders sagged. It had to be tacos. It'd be a long time before she could eat tacos without thinking about Ethan. A long time.

"I've got burritos and enchiladas too." Shannon's tone told her she hadn't hidden her reaction well. Amber was going to have to practice a whole new poker face.

"Good thing. I don't think I want tacos for a while."

If she could have seen their faces, she would have noticed the questioning glances and shrugs. As it was, she guessed from the silence. "Tacos equal Ethan."

"Ohh." Shannon and Jennifer echoed together.

Once they were all settled with food, Shannon popped open some locally bottled ginger ales and passed them around. All part of the tradition. Then she cleared her voice.

"We are gathered here today to commemorate Amber's going blind. This day would totally suck if we didn't have each other. Or God. Thanks for holding us tight, Father."

All three of them said, "Amen," in unison.

"So lift your glass and toast the day." They clinked their ginger ales together and drank.

"Oh, spicy." Jennifer coughed. She'd never been included in one of their commemorative days before, though she had heard of them.

"Yeah, that's part of it. The burning."

Amber clenched a hand to her chest. "And the after-burn later. Especially mixed with Mexican. It's going to be a Tums kind of night."

As they ate and talked, life seemed to spin into place. Amber pictured puzzle pieces all floating down to a huge tabletop. In the middle of an open space, settling in and finding a place, was her. A tip of sky, some flowery hill and a tiny piece of ocean.

Whenever talk turned more serious, she shifted it back to the light and silly. All she wanted to do was pretend things were normal. Strangely, they were beginning to feel like it already.

CHAPTER 39

L ife began to move into a familiar routine. Amber quit avoiding her group meetings. Maggie and she grew closer as she showed her how to adapt to the big changes. In the past, Amber used her ability to peek from her eyes as a crutch, or emergency exit, as Maggie coined the phrase. Now those exits were blocked and there weren't any more re-dos. No more crutches. No more cheating fate.

This group meeting was going to be different though. They'd all known she was partially sighted; some of them could see light or shadow. On occasion, off to the side, she'd still pick up something fuzzy, but it wasn't anything of consequence. In fact, she wished it would go away, making it easier still to adjust.

Tonight, she'd tell them all. It'd been two weeks since total blindness shifted her perspective. She hoped her life didn't hold any more shifts—but she sensed that wouldn't be the case. For now, Amber felt strong enough to go for it.

Maggie moved around in front of the class. "We'll have a guest in next week to show us how to manage our spices and cooking better. I know several of you have taken the cooking class, but this is more to do with practicality. And for those of you"—she cleared her throat in pointed exaggeration— "who have bothered to complete your advanced class in reading braille, you'll be happy to know the speaker will be bringing a variety of cookbooks with them."

The room filled with, "Oooo. She called you out."

Amber laughed it off. "Yeah, yeah. Life's been busy."

"Famous artist too good to learn to read?"

"Shoot, Sherri, that was harsh," Robert called back.

"I'm calling it like I see it."

They all chuckled.

Amber took this as her cue. She cleared her voice and said, "I've got something to say."

This signaled the rest of them to quiet down. Still, it took some time to override all the chortling and chiding going on.

"Let Amber speak, please." Maggie's voice grew closer toward her, and a hand landed on her shoulder, giving her a squeeze of encouragement.

"First, I want to say I'm sorry if I've been snotty to anyone here. Especially Sherri."

Sherri's quiet chatter faded. "Oh. Well. That's cool."

"Thanks. And second." She stopped, not sure how to proceed, not sure how they'd react. "Some of you know when I started this group, I could see most of you. You took me in and made this a safe place to share and get support."

There were murmurs of gratitude. "I want to let you know it's gone. All of it." The lighthearted attitude pervading the group dissipated. This wasn't what she wanted at all. She cleared her voice. "I'll start over. Let me introduce myself. Hi, I'm Amber, and I'm a blind person."

Several caught on. "Hi, Amber."

Someone grabbed her and pulled her into a hug. "You're okay, you know that?" Sherri.

"Thanks. You are too."

After the meeting, she helped clean up the place and put the chairs back in order. They'd stayed longer than they'd intended, sharing more personal anecdotes. Giving tips on how to adjust to no light at all. For the first time in her life, she felt included in a group setting. It was very strange, but very good.

"You did well tonight, you know?" Maggie tossed the doughnuts back in the box. "I'm going to give these to Daniel. You want any?"

"Who's Daniel?"

"He's the homeless guy who sits on the corner of the next block down. I thought maybe he was the one sneaking in here that night before all the fallout with Kyle."

"Oh. I didn't know his name. No, give them to him. I bet he'd like the coffee too."

"Probably. I don't have a thermos."

"I'll bring a couple next time. Then we can switch them out for him. He can give us the empty." She had two at home she never used.

"He'll lose it."

"I like the thrift store."

"We'll tell him tonight on the way to the bus." She picked up the box, and they moved out, switching off lights and the heating system as they went. Maggie locked the heavy double doors behind them, and they began walking.

"Any word from Ethan?" The question sounded innocent enough but Amber knew otherwise.

"No. There won't be. He's probably in Boston with his folks by now."

"You sure?"

Amber gave Maggie a look, then realized she couldn't see it. "I'm giving you my most sarcastic *you've got to be kidding me* look."

"Oh, thanks for letting me know. I'm giving you my *what?* face."

Laughing, Amber knocked shoulders with her. "Trust me, that ship has sailed. He made it clear by kicking me out of his life. I'm no doormat. If he doesn't want to stay friends, then there's nothing I can do about it. I'm certainly not going to beg."

"Are you sure that's it?"

"Yep." She wasn't. Not even close, but there wasn't another solution at hand, so she stuck with it. Her promise not to be wishy-washy went through her mind, but she shook it off. No one tried to be supportive more than she did. And he'd tossed her. So be it.

Maggie and Amber approached the corner, and Maggie called out. "You around, Daniel?"

"Daniel's here. Good ol' Daniel. He's always here."

"You want some doughnuts?"

"Love doughnuts."

"Next time I'll bring coffee too."

"Love coffee. Thanks, Miss Maggie."

Daniel's aroma was almost more than Amber could handle. They moved toward the bus stop to wait.

"How long has he lived on the corner?"

"He travels. He told me this is where he winters."

"Like snowbirds?" Amber chuckled. "Where does he summer?"

"Oh, down by the fountain I think. He's one of the walking wounded. He often mumbles about looking for someone."

"Why doesn't anyone help him?"

"We do." Maggie sighed. "He's been picked up and housed many times, but as soon as he's getting his feet under him, he stops his meds and spirals backward."

"Tough." Amber felt it was by the grace of God she'd been blessed with care and love. Then she stopped her thoughts. Someone might be looking at her blindness and thinking the same thing. She had to stop judging and start helping. This whole world was busted and everyone had a path to traverse. If they were open, they had God to walk it with them. If they weren't... She shuddered. In light of what God had done for her, it was for her to share it.

"How's your work going?"

"Rafe's got my stationery and prints up on a store online. He even got a couple local boutiques to carry them. He wants some more original work soon. I'm not sure what my focus will be yet. Before it was all about capturing the fleeting moment, to hold the light. But now... I don't know." A warming breeze washed over the budding trees nearby, carrying the scent of flowers and new growth.

"Spring is on the way." Amber took a deep breath, pulling it inside.

Their busses came, and they went their separate ways. She fiddled with her top, then her purse strap. She hadn't grown accustomed to being alone with her thoughts and no distractions yet. Conversations filtered to her from the other passengers. She tried not to hear, but that didn't work yet.

One man and his wife were fighting. The wife didn't think the husband was stepping up as a dad, and he didn't think she appreciated how hard he worked every day at a job he hated to keep them fed and housed. Another older couple (she could smell the liniment and mothballs) talked over their medical issues and the health of his colon. A girl and her boyfriend were kissing—kissing noises were the worst—and her friend, the odd-one out, kept trying to get them to look at something outside. She wasn't very successful.

Before she knew it, the bus driver called her street and she hopped off, heading to her apartment. As she entered her building, Maggie's words weighed heavily on her. What if Ethan had shut her down as part of a coping mechanism?

Amber climbed the stairs, not counting anymore because she sensed where they were. She let her cane guide her to her door and, once inside, showered and tumbled into bed. She didn't know what time it was. She closed her eyes and imagined the moonshine glowing through the bedroom window, lighting her floor with crisp shadows. She missed the moon. Instead of letting sleep claim her, she climbed from bed and set up her easel. It was the first time in these two weeks images called to her, and she didn't want to miss it or lose it to her dreams.

Amber felt the tubes for her marks and squeezed out the

paints she needed. She turned on her music, filling her apartment with classical piano. Then she sketched out her bedroom and the yellow-white moon low in the window, peering in like an old friend beckoning her to play. The shadows poured out of her brush like a cup spilling over its edges, the highlights crisp, all liquid silver and mercury bubbling, chasing moonbeam and revealing what was once hidden from view. Joy filled her soul as she made herself less and made the picture in her mind more. By the time the moon would have moved over her apartment, she'd finished, cleaned her bushes, and crawled wearily into bed.

Amber was never more alive, more like herself, than when she held a brush, smelled the paints, and felt the slide of colors and the roughness of the canvas surface as she transferred her vision. What more in life could she have? Now that she and God were on the same footing, her painting took on a new form, a new focus. She'd moved from chasing the light and capturing it on canvas to holding it gently in her mind. And letting Him hold her. There was nothing better in life than spending it with Him. Nothing. Satisfied of her place in the world, she drifted away.

CHAPTER 40

One day shifted into the next, the rhythm of her routine becoming solid once again. There were still the odd objects she tripped over, the slips of plates and spills of drinks, but for the most part, she'd normalized. As much as she was ever normal.

She entered Rafe's café, enjoying the aroma of a well-made cup of coffee, and moved toward what she'd come to think of as her booth. Rafe had the staff keep it empty for her. She'd come with her sketchpad and block out shapes and forms, a poetry all her own. Her former coffee shop held too many difficult memories. It was good to start somewhere new. Although, this one was six blocks farther away.

"Good morning." A cup of espresso was set down before her. Could anything smell better? The burnt-toast-met-cigar-and-chocolate richness swirled up to meet her nose, filling her with the energy for the day before her lips tasted a drop.

"Good morning." She smiled across the table as Rafe sat down.

"Good news. We've sold all your latest ocean scenes. Oh, and one of the bridge down by the river. And your latest moonshine-dancing print."

"Moonshine dancing?"

"That's what a sweet little girl named Katie called it."

"Oh, was Katie here?" The idea thrilled her. She'd not been back to the school since losing her sight altogether. She should go. She'd have Justin take her, and she'd sit in on one of his classes. Maybe next week.

"They bought a print of it for her room."

"Who bought the original?"

"A young gentleman. He seemed particularly moved. He also purchased an ocean scene. Stood in front of it for ages. I thought he'd go for the print but he bought the original."

"I'm glad it connected with someone." It'd been the last of those ocean paintings she'd done. She didn't want any extra reminders of what was in the past. "How many gaps do you have?"

"Four. A sweet little old lady visited yesterday and asked for a picture of a sunflower."

Amber smiled. She'd never done a sunflower. Maybe Shannon could drive her to a field where she could touch them and smell them and walk among them, studying their shape and design for a day. "I could try." Even as she thought about it, the flower grew in her mind, rough and dry at the center, soft and pliable, cool yellow petals. Yes.

Rafe stepped away to help with a customer, leaving her to her own devices.

She sipped at her espresso, her heart singing to the new ideas forming in her head. She'd been greatly blessed. Funny how God had given her an ability she could cling to during her trial. No, not *funny*. A different word. Amazing. Incredible. Spirit-lifting. Gift. A gift worth clinging to. A gift worth holding. A gift meeting her where she was, guiding her where she needed to go, filling her with hope and all the while pointing back to her Creator. Huge.

There were too many words.

Rafe sat back down. "Tell me, lovely, what are you doing tonight?"

"I think," she paused, "nothing. Nothing on my agenda tonight."

"Have dinner with me?"

Amber thought it over. "Sure. Here? What did you want to talk about? Marketing a new line of T-shirts? I'll say this up front—I don't do fish prints."

"Fish prints?"

"Yeah, you know where the artist would paint a fish and then slap it on paper."

"No fish. Okay." He sounded perplexed.

"Of course, in my case, it'd be like my face or maybe Mocha's face. And that's just not cool with me." She giggled. "Sorry. What shall we talk about?"

"I meant dinner. You know, where we go out and share thoughts and have food."

Amber quit her sketching and looked up in his general direction. *Poker face, poker face.* "Wait, like a date?"

"Exactly like a date."

She frowned.

"I take it from your expression that that is distasteful?"

So much for her poker face. She needed to practice more on Shannon. "No, not distasteful. I've never thought of you like that. You're my agent."

"Business, right? Not good to mix things up?"

Relief flooded her at the suggestion. "Absolutely."

"I understand. So, if I quit being your agent, then you'd date me?"

"Well..." she stopped.

"Another unsure look. I get it. We'll keep things the way they are." He sounded hurt. "Can I ask you something, Rafe?"

"Sure." She could hear him fiddling with his cup and spoon. Not really mixing. Maybe balancing it.

"What do you see in me?"

The spoon clattered across the table and onto the floor. His server grabbed it and gave him a new one before he could ask.

"What do I see in you? Why, lovely, you are just that. Beautiful. You see life like no one I've ever met. And yes, I mean *see.* You see more than most with sighted eyes. Not to mention you can see right through me, so I don't bother pretending to be someone I'm not when I'm with you. It's liberating, if not a bit terrifying."

She felt her face flush with pleasure and embarrassment. She'd never been admired so much before. Rafe, despite being handsome and influential, wasn't really her type. Amber liked a man she could be herself with—and not worry about what she'd said or what she wore. As soon as Rafe opened his mouth the very first time they'd met, she knew he was not in that category of guy. Of course, her record in finding such a man wasn't great, and there probably wasn't such a person in her future. Not now.

"You have no idea what that means to me. I'll remember it always."

Rafe gave a chuckle. "Glad to help." He moved from the bench seat and leaned over. "I'll be searching for a new agent for you now, you know." He moved away from her, his footsteps retreating through the café.

She suddenly saw their canceled cross-country train excursion very differently. He was teasing her...mostly. She'd move very carefully with him in the future. The waiter came over.

"Your usual salad today, Miss Kirk?"

"Let's shake things up. How's your tuna on rye?"

"You won't regret it. We add grilled onion and toast it with gruyère cheese. The best melt ever."

"Oh, I'm sold." She sighed. "Speaking of sold, do you know who purchased the ocean and moonshine paintings? Rafe didn't remember his name."

"I'm not sure. Let me go ask Rhonda. She does most of the print and painting sales when I'm not here."

Moments later, Rhonda came by. "You were wondering about some sales?" Amber heard her shifting through a ledger.

"Yes, the last ocean and moonshine originals." Amber picked up her cup for a sip.

"Oh, him. I don't need to look that up. He paid cash, so I don't have his name, but he had the bluest eyes. Honey colored skin. Super short cropped black hair with a touch of gray at the temples. Oh, and he walked with crutches. Must have had an accident. I flirted my best, but didn't get anything out of him. Hope he comes back."

Amber held her cup mid-sip, shock and surprise shooting through her nervous system.

It couldn't be. And if it was, why?

CHAPTER 41

"He's got no business shutting me out and then buying those paintings." Amber paced in her apartment.

"Would you sit down for a minute?" Shannon had obviously lost patience with Amber after watching her walk back and forth across her apartment for the past forty minutes, ranting. "Sit. Down. Now."

Amber threw herself on the couch.

"He's got a right like everyone else to buy whatever he wants. They obviously mean something to him. Let him have them."

"But *why* does he want them? And what is he doing here, anyway? He's supposed to have moved to Boston."

"What's bothering you more? That he bought your paintings, or that he didn't leave town when he said he did?"

"I'm saying if a person tells you they're moving, they should move." Amber tossed a pillow across the room.

"Or at least call you and tell you they've changed their mind?"

"Exactly!"

They sat together, Amber huffing, Shannon humming nonsensical tunes for several minutes before Amber realized what she was doing.

"Quit it."

"What?" Shannon hummed some more, goading Amber.

"That humming thing. You don't know what you think you know."

"I'm sorry? That was super convoluted."

"You know what I mean."

"Sure thing." Shannon flipped through a magazine.

"That's outdated, isn't it?"

"What? I can't even read a magazine without annoying you?"

Amber, defeated, groaned in frustration. "I don't know what's wrong with me."

"You're hurt."

"Yeah. I'm hurt. I've been hurt before, and I'm sure this won't be the last time. I guess I thought I could ignore it." She pulled a pillow over her face.

"I think you should go see him."

As Amber sat bolt upright, the pillow went flying, startling Mocha, who skittered in the direction of the table. "And have him kick me out again?"

"Maybe. At least you wouldn't have these unanswered questions in your mind."

Shannon had more baggage with rejection than she did. At least, Amber thought so. "You'd go?"

Shannon went still. "Yeah. I think I would."

"I'll consider it." She really wouldn't. Why should she go and put herself out there again just to get smacked down?

"Meanwhile, what's your next series? I've been itching to get out of town. I'll take you wherever you want to go."

"I'm going to do a series on sunflowers, but that'll be in the middle of summer. I'd love to go to the tulip festival. It opens tomorrow."

"Perfect."

Amber looked up, alerted that something was off with Shannon. Despite her outward artsy appearance, Shannon wasn't much for being spontaneous.

"What's up?"

Shannon tossed what she was reading. Amber felt in front of her and straightened up the magazines, feeling the crumbs from their dinner of croissant sandwiches getting under her fingernails. She really needed to practice the cleaning thing.

"My dad might be in town."

"How do you know?"

"One of his buddies saw him and called me at work. He looks bad, I guess."

"How long has it been since you've seen him?" Amber didn't want to press her. Whenever the subject of her father came up, it'd throw her into a depression—sometimes for weeks. It became the topic they never spoke of. He whose name must not be uttered.

"Over fifteen years. Maybe longer. I used to count the days, then the years. And then one day, I decided to let him go. Like I let my mom go. She's dead. I figured he would be too."

"He wasn't an addict like her, though."

"He might as well be." Shannon sighed aloud. "He put his own desires ahead of everyone else for his entire life. That's what an addict does. He told everyone he can't help himself. *Check.* He told everyone how he was so strong and didn't need anyone else. *Check.* He told everyone how he could change at any moment. *Check.* He gave up everything he had to live alone on the streets. *Quadruple check.*" Her voice rose at the end, angry.

"But he's mentally ill."

"He's had choices. He could have taken his meds. He could have stayed in a facility that would help him. But no. When he's on his meds, he's great and decides he's finally cured, but he won't stay on them. Maybe he thinks he doesn't need them anymore, maybe it's the money, maybe sometimes they make him feel like garbage—I've heard every excuse. Well, what about how everyone else feels around him when he's off them?" Shannon pushed the chair back and headed into the kitchen. Amber heard her washing up.

"I can do those."

"I want to."

Amber heard the *need to* in Shannon's voice, so she decided to sit at the kitchen table behind her and let her at them.

"He's selfish." She clunked a plate in the drainer.

Amber had never heard Shannon so animated and pointed when it came to her father.

"He can't help how he behaves, Shannon."

She slammed a pan into the sink. "Don't tell me that. He's always put himself first. Always. If someone told me I could have my kid back if I stayed on my meds, can you imagine me saying anything but yes? Can you see me doing anything to jeopardize that?"

Amber went still. "I..." She swallowed down the emotions welling in her throat. "I didn't have any idea." All those years, Shannon had ached for her father. Prayed for him to come for her. Amber didn't know it was in *his* hands the whole time. "I don't know what to say. I'm so sorry."

"Forget it. I shouldn't have said anything." She turned off the water, and Amber heard her rustling around. "I'm going to go, okay? Don't forget to lock up after I leave."

"Okay." She knew Shannon well enough to respect her space and let her figure things out on her own. She would. She always did. When she heard Shannon leave, Amber went to the door, locking it tight.

Hours later, she lay in her bed, wondering. Rejection messed with her self-confidence more than anything. Personal rejection, that was. She'd grown accustomed to having her work rejected. One person's ideas didn't necessarily connect to another—artistic expression could be fickle. But what about Shannon and her dad? Why did people have to be so awful to one another?

Turning over and punching her pillow into submission, she scrunched down, trying to sleep. She tried to shut out her thoughts. Nearly every person she'd ever trusted had left her. Like a switch turned off, they found someone else to confide in. For most of them, she'd never even known what she'd done wrong. What she wouldn't do to be one of those secure people who would let people walk away easily and find new people to replace the old ones with like they'd done to her. But she wasn't that way. She'd never be that way.

And Kyle. What a case he was. Scary. She sure could pick them. He was in the state prison, awaiting a mental competency hearing. Maybe she sucked at picking people?

She always trusted the wrong ones. Except Shannon. But what about Ethan?

Ethan. He'd seemed different. He'd *seemed* real. That's the part she couldn't get over. Even after he'd pushed her out, she still worried about him. Cared about him.

She turned onto her other side, wondering how late it'd gotten. Without the passage of light through the apartment from the moon and streetlights, and the digital glow of the clock, her sense of time had gotten completely turned upside down. She knew it could happen. She'd read about it and even heard a couple people in her group talking about it. It truly was strange. Humans were made for visual cues—made for light.

"God? Help me be more careful in the future, okay? I know I'm supposed to love people and care for them. But it'd sure be great not to be crushed so often." She got the impression that wasn't how it worked. Everything worthwhile involved risks, especially when dealing with people. Her only alternative to being left was to cut herself off from people entirely, and she wasn't willing to do that. "Would you please comfort Shannon tonight too? She's really hurting." If Amber could, she'd pick Shannon up out of her life and put her in one where she'd never get hurt. She wished she could cushion everyone she cared about, keep them all protected.

Again, she got the impression that wasn't how life was supposed to work either.

Mocha raced through the apartment, chasing after something

Amber hoped wasn't a mouse. Or a cockroach. Her housekeeping skills were awful. She'd probably missed corners. She'd definitely left food on the counter or table multiple times. Mocha usually found that, though.

Without warning, he leapt onto her belly, surprising her, and began to knead the blankets before settling down. She ran her fingernails down his back, then curled around his tail. She sure loved this ridiculous cat.

Amber took stock. She had two moms, her best friend, and this cat. Justin by extension. She didn't need anyone else to confide in.

Mocha purred and rolled over for her to rub his tummy, stretching out under her hand, purring louder. So much for getting a seeing eye dog. Even though the training school was less than an hour away, she'd never gone. Maybe one day. Right now, it was too much change all at once—and she was sure Mocha would resist the idea. An idea flashed through her mind. She could always get a halter and train Mocha.

Mocha's ears twitched under her hand at an imagined victim. He wound himself up and launched to the floor, pouncing and hissing. The jingle of his toy mouse filled the apartment.

Strangely, there weren't seeing-eye-cat schools advertised.

A cup on the counter crashed to the floor.

Probably for the best.

CHAPTER 42

The March sun warmed her head and back, chasing off the chill of the day. Amber crouched down in the midst of the field where the owner said she could go. Back on the dirt access road, Shannon would be setting up Amber's easel and taking photographs for herself of the tulip festival and row after row of brightly colored flowers and their admirers. Shannon brought her sketchbook too, for a later sculpture she was working on.

It relieved Amber to know that Shannon got something out of driving her around. She never wanted to be a burden on her friend. Since they both used their time on outings for research on their own projects, it took that pressure off.

"It's like Easter threw up out here." Shannon laughed.

"Great visual, thanks!" The sweet, new-growth aroma of the tulips mixed with the warming soil underneath. She inhaled deeply and committed it to memory. Amber reached out her hands, gently brushing the cool petals, feeling them flip past her palms. They reminded her of feathers. She caressed a petal, and the spoon shape bent, pliable under the pressure of her fingers.

Amber measured the size and shape in comparison to her hand, then she leaned down and felt them against her face. Not feathers—more like thin leather. She pressed a loose petal against her lips.

She listened to the birds in the distance, heard the squeals of children nearer the front of the gardens, and the laughter of older people, enjoying what had to be thousands of newly opened buds, all colors of the rainbow, suspended on tall, stiff stalks of green.

Amber put her hand up to her mouth, and aimed in the direction she thought Shannon sat. "I'm ready."

"Be right there."

She heard the swooshing of flowers against Shannon's pant legs.

"What do you see?" Amber moved her head one way, then the other, drawing in the scents, the sounds, the tickle of breeze, the picture forming in her mind like colored chalk on a blackboard.

"Orange, pink, splashes of magenta. Yellow, white, peach, blue. Even black."

"Wow."

"Very wow. Some ruffled, some smooth, some ragged and striped." Shannon led her to her chair, and she set up her paints and canvas, marking off the areas, sensing her way. She spread the paint on thickly, then pushed it back in places with other brushes before slathering on more. She moved like the waves on the ocean, like the waves of the fields with the flowers bending to the winds of change. After two hours, she put her brush down.

"Well?" she called to Shannon, who came back over to her.

"It's like a sea of color. Waves of movement, shifting, full of depth."

"Good."

Amber started and finished another. Then, as the heat of the day pressed upon them, they packed it up and hiked back to the car. Shannon loaded everything inside on makeshift racks, and Amber loaded herself. During the drive back into Portland, Amber kept her ideas to herself, remembering the shapes, the sensation of it all. She'd be able to paint four more on her own. Then the emotions, the smells, and the sounds would fade, as they always did.

Amber felt the car slow and measured the turns. "Are we downtown?"

"Yes. Let's stop for lunch at the café, okay? We'll drop these off in the back, and it'll save a trip."

"Sounds good." Amber took her phone from her pocket and called in to have one of Rafe's employees meet them out front with lunch in a sack and to report they'd be dropping off the paintings. Instead, Rafe answered.

"I'm glad you're coming. I have a client who's requested a large painting of the Burnside Bridge. He wanted to know if you could get it done today."

"No. I'm exhausted. I've been up since six and out in the tulip fields all day."

"He'll pay double the price."

Amber could sure use the money. Mocha was due for shots and a checkup at the vet's. And she'd had her eye on a new climbing toy and a halter. More and more she became convinced she'd be able to train Mocha to walk on a lead. And then...who knew?

Besides, starving as an artist wasn't all it was cut out to be. "Fine. But only if Shannon agrees." She covered the microphone and filled Shannon in. Shannon agreed.

"She says fine. But she wants to be paid too."

"In food?"

"Yes. Food."

Shannon called toward the phone. "We're here."

Moments later, Amber heard men—two of them—come out. They collected the paintings and loaded something in the backseat—likely a picnic hamper. The car filled with the aroma of garlic, onions, and corned beef.

"Okay, off to Burnside. Parking is going to suck, though."

Luckily, they found a disabled spot, so Shannon put up Amber's placard, and they unloaded the car. Amber held the handcart with one hand and carried their lunch with the other. They shook out a blanket and put out the food. Then she set up her easel.

Amber loved it here. The aromas, the sounds. All of it. Even if it had been Ethan's spot, he couldn't claim the river all to himself. She heard a boat in the distance, listened to the gulls, and heard the water lapping on the rocks.

After eating her lunch, she started sketching and blocking. She heard Shannon move away, her digital camera rapidly clicking.

Nothing filled Amber with satisfaction like painting did. She'd been so afraid of losing her sight, of losing her connection with creation—and thus the Creator. Instead, she was learning to see all over again in a way so full of depth she'd never be able to investigate it fully. Her throat ached with emotion and gratitude.

Losing her sight had been horrible, and she didn't feel glad about it—but somehow God was making something worth being thankful for in the midst of her pain, her grief, her loss. She could still use her gifts, but not in a way she'd ever imagined. The more she gave up her ideas and plans and trusted the Father for what the day might hold, the less painful the transition became. This was...better. Not fun or easy—but better. Deep in her core, the idea resonated truth. She hoped she'd remember it the next time she got on the wrong bus or stubbed her toe on an unseen object.

Today she was doing what she loved, hanging out with her best friend, and lo and behold, the sun was out in the rainy northwest. Best day ever. She slathered blue and green together on her pallet, and began to dash it on the canvas before her, creating a scene only she had sight for, preparing the sky and the river to receive the manmade bridge to come. Embracing light and shadow both.

"I love that shade of blue." His voice broke into her thoughts.

Amber went still.

"I've got another painting very similar. It's at home on my wall. In fact, I have two others. One the artist made especially for me. It's in my bedroom, where I can see it every morning." She heard scraping sounds and the drag of crutches over sidewalk and then grassy turf. "It gives me hope on bad days. It reminds me of where I've been and gives me the courage to keep my eyes on where I have to go and Whom I should be following."

He stood beside her now, blocking the sun, giving her shade and coolness to match the color in her head. The color she saw when she painted this spot.

The color of his eyes in her memories.

"I'm afraid you're interrupting my work. I've got a client who ordered this right away."

"I know." His tone went low with significance.

"*You're* the client?"

The warm timbre of his voice and spicy scent of his aftershave surrounded her. "I am."

She began to paint again, not trusting herself to say or do anything else. She painted in the river, lit the waves with sunlight sparkles, splashed the breakers on the rocks, scuttled the boats into slips. She reached for the nimbus gray and burnt umber, blocking out the bridge's structure. She meant to ask Shannon to help her with the support counts. For now, though, this was enough.

As her arm moved, her mind hoped, and her heart waited.

"I saw the ocean paintings in the gallery. I bought one."

"I know." Her voice came out in a whisper.

"It's in the living room."

"Your living room in Boston?" Oh, she'd found her tongue now. "I didn't move."

"And didn't think to call me." Her hand jerked, and she knew she would have an error to fix.

"I needed to see how things went."

She stopped painting. She didn't want to ruin it with her anger, and if she continued, the painting would be black and red, obliterating all the life, beauty, and promise it'd held. She tossed her brush into the glass and turned to face him.

"Why are you here, Ethan?"

"I'd meant to move. Promised myself I would. But the doctor convinced me to finish my treatment here so there wouldn't be anything left to chance or lost in the transfer of care. And Sam got me up on my prosthetics. She'd put in so much work, so much time, I didn't want to leave until she'd signed me off."

"Thanks for keeping me in the loop." Nothing said about her and her support or her help. Or her friendship.

He continued. "And then, I couldn't find a job in Boston. I didn't want to be a burden to my parents. Maggie kept calling me and telling me there was no one to fill my place here. She said you agreed with her."

"She's my mom, did you know that?"

"I did." He didn't sound surprised. He didn't even sound like this was recent knowledge.

"How long have you known?"

"I started to put things together a while back. Maggie told me her story years ago. And then you mentioned your adoption to me, and I realized you and Maggie's daughter shared a name. That pretty much cinched it for me."

"Thanks for telling me that too."

"If you'd listen..."

She held up her hand to keep the words *to reason* from emitting from his mouth.

"It's too late, Ethan. I'm tired of putting myself out there only to have you push me away. I've got better things to do."

He put a hand on her shoulder, but she wrenched away, pulled out her cane and headed toward the water's edge. She heard boats tearing up the river, fishermen on the rocks calling to one another. She kept walking, feeling the grass under her feet give way to pavement, until she heard the screech of bike brakes and felt the hard yank of a hand and fell backward into a heap of legs and crutches and man.

A very angry woman yelled at them. "Watch it! What are you, blind?"

If she'd still had her cane in her hand, she'd have waved it at the bicyclist—or chucked it at her. As it was, Amber sat defeated on the grass. Ethan lay next to her.

"I can't believe that woman. And you, what were *you* thinking, storming right in front of her like that? You could have both been hurt." His tone condemned her for stupidity, and she realized, for once, *she* knew more than he did. He didn't know about her sight.

"I can't believe this." Now he sounded embarrassed, ashamed. "Nothing ever works the way I think it will." He shifted and pulled, and she realized she'd been sitting on one of his crutches. She slipped off of it and onto the grass as he continued his rant. "You know. You're probably right. This was stupid. I don't know what I was thinking setting this up."

"Quitter." She was done being nice. She was done being understanding. She wanted to call him a chicken on top of it all.

"You don't know what you're talking about. I've done nothing but work my tail off to get well, to get upright. To stand, as it were, on my own two feet. I never..." He paused for breath. "...ever wanted you to see me like I was again. Like *this*."

"Don't worry. I can't."

She heard him wrestling with something, the clack of plastic, the smack of wood, distracted. "Can't what?"

"Can't see you like this."

Everything went still. She sensed his eyes on her. She gave him a brave smile and then waved her hand in front of her eyes. "All's dark on the western front."

"Oh, God." As with Shannon, when Ethan used God's name, he was actually addressing Him—not cursing. Ethan pulled her to him, crushing her against his chest, drawing her as close as he could. "I didn't know. Maggie never said." He started rocking her, but she could tell he was comforting himself as much as her. And she knew something else too. It wasn't about him rejecting her after all. It'd been about ego.

Ego, she could handle.

Amber leaned into him, wrapping her arms around his waist, supporting him. "I'm okay. Or I'm learning to be okay."

"It's not fair."

She smiled into his shoulder. "Little in life is. Tell me one thing— are you cancer free?" She held her breath, waiting for his answer.

"For now. I'm in remission. There's no guarantee."

Remission. She could handle remission too.

"There's only one guarantee we can rest in. Jesus has that wrapped up." It was then she felt his lips kiss the top of her head, then move to her temple, her cheek, and finally coming to rest, sweetly, against her lips. The gentle reverence of his mouth on hers, the warmth of his arms encircling her, protecting her, the breeze washing over them, the scent of his cologne—all of it overpowered her, and she melted into his embrace.

Someone nearby made a whooping sound. It got closer and closer. Shannon had found them. Amber tried to imagine the spectacle they made, but even *her* imagination couldn't quite do it justice compared to Shannon's giggles of glee.

In her mind's eye, she pictured Ethan's prostheses and crutches littered around them like a mannequin accident scene. Her cane in shards—scattered along the bike path. Her paint-covered shirt messing up his clothes, and her hands leaving trails of blue-green over his cheeks, where she held his face as she brushed away his tears and felt the laughter on his lips in between their kisses. Maybe one day she'd ask Shannon how it really looked.

For now, living it was much more important than recording it.

AUTHOR'S NOTES

When conceiving the plot for *Hold the Light*, I wanted to share about disability or illness in a way that would connect to the reader immediately. While I suffer a disability due to illness, that is a hard subject for many to connect with, and I knew I needed to find another avenue.

I've found that a loss most people have worried about is their sight. Even now I have a friend who is in the middle of this trial, trying to come to terms with what her life will be like without her vision. The unknown is scary. Any new condition or illness can cause us to rethink our purpose in the world, shift our values, and redirect our focus. It brings grief and hardship and a reordering of our lives before we can find acceptance and joy in the midst of sorrow.

Macular degeneration is one of the most common forms of blindness. For some sufferers, it takes years for the disease to progress, but for a select few, it's very fast. It is rare to lose complete sight, as Amber did. Most people are left with a fuzzy peripheral vision, inhibiting reading, driving, and daily tasks. The greatest population that succumbs to macular degeneration is those over sixty.

A smaller number of people—1 in 10,000—is born with a genetic hereditary condition called early onset, or middle onset, macular degeneration, affecting those aged five to twenty and even into their thirties. For the sake of the story's timeline, I took the liberty of increasing Amber's vision loss over a shortened period. It is not unheard of, however, for children to be diagnosed at age ten and not experience full vision loss until their mid-twenties or thirties.

For more information on blindness, blindness aids, or governmental assistance, please contact http://www.oregon.gov/blind.

I hope and pray I did justice to the challenges, trials and triumphs those who deal with blindness face.

ACKNOWLEDGMENTS

First, I want to thank Vinnie Gwozdz at the Oregon Commission for the Blind (http://www.oregon.gov/blind) for answering all my questions and being so encouraging in my writing about blindness and the challenges those with the condition face and overcome daily.

Next, I want to thank JoAnn Northcutt, a sweet lady who invited me into her home and shared openly with me the daily challenges she's faced in losing her sight from macular degeneration.

A huge thanks to Roseanna White and the entire WhiteFire Publishing family. I'm so blessed to be part of a house that promotes transparency of faith, that prays for me, and that encourages me. Thanks for this book-baby. She's so pretty. I couldn't have done it without you.

Now for the personal mushy stuff. My illness comes with dark days that cause me to think of those in my life with a deep tenderness and tremendous gratefulness—and to make sure they know how I feel because we never know what the next moment will hold. And since I'm a writer, I get to do it publicly:

To Jesus: It's all for you. Every day. Always. My heart, my gifts, my dreams, my everything for my Lord, King, Savior.

To my family, Ken, Madeline, and Seth: You give me the courage to face the hard days, the peace to know I can curl up and rest when I need to without guilt, and the encouragement to keep going in this writing life when days go by without my ability to sit at the computer. I am so thankful to our Lord to be part of your lives. Every day with you is a gift.

To my dear friend and sister-by-choice, Janet Hewitt: You are the best PA (personal assistant) in the world. You've intuitively helped me at book signings and speaking engagements. You have driven me to doctor's appointments and held my hand when I've gotten bad news. Thank you for praying for me every day and for knowing just what to say on crummy days as well as the joyful ones. You bless my life.

To my parents, who are the best marketing team and cheering section EVER: Allan and Carol Solstad, and Richard and Andrea Johnson. You have always encouraged me to reach and grow in faith and dreams. THANK YOU.

To my sister, Joy: I'm so grateful to have married into your life. You bless me with your love, support and sweetness. The times we spend together are invaluable and precious.

To my amazing critique partners and sisters on this demanding, exhilarating, emotional roller coaster: Danika Cooley and Melody Roberts. I don't know what I'd do without you ladies. You are consistently encouraging, incredibly talented, and so patient with me (all the adverbs)! You lead faithfully by example. Thanks for not letting me quit (yes, dear reader, writers want to quit often) on those hard days and for praying me onward.

To my critique group, The Encouragers: Every writer needs a critique group, and ours is chock full of talent and amazingness—iron sharpens iron! Sandra Bensman, Danika Cooley, Louise Dunlap, Kelly Fritz, April Lesher, Jac Nelson, Nora Peacock, Kendy Pearson, Melody Roberts, Rachel Russell, and Julie Streit.

To my lifelong buddies, LeeAnn Macklin and LeAnna Murray: I love you. Thanks for hanging in there.

To my thoughtful, supportive, girlfriend-tribe, THANK YOU for being there in the gap countless times: Chris Collier, Susan Creer,

Billie Jo Robbins, Tammy Schwartz, Lynn Trachte, Laurene Wells, and Beth Zulaski.

And to my spiritual mentors Debbie Carpenter, Valerie Becker, and Janice Moss: You ladies battle harder, pray harder, and love harder than anyone I know. You amaze me.

MUST-SEE CONTEST ENTRIES

Thanks so much for sharing your Must-See List with me. I made sure to use them all!

Listed by entry date:

Chris Collier, Louise Dunlap, Bonnie Steinborn, Madeline McGowan, Kim Morris, Stephanie Spath—WINNER of gift card, Janet Hewitt, Nancy Meacham-Cole, Billie Jo Robbins, Sara Goff, Urailak "A" Liljequist, Joan Leotta, Gail Kittleson, June Foster, Ruth Ann Dell, Melody Roberts, Jac Nelson, Johnnie Alexander, amethyst212, Janice Moss, Valerie Becker

DISCUSSION QUESTIONS
FOR GROUPS

1. Amber faces a significant loss early in the story. Have you or a loved one ever faced an illness or injury? How did you/ they get through it?

2. Shannon is Amber's fierce supporter and protector. Have you ever had a friend look out for you like that? Is there a time you'd like to share about? How did it make you feel when they came to your rescue?

3. Amber's mother loves her dearly but finds it hard to express in a way that Amber can see. Have you ever had trouble connecting with a loved one? What did you do?

4. Kyle turns out to be not only damaging but dangerous. What do you think you'd do in that situation?

5. Loss always carries grief—and grief can be tricky. Sometimes it can revisit you when you least expect it. If you've experienced a loss, have you found a way to cope during those sneak-attacks?

6. Sometimes people can hurt us with their words. Amber finds this at a place that should be the most supportive and safe—church. Has anyone ever been thoughtless with their advice to you? How did you deal with it?

7. Do you know someone with a disability, physical challenge, or illness? How do you support them? What have they said has been the most helpful to them?

8. Sometimes God doesn't answer our prayers the way we hope He would. Sometimes He brings us to and through hard times rather than removing us from it. How do you get through those times?

9. Have you faced a time where you just had to accept a situation instead of changing it? What did you learn from that?

10. Can you share about a time where God met you where you were and carried you through a trial?

11. Ethan lets his ego get in the way of reaching out for help. Has there been a time in your life you were unwilling to lean on another or even ask for help? Did you learn to be or are you still independent? What do you think is better?

12. There were many moments in the story where people showed up for Amber and helped her. They became the hands and feet of Jesus. Can you make a list of ways to help a hurting person in your life? What's the best way to know how to help?

ALSO BY APRIL MCGOWAN

MACY

Independent...or Alone?

Macy longed for independence her whole life. Maybe marrying Arthur to escape her home hadn t been the best plan, but it seemed good enough at the time. Now, pregnant and abandoned in a diner far from anyone she knows, Macy must start life all over again. Relying on the mercy of the diner's owners, she begins to put things back together. Macy must make her own decisions for the first time in her adult life but it isn't all it's cracked up to be. And with the too-alluring Toby at her side instead of her husband, she s discovering those decisions harder to make than ever.

JASMINE

She survived her past but how can she face it?

Jasmine is a survivor. She's lived through the abuse of her father, running away at age fourteen, living on the streets, and now she counsels at risk young women giving them a second chance at life.

But when her mother dies, can she go home again and face the past she's forced herself to forget for the last twenty years? Or will the past she's now forgotten take over her present once again?

CPSIA information can be obtained
at www.ICGtesting.com
Printed in the USA
FFOW03n1041131117
43455446-42109FF